THE Arabian Nights

BASED ON THE TRANSLATION ♦ FROM THE ARABIC BY ♦ EDWARD WILLIAM LANE

SELECTED, EDITED AND ARRANGED ♦ FOR YOUNG PEOPLE BY ♦ FRANCES JENKINS OLCOTT

ILLUSTRATIONS AND ♦ DECORATIONS BY ♦ MONRO S. ORR

Editor's Preface

OF all the folk-literature adapted for children, none is more richly imaginative, warm in colour, and full of varied adventures than the "Arabian Nights' Entertainments," for which reason a volume of selections from the same should be in every child's own library.

This edition of selected tales edited for young people is based on the version of the Oriental scholar, Edward William Lane. His translation from the Cairo text, although it is the standard, classic household version for adults, may not be given unexpurgated to children as it contains much that is unfit for them to read. It has, however, great educational values, the chief of which lie in its epic treatment, so characteristic of primitive people; in its thrilling adventures, related with convincing details; and in its dignified style, resembling that of Bible narrative. Its educational values are increased by Lane's painting, as with a large, free brush, desert scenes, and life in the great Oriental cities; and in his depicting Eastern customs and religious beliefs which control the "faithful" Mohammedan's daily actions.

The tales abound in Genii with their heads in the clouds, their feet resting upon the earth, their heads like domes, their hands like winnowing-forks, their legs like masts, their mouths like caverns, their nostrils like trumpets, their eyes resembling lamps, and hair dust-coloured and dishevelled; and with damsels as beautiful as the shining moon, with eyes like those of gazelles, cheeks like anemonies, mouths like the seal of Solomon, and figures like the waving branch. The stories also describe Oriental cities crowned with domes and minarets, subterranean abodes, flying Genii; and verdant gardens in which are flowing rivers, blossoming flowers, and trees full of birds proclaiming the praises of Allah the One, the Omnipotent.

The pages of the original Lane edition are illustrated with the delicate drawings of William Harvey, who in true Oriental spirit depicts the buildings, costumes and life of Mohammedans. As it is almost impossible to reproduce satisfactorily these old engravings, coloured illustrations are here substituted for the Harvey drawings.

Several of the stories included will be new to most children. Of these are "The Story of the City of Brass," which relates the search for bottled Genii; "The Adventures of Hassan of Balsora," which describes the wonders of the enchanted Islands of Wak Wak, and the humorous story of "Caliph the Fisherman."

Two stories, "Aladdin" and "Ali Baba," are not included in the Cairo text, and as an edition for children of the Arabian Nights would be incomplete without these tales I have added them; editing the versions of Jonathan Scott, translated from the French of Galland.

In rendering these stories I have retained the original language as far as possible. The familiar forms of proper names are given instead of Lane's more accurate but uninteresting transliterations, and English equivalents have been substituted for some Arabic words. Long sentences are shortened, tedious conversations condensed, and lengthy stories broken into chapters. Those parts of the stories unsuitable for children are removed, which in a few cases necessitates slight changes in the plots. I have, however, conscientiously tried to preserve the original matter, and the genius and customs of the Arabians, making only such alterations as the interests of the children demand.

FRANCES JENKINS OLCOTT.

July, 1913.

Contents

Contents

Contents

Chapter VI

Chapter VII

Chapter VIII

Chapter IX

Conclusion

List of Illustrations

Shahriar and Sheherazade

THERE was in ancient times a King of India and China, possessing numerous troops and guards and servants, and he had two sons. Both of these princes were brave horsemen, but especially the elder, who inherited the kingdom of his father, and governed his subjects with such justice that the inhabitants of his country and whole empire loved him. He was called King Shahriar. His younger brother was named Shahzeman, and was King of Samarcand. Each of them ruled over his subjects with justice for the period of twenty years with the utmost enjoyment and happiness.

At the end of twenty years the elder King felt a strong desire to see his brother and ordered his Vizier to repair to him, and bring him. He prepared for his brother handsome presents, such as horses adorned with gold and costly jewels, and also memlooks, and female slaves and expensive stuffs. He then wrote a letter to King Shahzeman, expressing his great desire to see him, and having sealed it, and given it to the Vizier, together with the presents, he ordered him to strain his nerves, and tuck up his skirts, and make haste to go and return.

The Vizier answered: "I hear and obey," and forthwith prepared for the journey. He proceeded night and day over deserts and wastes, until he drew near to the city of Samarcand, when he sent forth a messenger to inform King Shahzeman of his approach. Whereupon the King ordered the chief officers of his court, and the great men of his kingdom, to go forth a day's journey to meet him, and they did so, and walked by his stirrups until they returned to the city. The Vizier presented himself before King Shahzeman, greeted him with a prayer for the continuance of his power and blessing, kissed the ground before him, and handed him the letter. The King took it, and read it, and said to the Vizier: "I will not go until I have entertained thee three days." Accordingly he lodged him in a palace befitting his rank, accommodated his troops in tents, and so they remained three days.

On the fourth day the King equipped himself for the journey, made ready his baggage, and collected costly presents for his brother. He then sent forth his tents, camels and mules and servants, appointed his Vizier to be governor of the country during his absence, and set out towards his brother's dominion. King Shahriar, rejoicing at the tidings of his approach, went forth to meet him, saluted him, and welcomed him with the utmost delight. He ordered that the houses and shops should be decorated on the occasion, and, escorting his brother into the city, entertained him with sports, mirth and hunting.

Now it happened one day that the two Kings went forth alone, from a private door of the palace to walk by the sea. They walked until they arrived at a tree in the midst of a meadow, by a spring of water, on the sea shore. They drank of this spring, and sat down to rest, and, lo, the sea became troubled, and there arose from it a black pillar, ascending towards the sky, and approaching the meadow. Struck with fear at the sight, they climbed up into the tree, which was lofty; and, behold, the black pillar was a Genie of gigantic stature, broad-fronted and bulky, bearing on his head a chest.

The Genie landed, and came to the tree into which the two Kings had climbed, and having seated himself beneath it, opened the chest, and took out of it another box, which he also opened. There came forth from it a young woman fair and beautiful like the shining sun. When the Genie cast his eye upon her he said: "O Lady of noble race, whom I carried off on thy wedding-night, I desire to sleep a little." And he placed his head upon her knee and slept.

The damsel raised her head and saw the two Kings in the tree. She removed the head of the Genie from her knee, and, having placed it on the ground, stood under the tree, and made signs to the two men, saying: "Come down, fear not this Afrite. But if ye do not come down I will rouse him, and he shall put you to a cruel death!" So, being afraid, the Kings came down to her. She then took from her pocket a purse, and drew from this a string upon which were ninety-eight seal rings. "Know," said she, "that the owners of these rings, unknown to this foolish Afrite, gave me all these, therefore give me your two rings, ye brothers!" So they gave her their two rings from their fingers. Then said she to them, "This evil Afrite whom I hate, carried me off on my wedding-night, and put me in this box, and placed the box in the chest, and affixed to the chest seven locks, and deposited me, thus imprisoned, in the bottom of the roaring sea, beneath the dashing waves, not knowing that some day, while he sleeps, I shall surely slay him! In accordance with this says one of the poets:

'Never trust in women, nor rely upon their vows.
They offer a false affection, for perfidy lurks within their clothing.
For greatly indeed to be wondered at is he who hath kept himself safe from woman's artifice!'"

When the two Kings heard these words from her lips they said one to the other: "If this Afrite hath so great a calamity, what will befall us if we have aught to do with women? From now on let us keep ourselves safe from the artifice of women!" And immediately they departed and returned to the city.

As soon as they had entered the palace, King Shahriar caused his wife to be beheaded. And henceforth he took a new wife every day and he ordered her to be killed the morning after the marriage festivities. Thus he continued to do for three years, and the people raised an outcry against him, and fled with their daughters. Such was the case when one day the King ordered the Vizier to bring him a bride according to custom. The Vizier went forth, and searched, and found none, and went back to his house in great fear of what the King might do to him.

Now the Vizier had two daughters, the elder of whom was called Sheherazade, and the younger Dinarzade. The elder daughter, seeing her father sorrowful, said: "Why do I see thee thus changed and oppressed with solicitude?" When the Vizier heard these words from his daughter he related to her all that had happened. "O my father," said Sheherazade, "give me in marriage to this King, and either I shall die, and be a ransom

THE PEOPLE FLED WITH THEIR DAUGHTERS

for one of the daughters of my people, or I shall live and be the cause of their deliverance from him." "I conjure thee," exclaimed her father, "that thou expose not thyself to such peril!" But Sheherazade persisted in her determination and persuaded him until he arrayed her and took her in to King Shahriar.

Now Sheherazade had read many histories of ancient Kings and works of poets, and before going to King Shahriar she gave directions to her younger sister saying to her: "When I have gone to the King I will send to request thee to come. When thou comest do thou say: 'O my sister, relate to me some strange story to beguile our waking hours,' and I will relate a story that shall, if it be the will of Allah, deliver me from death."

So her father the Vizier took Sheherazade to the King, who, when he saw her, rejoiced because of her goodness and beauty. But Sheherazade wept and said: "O King, I have a young sister, and I wish to take leave of her." So the King sent for Dinarzade and she came to her sister and embraced her, and after she had waited for a proper opportunity, she said: "O my sister, relate to us a story to beguile the waking hours of our night." "Most willingly," answered Sheherazade: "if this virtuous King permit me." The King hearing these words and being restless was pleased with the idea of listening to a story, and thus on the first night of the thousand and one, Sheherazade commenced her story-telling.

Chapter I

THE STORY OF THE FISHERMAN AND THE GENIE

THERE was a certain poor fisherman, who had a wife and three children. It was his custom to cast his net every day no more than four times. One day he went forth at the hour of noon to the shore of the sea, and put down his basket, and cast his net, and waited until it was motionless in the water, when he drew together the strings, and found it to be heavy. He pulled but could not draw it up. He then stripped himself, and dived around the net, and pulled until he drew it out. But when he came to examine the net he found in it the carcass of an ass.

He then disencumbered his net of the dead ass, and descending into the sea, cast the net again, and waited until it had sunk and was still, when he pulled it, and found it more heavy than before. He therefore concluded that it was full of fish, so he stripped, and plunged, and dived, and pulled until he raised it, and drew it upon the shore, when he found in it only a large jar full of sand and mud.

He threw the jar aside, cleansed his net, and begging the forgiveness of Allah for his impatience, returned to the sea the third time, and threw his net. He waited until it had sunk and was motionless, he then drew it out, and found in it only a quantity of broken jars and pots.

Upon this he raised his head towards Heaven, and said: "O Allah, thou knowest that I cast my net not more than four times, and I have now cast it three times!" Then exclaiming, "In the name of Allah!" he cast the net again into the sea, and waited until it was still. When he attempted to draw it up he could not, for it clung to the bottom, so he dived again and raised it to the shore. When he opened it he found in it a bottle of brass, filled with something, and having its mouth closed with a stopper of lead, bearing the impression of the seal of our lord Solomon.

At the sight of this, the fisherman was rejoiced. He shook the bottle and found it to be heavy, and said: "I must open it, and see what is in it, and then I will sell the bottle in the copper-market for it is worth ten pieces of gold!" So he took out a knife, and picked at the lead until he extracted it from the bottle. He then laid the bottle on the ground and shook it, but there came forth from it nothing but smoke, which ascended to the sky, and spread over the face of the earth. And after a little while the smoke collected, and became an Afrite whose head was in the clouds, while his feet rested upon the earth. His head was like a dome, his hands were like winnowing-forks, his legs like masts, his mouth resembled a cavern, his teeth were like stones, his nostrils like trumpets, and his eyes like lamps, and he had dishevelled and dust-coloured hair.

When the fisherman beheld this Afrite, the muscles of his side quivered, his teeth were locked together, his spittle dried up, and he saw not his way. But the Afrite, as soon as he perceived him, exclaimed: "There is no deity but Allah! Solomon is the Prophet of Allah! O Prophet of Allah, slay me not, for I will never again oppose thee in word, or rebel against thee in deed!" "O evil Genie," said the fisherman, "Solomon hath been dead a thousand and eight hundred years. What is thy history, and what is thy tale, and what was the cause of thy entering this bottle?"

When the Afrite heard these words of the fisherman he said: "There is no deity but Allah! Receive news, O fisherman, of thy being instantly put to a most cruel death." "Wherefore," exclaimed the fisherman, "wouldst thou kill me, when I have liberated thee from the bottle, rescued thee from the bottom of the sea, and brought thee up on dry land?" The Afrite answered: "Choose what kind of death thou wilt die, and in what manner thou shalt be killed." "What is my offence," said the fisherman, "that this should be my reward from thee?" "Hear my story, O fisherman," the Afrite replied. "Tell it then," said the fisherman, "and short be thy words, for my soul hath sunk to my feet."

"Know then," said the Afrite, "that I am one of the heretical Genii. I rebelled against Solomon the son of David, and he sent to me his Vizier, who came upon me forcibly, and took me to him in bonds, and placed me before him. When Solomon saw me he offered up a prayer for protection against me, and exhorted me to embrace the faith, but I refused. Upon which he called for this bottle and confined me in it, and closed it with a leaden stopper, which he stamped with the Most Great Name. He then gave orders to a Genie, who carried me away, and threw me into the midst of the sea. There I remained a hundred years, and I said in

THE SMOKE COLLECTED AND BECAME AN AFRITE

my heart, Whosoever shall liberate me, I will enrich him for ever! But the hundred years passed over, and no one liberated me. I entered upon another hundred years, and I said: Whosoever shall liberate me, I will open to him the treasures of the earth! But no one did so. And four hundred years passed over me, and I said, Whosoever shall liberate me, I will perform for him three wishes! But still no one liberated me. I then fell in a rage and said within myself: Whosoever shall liberate me now, I will kill him. I will only suffer him to choose in what manner he shall die! And, lo, now thou hast liberated me, and I have given thee thy choice of the manner in which thou shalt die."

When the fisherman heard the story of the Afrite he said within himself: "This is a Genie, and I am a man, and Allah hath given me sound reason, therefore I will now plot the destruction of this evil one with my reason and my art." So he said to the Afrite, "By the Most Great Name engraved upon the seal of Solomon, I will ask thee one question, and wilt thou answer it to me truly?" On hearing the mention of the Most Great Name, the Afrite trembled and replied: "Yes, ask and be brief." The fisherman then said: "How wast thou in this bottle? It will not contain thy hand or thy foot, how then can it contain thy whole body?" "Dost thou not believe that I was in it?" exclaimed the Afrite, and he shook and became converted again into smoke, which rose to the sky, and then became condensed, and entered the bottle little by little, until it was all enclosed. The fisherman hastily snatched the leaden stopper, and having replaced it in the mouth of the bottle, called out to the Afrite: "Choose what manner of death thou wilt die!"

On hearing these words of the fisherman, the Afrite endeavoured to escape, but could not. The fisherman then took the bottle to the brink of the sea, saying: "I will assuredly throw thee here into the sea." The Afrite exclaimed: "Nay, nay!" To which the fisherman answered, "Yea, without fail. I will throw thee into the sea, and if thou hast been there a thousand and eight hundred years, I will make thee to remain there until the hour of judgment!" "Open to me," said the Afrite, "that I may confer benefits upon thee." The fisherman replied, "Thou liest, thou accursed. I and thou are like the Vizier of the Grecian King and the sage Douban." "What," said the Afrite, "was the case of the Vizier of the Grecian King, and the sage Douban, and what is their story?" The fisherman answered as follows:

STORY OF THE GRECIAN KING AND THE SAGE DOUBAN

KNOW, O Afrite, there was in former times, a monarch who was King of the Grecians, possessing great treasure, and numerous and valiant forces, and troops of every description. But he was afflicted with leprosy, which the physicians and sages had failed to cure, neither their potions nor powders, nor ointments were of any benefit to him.

At length there arrived at the city of this King a great sage, stricken in years, called the sage Douban. He was acquainted with languages, medicine and astrology, as well as with the properties of plants, dried and fresh, and he was versed in the wisdom of the philosophers.

After the sage had arrived in the city he heard of the King, and of the leprosy which afflicted him. So one morning he attired himself in the richest of his apparel, and presented himself before the King. He kissed the ground before him and said, "O King, I have heard of the disease which hath attacked thee, and I will cure thee without giving thee to drink any potion, or anointing thee with ointment."

When the King heard his words he said: "Verily, if thou cure me, I will enrich thee and thy children's children! I will heap favours upon thee, and whatsoever thou shalt desire shall be thine, and thou shalt be my companion and friend." He then bestowed upon the sage a robe of honour and other presents.

The sage went out from the presence of the King and returned to his abode. He selected certain medicines and drugs, and made a golf-stick, with a hollow handle, into which he put the medicines and drugs. He then made a ball, skilfully formed. The following day he went again to the King, and kissed the ground before him and directed him to repair to the horse-course, and to play with ball and golf-stick. The King attended by his Emirs, and Viziers, went thither. As soon as he arrived there the sage Douban handed him the golf-stick saying: "Take this golf-stick, grasp it thus, and ride along the horse-course, and strike the ball with all thy force, until the palm of thy hand becomes moist, when the medicines will penetrate into thy hand, and pervade thy whole body, then shalt thou find thyself cured, and peace be on thee." So the King did as the sage directed, and the leprosy left him, and his skin was clear as white silver.

On the following morning the King entered the council-chamber, and sat upon his throne, and the chamberlains and other great officers of his court came before him. The sage Douban also presented himself, and when the King saw him he rose in haste, and seated him by his side. And food was set before them, and the sage ate with the King, and remained as his guest all day. And the King made him his companion and familiar friend, and gave him two thousand pieces of gold, besides dresses of honour and other presents, and mounted him on his own horse, and so the sage returned to his house.

Now there was among the King's Viziers, one of ill aspect, and of evil star, sordid, avaricious, and of an envious and malicious disposition. When he saw that the King had made the sage Douban his friend, he envied him, and meditated evil against him. So he approached the King, and kissed the ground before him, and said: "O glorious King! It hath been said by the ancients:

> 'He who looketh not to results,
> Fortune will not attend him.'

Now I have seen that the King is in a way that is not right since he hath bestowed favours upon his enemy, and upon him who desireth the downfall of his dominion. He hath treated him with kindness, and made him his friend. I fear therefore for the King, the consequence of this conduct."

At this the King was troubled: "Who," asked he, "is mine enemy, to whom I show kindness?" "O King,"

THERE ARRIVED A GREAT SAGE VERSED IN THE WISDOM OF THE PHILOSOPHERS

replied the Vizier, "if thou hast been asleep, awake! I allude to the sage Douban. If thou trust in this sage, he will kill thee in the foulest manner. He cured thee by the means of a thing thou heldest in thy hand. What will prevent him from killing thee by a thing that thou shalt hold in the like manner?" The King answered: "Thou hast spoken the truth! It is probable that this sage came as a spy to accomplish my death. What then, O Vizier, shall be done to him?" The Vizier answered: "Send for him immediately, and strike off his head. Betray him, before he betray thee!"

The King immediately sent for the sage, who came full of joy, not knowing what was decreed to befall him. "Knowest thou," said the King, "wherefore I have summoned thee?" The sage answered: "None knoweth what is secret but Allah, whose name be exalted!" Then said the King, "I have summoned thee that I might take thy life away. It hath been told me that thou art a spy, and that thou hast come hither to kill me, but I will prevent thee, by killing thee first!" and so saying, he called out to the executioner: "Strike off the head of this traitor, and relieve me from his wickedness." The executioner then advanced, and bandaged the eyes of the sage, and having drawn his sword waited for the signal of the King.

"Spare me!" said the sage, "spare me, and so may Allah spare thee, and destroy me not lest Allah destroy thee! Wherefore wouldst thou kill me, and what offence hath been committed by me? Wouldst thou return me the recompense of the crocodile?" "What," said the King, "is the story of the crocodile?" "I cannot relate it while in this condition," the sage answered, "but I conjure thee by Allah to spare me, and so may He spare thee!" And he wept bitterly. Then one of the chief officers of the King arose, and said: "O King, give up to me the blood of this sage. We have not seen him commit any offence against thee, but he cured thee of thy disease." "He is a spy," the King answered, "that hath come hither to kill me. I must therefore kill him, and then I shall feel myself safe."

Now when the sage Douban heard these words he knew there was no escape for him, so he said: "O King, grant me some respite so that I may return to my house, and give directions to my family and neighbours to bury me, and dispose of my medical books. Among my books is one of especial value which I offer as a present to thee. When thou hast cut off my head, if thou open this book, and count three leaves, and then read three lines on the page to the left, the head will speak to thee, and answer whatever thou shalt ask."

At this the King was excessively astonished and shook with delight, and he sent the sage in the custody of guards, bidding him descend to his house, to settle with all speed his affairs. On the following day he went up to the court, and the Emirs, and Viziers and all the great officers of the state went thither also, and the court resembled a flower-garden.

When the sage had entered he presented himself before the King bearing an old book, and a small pot containing a powder. He sat down, and said, "Bring me a tray." So they brought one, and he poured out the powder in it, and spread it. Then said he: "O King, take this book and when thou hast cut off my head, place it upon this tray, and press it down upon the powder, then open the book." As soon as the sage had said that the King gave orders to strike off his head, and it was done.

The King then took the sage's head, placed it on a tray, opened the book, and found that its pages were stuck together, so he put his finger to his mouth, and moistened it, and opened the first leaf and the second and the third. He opened six leaves, and looked at them, but found on them no writing. So he said: "O sage, there is nothing written in it." The head of the sage answered, "Turn over more pages." The King did so, and in a little while poison from the leaves penetrated his body, for the book was poisoned, and the King fell back and cried out. Upon this the head of the sage said:

"Thou madest use of thy power, and used it tyrannically. Soon it became as though it never had existed!
    This is the reward of thy conduct, and Fortune is blameless!"

When the head of the sage Douban had uttered these words, the King immediately fell down dead.

   *   *   *   *   *   *   *   *   *

Here Sheherazade perceived the light of day, and discontinued her story. "How excellent, how pleasant is thy story!" said Dinarzade her sister. "It is nothing," answered Sheherazade, "compared to the story I will tell to-night, if I live and the King spare me!" "Verily," exclaimed the King, "I will not kill thee until I hear the remainder of thy story!"

When the King went forth to the hall of judgment, the Vizier went thither with his daughter's grave-clothes under his arm. But the King gave judgment, and transacted the business of his empire, without ordering

Sheherazade to be put to death, and the Vizier was much astonished. The court then dissolved, and the King returned to the privacy of his palace.

When night was come, Sheherazade again commenced her story-telling, and related as follows:

CONTINUATION OF THE STORY OF THE FISHERMAN AND THE GENIE

NOW, O Afrite," continued the fisherman, "know that if the King of the Grecians had spared the sage Douban, Allah had spared him. But he refused to spare the sage, therefore Allah destroyed him, and thou Afrite, if thou hadst spared me, Allah had spared thee, and I had spared thee. But thou desiredst my death, therefore will I put thee to death, imprisoned in this bottle, and will throw thee here into the sea."

The Afrite, upon this, cried out: "I conjure thee by Allah, O fisherman, that thou do it not! Spare me in generosity, and be not angry with me for what I did! Display humanity and liberate me, and I vow to thee that I will never do thee harm, but, on the contrary, I will enrich thee forever!"

Upon this the fisherman bound the Afrite by oaths and vows, and made him swear by the Most Great Name of Allah, that he would do him no harm. Then the fisherman opened the bottle and the smoke ascended and collected, and became as before an Afrite of hideous form, and the Afrite kicked the bottle into the sea. When the fisherman saw this he was filled with fear, but the Afrite laughed, and walking on before him, said: "O fisherman, follow me." The fisherman did so, not believing in his escape. They quitted the neighbourhood of the city, and ascended a mountain, and descended into a wide desert tract, in the midst of which was a lake of water. Here the Afrite stopped and ordered the fisherman to cast his net and take some fish.

And the fisherman looking into the lake saw in it fish of different colours, white and red and blue and yellow. He cast his net, and drew it in, and found in it four fish, each of a different colour. The Afrite then said: "Take them to the Sultan, and present them to him, and he will give thee what will enrich thee. At present I know of no other way of rewarding thee, having been in the sea a thousand and eight hundred years, and not having seen the surface of the earth until now. Take not the fish from the lake more than once each day, and now I commend thee to the care of Allah." Having said thus he struck the earth with his foot, and it clove asunder, and swallowed him.

The fisherman then went back to the city, and going up unto the King he presented him with the fish. The King in return gave him four hundred pieces of gold, and the fisherman took them in his lap, and returned to his wife joyful and happy. The King was excessively astonished at the fish, for he had never seen any like them in the course of his life, and he said: "Give these to the slave cook-maid and bid her prepare them for me." Now this maid had been sent as a present to him by the King of the Grecians, three days before, and he had not yet tried her skill. The Vizier therefore gave her the fish and ordered her to fry them.

The cook-maid took the fish, cleaned them, and arranged them in the frying-pan, and left them until one side was cooked, and turned them over on the other side. And, lo, the wall of the kitchen clove asunder, and there came forth from it a tall damsel, smooth-cheeked and beautiful in countenance, wearing on her head a blue handkerchief, and rings in her ears, and bracelets on her wrists, and rings set with precious jewels on her fingers. She dipped the end of a rod in the frying-pan and said: "O fish, O fish, are ye remaining faithful to your covenant?" The fish raised their heads from the frying-pan and answered:

"Yes, yes! If thou return, we return. If thou come, we
   come.
   If thou forsake, we verily do the same."

Then the damsel overturned the frying-pan and departed by the way she had entered, and the wall of the kitchen closed up again.

The cook-maid, terrified, arose, and, behold, the four fish were burnt like charcoal! As she sat reproaching herself, the Vizier approached and said to her: "Bring the fish to the Sultan." And the maid wept and told him what had happened. The Vizier was astonished, and sending for the fisherman ordered him to bring four more fish like the others.

The fisherman accordingly went to the lake, and threw his net, and, when he had drawn it, found in it four fish as before. He took them to the Vizier who went with them to the maid, and bade her fry them in his presence. The maid prepared the fish, and put them in the frying-pan, left them until one side was cooked, then turned them over. In a little while the wall clove asunder, and the damsel appeared, clad as before, and holding the rod. She dipped the end of the rod into the frying-pan, and said: "O fish, O fish, are ye remaining faithful to your convenant?" The fish raised their heads and answered as before:

"Yes, yes! If thou return, we return. If thou come, we
  come.
  If thou forsake, we verily do the same."

And the damsel overturned the frying-pan with the rod and returned by the way she had entered, and the wall closed up again.

The Vizier astonished went to the King, and informed him of what had happened. The King said: "I must see with mine own eyes." He sent therefore to the fisherman commanding him to bring four fish like the former. The next day the fisherman repaired to the lake, and brought the fish hence to the King, who gave him again four hundred pieces of gold. The King then ordered the Vizier to cook the fish in his presence, and he replied: "I hear and obey."

The Vizier brought the frying-pan, and, after he had cleaned the fish, he threw them into it. As soon as he had turned them over, the wall clove asunder, and there came forth from it a negro, as big as a bull, holding in his hand a branch of a green tree, and he said in a terrible voice: "O fish, O fish, are ye remaining faithful to your covenant?" And the fish raised their heads and answered:

"Yes, yes! If thou return, we return. If thou come, we
  come.
  If thou forsake, we verily do the same."

The black then approached the frying-pan and over-turned it, and the fish became like charcoal, and he went away through the wall, which closed again as before.

Then said the King: "There must be some strange tale connected with these fish." So he sent for the fisherman and asked him whence the fish came. "From a lake between four mountains," the fisherman answered, "about half an hour's journey from this city." At this the King was astonished, and ordering his troops, he set out immediately with them and the fisherman. They ascended the mountain and descended into a wide valley tract, which they had never seen before in all their lives. And between four mountains was a lake, and in it fish red and white and yellow and blue. The King paused in astonishment, and said to his troops: "Have any of you seen this lake before?" They all answered: "No." Then said the King: "Verily, I will not enter my city, nor will I sit upon my throne, until I know the true history of this lake and of its fish."

And having called for his Vizier, the King gave him charge of all the troops. He then disguised himself, and slung on his sword, and departed secretly by night. He journeyed night and day for the space of two days, when there appeared in the distance a black object. He approached, and found it to be a palace built of black stone, overlaid with iron. One of the leaves of its door was open, the other shut.

The King knocked gently, but heard no answer. He knocked a second and a third time, but again heard no answer. He knocked a fourth time with violence, but no one answered. Thinking the palace was empty, he took courage, and entered the passage, and passed into the court which was in the midst of the palace, and he found no one there. The court was magnificently furnished, and in the centre was a fountain with four lions of red gold, which poured forth water from their mouths, like pearls and jewels. Around the fountain were birds and over the top of the court was extended a net, which prevented their flying out. But he saw no person whom he could ask about the lake, and the fish, and the mountain, and the palace.

While he was reflecting upon these things, he heard a voice of lamentation, and sorrow, which proceeded from the direction of a curtain suspended before the door of a chamber. He raised the curtain and beheld a young man sitting on a sofa. He was a handsome youth, of pleasant voice and rosy cheeks, and was clad in a vest of silk embroidered with gold. The King saluted him, and the young man returned the salutation, saying: "O my master, excuse my not rising!" "O youth," answered the King, "tell me the meaning of the lake, and of its fish of various colours, and of this palace, and of the reason of thy being alone, and of thy lamentation!"

When the young man heard these words he wept bitterly. He stretched forth his hand, and lifted up the skirts of his clothes, and, lo, half of him, from his waist to the soles of his feet, was stone. He then said: "Know, O King, that the story of the fish is extraordinary!" and he related as follows:

THE STORY OF THE YOUNG KING OF THE BLACK ISLES

MY father was king of the city which was situated here. His name was Mahmoud, and he was lord of the Black Isles, and of the four mountains. After a reign of seventy years he died, and I succeeded to his throne. Whereupon I took as my wife the daughter of my uncle, and we lived together happily for five years.

One day my wife went to the bath. I commanded the cook to prepare the supper, and entered this palace and lay down to sleep. I had ordered two maids to fan me, and one of them sat at my head and the other at my feet. But I was restless and could not sleep, my eyes were closed, but my spirit was awake, and I heard the maid at my head say to her at my feet: "Verily our lord is unfortunate, and what a pity it is that he should have such a wicked wife! For every night when he drinketh his cup of wine, she putteth a sleeping potion into it, in consequence he sleepeth so soundly that he knoweth not what happeneth. After she hath given him the wine to drink, she dresseth herself, and goeth out, and is absent until daybreak. When she returneth, she burneth a perfume under his nose, and he waketh from his sleep."

When I heard these words, the light became darkness before my face, and I was overcome with horror. My wife returned from the bath, the table was prepared, and we ate and drank as usual. I then called for the wine which I was accustomed to drink before I lay down to sleep. She handed me the cup, but I turned away, and, pretending to drink it, poured it into my bosom, and immediately lay down, and closed my eyes. Then said she: "Sleep on! I wish that thou wouldst never wake again! I abhor thee, and abhor thy person, and my soul is weary of thy company!"

She then arose and attired herself in her most magnificent apparel, and having perfumed herself, and slung on her sword, opened the door of the palace and went out. I got up immediately, and followed her through the streets to the city gates. She pronounced some words which I understood not, and the locks fell off, and the gates opened. She went out, I still following her without her knowledge. She proceeded until she came to a building, made of mud, and having a dome. She entered and I climbed upon the roof of the building, and, looking down through an aperture, I beheld there a black slave, whose large lips, one of which overlapped the other, gathered up the sand from the pebbly floor, while he lay upon a few stalks of sugar-cane.

My wife entered, and kissed the ground before this slave, and he raised his head towards her and said: "Woe unto thee, thou miserable woman! Wherefore hast thou remained away until this hour? Prepare me something to eat. Uncover the dough-pan. It contains some cooked rats' bones. Bring to me then the earthen pot of barley-beer."

So she arose, and uncovered the dough-pan, and gave him to eat of the cooked rats' bones, and brought to him the earthen pot of barley-beer, and she waited on him like a slave. When I saw her do this I became filled with rage. I descended from the roof of the building, entered, concealed my face in my cloak, and lifting my sword, I struck the slave a blow upon his neck. I thought I had killed him, but the blow instead of severing his neck, only cut the gullet and skin and flesh. When I thought that I had disposed of him I returned to my palace, and lay down upon my bed.

On the following day, I observed that my wife had cut off her hair and put on mourning apparel, and she said to me: "O my husband, blame me not for what I do, for I have received news that my mother is dead, and that my father hath been slain, and that one of my two brothers hath died of a poisonous sting, and the other by the fall of a house. It is natural, therefore, that I should weep and mourn!" Accordingly she continued mourning and weeping and wailing a whole year. After which she said to me: "I wish to build in thy palace a tomb, that I may repair thither to mourn alone." I replied: "Do what thou seest fit."

So she built a tomb, after which she removed thither the slave, and there she lodged him. He was excessively weak, for from the day on which I had wounded him, he had never spoken. My wife visited him every day, to weep and mourn over him, and took him wine to drink and boiled meats. When I discovered this I entered her apartment with a drawn sword in my hand, and I was about to strike off her head, but she arose and standing before me, pronounced some words which I understood not, and said: "May Allah by means of my enchantment make thee to be half of stone and half of flesh." Whereupon I became as thou seest, unable to move, neither dead nor alive! She enchanted the city and its markets and fields. The inhabitants of our city were Mohammetans, and Christians, and Jews, and Magians, and she transformed them into fish. The white are Mohammetans, the red the Magians, the blue the Christians, and the yellow the Jews. She also transformed the four islands into four mountains and placed them around the lake. Every day she tortures me, inflicting upon me a hundred lashes with a leather whip, until the blood flows from my wounds. Having said thus the young man wept and lamented aloud.

The King on hearing this story was filled with rage. He arose and slung on his sword, and went to the place where the slave lay. After remarking the candles and lamps and perfumes and ointments, he approached the slave, and with a blow of his sword slew him. He then carried him on his back, and threw him into a well, which he found in the palace. Returning to the tomb, he clad himself in the slave's clothes, and lay down with the drawn sword by his side.

Soon after the vile enchantress came to her husband, and having pulled off his clothes, took the whip and regardless of his cries beat him. She then put on his garments, and repaired to the slave with a cup of wine and a bowl of boiled meat. Entering the tomb she wept and wailed, exclaiming: "O my master, answer me! O my master, speak to me!" Upon this the King speaking in a low voice ejaculated: "Ah, ah, there is no strength nor power but in Allah!" On hearing these words she screamed with joy, exclaiming: "Possibly my master is restored to health!" The King again lowering his voice, replied: "Thou wretched woman! Thou deservest not that I should address thee because all day long thou tormentest thy husband, while he calleth out and imploreth the aid of Allah." "Then, with thy permission," she replied, "I will liberate him from his sufferings." "Liberate him," said the King, "and return here to me."

She replied: "I hear and obey," and immediately arose, and, taking a cup of water, pronounced certain words over it, upon which it began to boil like a cauldron. She then went to her husband, sprinkled some of it upon him, saying: "By virtue of what I have uttered, be changed from stone to flesh!" And instantly he shook, and stood upon his feet rejoicing in his liberation. And she cried out in his face: "Depart, and return not hither, or I will kill thee!" **And he departed.**

She returned to the tomb and said: "O my master, I have accomplished thy desire. Come forth to me that I may see thee." "The people of this city," the King replied, "are still enchanted. Every night, at the middle hour, the fish raise their heads, and imprecate vengeance upon thee. Liberate them, then come and take my hand and raise me." On hearing these words she sprang up full of happiness, and hastened to the lake, where taking a little of the water she pronounced some words over it, whereupon the fish raised their heads, and immediately became men again. The enchantment was removed from the city, and the mountains also became changed into islands as they were at first.

The enchantress returned to the King, whom she still imagined to be the slave, and said to him: "O my beloved, stretch forth thy honoured hand that I may kiss it!" But the King having his keen-edged sword ready in his hand, thrust it into her bosom, and clove her in twain.

He then went forth, and found the young man who had been enchanted, waiting for his return. The young Prince kissed his hand and thanked him, then said the King, "Wilt thou remain in thy city or come with me to my capital?" "O King of the age," answered the young man, "dost thou know that between thee and thy city is a distance of a year's journey? Thou camest in two days and a half only because the city was enchanted. But, O King, I will never quit thee for the twinkling of an eye!"

The King rejoiced at his words and said, "Praise be

to Allah, who hath given thee to me! Thou art my son, for I have never been blessed with a son!" And they embraced each other. The young Prince, who had been enchanted, then went to his palace, arranged the affairs of his kingdom and prepared everything needful for a journey, and he departed with the King, whose heart burned with desire to see again his own country.

They continued their journey night and day for a whole year until they drew near to the city of the King. The Vizier and the troops, who had lost all hopes of his return, came forth joyfully to meet him, and he entered his city and sat upon his throne.

And when all things were restored to order, the King said to his Vizier: "Bring hither the fisherman who presented to me the fish." So the fisherman came, and the King invested him with a dress of honour, and asked if he had any children. The fisherman informed him that he had a son and two daughters. The King on hearing this took as his wife one of the daughters, and the young Prince married the other. The King also conferred upon the son the office of treasurer. He then sent the Vizier to the city of the young prince, the capital of the Black Isles, and invested him with its sovereignty. As to the fisherman he became the wealthiest of the people of his age, and his daughters continued to be the wives of the King and the Prince until they died.

* * * * * * * * *

"But this," added Sheherazade, "is not more wonderful than what happened to the porter."

Chapter II

STORY OF THE PORTER AND THE LADIES OF BAGDAD AND THE THREE ROYAL MENDICANTS

THERE was in the days of the Caliph Haroun Er Raschid a man who was a porter of the city of Bagdad, and one day as he sat in the market, reclining against his crate, there came to him a lady wrapped in a mantle of gold embroidered silk, with a border of gold lace. She raised her face-veil and displayed beneath it a pair of black eyes with long lashes, and features of perfect beauty. She said, with a sweet voice: "Bring thy crate and follow me."

The porter took up his crate and followed her to a shop, where she bought for a piece of gold a quantity of olives and two large vessels of wine, which she placed in the crate, saying to the porter: "Take it up and follow me." He took up the crate and followed her to the shop of a fruiterer where she bought Syrian apples, and Othmanee quinces, and peaches of Oman, and jasmine of Aleppo, and water-lilies of Damascus, and Sultanee citrons, and cucumbers and limes of the Nile. She bought also sweet-scented myrtle, and sprigs of the henna-tree, and chamomile, anemonies, violets, and pomegranate-flowers and eglantine. All these she put into the porter's crate, and said to him: "Take it up, and follow me."

So he took it up and followed her until she stopped at the shop of a butcher, to whom she said: "Cut off ten pounds of meat." The butcher cut it off for her, and she wrapped it in a banana leaf, and put it in the crate, and said again: "Take it up, O porter." He did so, and followed her to the shop of a confectioner, where she bought a dish and filled it with sweets of every kind, and put it into the crate. Then said the porter, "If thou hadst told me beforehand I would have brought a mule to carry all these things!" The lady smiled at this remark, and next stopped at a perfumer's, where she bought ten kinds of scented waters, rose-water, orange-flower-water, willow-flower-water, together with sugar, and a sprinkling-bottle of rose-water infused with musk. She bought also frankincense, aloes-wood, ambergris, and musk, and wax candles, and placing these in the crate she said: "Take up thy crate, and follow me."

The porter, therefore, took up his crate, and followed her until she came to a handsome and lofty house, with an ebony door, overlaid with plates of red gold. The lady knocked, whereupon the door was opened by a portress, who was a damsel tall and fair and beautiful and of elegant form, with a forehead like the bright new moon, eyes like those of gazelles, cheeks like anemonies, and a mouth like the seal of Solomon. When the porter beheld her he was overcome by her beauty, and the crate nearly fell from his head.

The portress, standing within the door said to the cateress and the porter: "Ye are welcome." And they entered, and followed her into a spacious saloon, decorated with various colours, and carved wood-work, and fountains, and benches, and closets with curtains hanging before them. At the upper end of the saloon was a sofa of alabaster, inlaid with large pearls and jewels, with a curtain of red satin suspended over it, and on this sofa was seated a young lady of the most extraordinary beauty.

This third lady, rising from the sofa, advanced with a slow and elegant gait to the middle of the saloon. "O my sisters," said she, "why stand ye still? Lift down the burden from the head of this poor porter." Then the cateress placed herself before him, and the portress behind him, and the third lady assisting them, they lifted the crate down from his head. They then took the things out of the crate and gave the porter two pieces of gold, saying, "Depart, O porter."

But the porter stood looking at the ladies and admiring their beauty, for he had never seen any more handsome. When he saw that they had not a man among them, and when he gazed on the wine and fruits and sweet-scented flowers, he was full of astonishment, and hesitated to go out. Then said one of the ladies to him: "Why dost thou not go? Is thy hire too little?" "Verily, O my mistress," exclaimed the porter, "I am satisfied with my hire, but I wonder at seeing no man among you, to amuse you with his company. Ye are three only and have need of a fourth, who should be a man of sense, discreet, and a concealer of secrets." "We are maidens," they replied, "who fear to impart our secret to him who will not keep it, for we have read in a certain book this verse:

'Guard thy secret from another, intrust it not,
For he who intrusteth a secret hath lost it.'"

"By your existence," said the porter, "I am a man of sense and act in accordance with the saying of the poet:

'A secret is with me as a house with a lock,
Whose key is lost and whose door is sealed.'"

When the ladies heard these words they consulted together and then said to the porter: "Stay, thou art welcome, but first read what is inscribed upon the door." Accordingly he went to the door and found written upon it in letters of gold,

Speak not of that which concerns thee not!
Lest thou hear that which will not please thee!

Then said the porter: "Bear witness to my promise that I will not speak of that which does not concern me."

The cateress arose, and prepared the table by the pool of the fountain. She strained the wine and arranged the bottles, and lighted the candles and burned some aloes-wood. She made ready the feast and they sat down to the table, the porter, sitting with them, thinking that he was in a dream!

While they were eating and drinking they heard a knock at the door, and, lo, there stood without three foreigners, each blind of the left eye, and they begged a night's lodging. The ladies consulted together, then the mistress of the house said: "Let them enter on condition that they speak not of that which concerns them not, lest they hear that which will not please them."

So the portress brought in the three men, each blind of one eye, and being mendicants they drew back and saluted, but the ladies arose, and seated them, and handed to them food and drink. When they were satis-

fied the portress brought a tambourine, a lute and a
Persian harp, and the mendicants arose, one took the
tambourine, another the lute and the third the harp,
and they played, while the ladies accompanied them
with songs. While they were thus amusing themselves
somebody knocked at the door, and the portress went
to see who was there. Now the cause of the knocking
was this.

The Caliph Haroun Er Raschid had gone forth this
night in search of adventure, accompanied by Jaafar
his Vizier and Mesrour his chief executioner. He was
disguised as a merchant, and as he went through the
city he happened to pass the house of these ladies and
hearing the sound of music and jollity he said to Jaafar,
"I wish to enter this house, and to see who is giving this
concert." Jaafar therefore knocked at the door, and
when the portress opened it, he begged for food and a
night's lodging. The portress seeing them dressed like
merchants and that they had a respectable air, returned, and consulted her sisters, and they said: "Admit
them."

So the Caliph entered, with Jaafar and Mesrour, and
the ladies saluted them saying: "Welcome are our
guests, but we have a condition to impose upon you,
that ye speak not of that which concerns you not, lest
ye hear that which will not please you." "Good,"
they answered, "we accept the condition."

And they all sat down to feast and make merry.
And the ladies brought wine to the Caliph, but he drew
back and refused it, saying: "I drink not wine for I
have a vow." Whereupon the portress spread before
him an embroidered cloth, and placed upon it a china
bottle of willow-flower-water. She added to it a lump

of ice, and sweetened it with sugar. The Caliph thanked her, and said to himself: "To-morrow I will reward her for this kind act."

After a while the mistress of the house arose, and said to the cateress: "Arise, O my sister, and let us fulfil our debt." The cateress left the saloon, and soon returned leading two black hounds, with chains around their necks. She dragged them into the midst of the saloon, and the mistress of the house tucked up her sleeves above her wrist, and taking a whip, fell to beating one of the hounds who whined, and howled and shed tears. Then the lady threw down the whip, and pressed the hound to her bosom, and wiped away its tears, and kissed its head. She then said to the cateress: "Take her back, and give me the other." And she whipped it even as she had whipped the first.

The mistress of the house then seated herself upon a sofa of alabaster, overlaid with gold and silver, and said to the portress and cateress: "Now perform your parts." The portress seated herself upon the sofa, and the cateress brought from a closet a bag of satin, with green fringe, and took from it a lute. She tuned the lute, and played upon it a plaintive air accompanying it with a song, and as soon as the portress heard the song, she cried out, rent her clothes, and fell fainting on the floor, and the Caliph perceived upon her bosom marks of beatings. The cateress sprinkled rose-water on her face and she recovered.

The Caliph was filled with astonishment at all he saw, and said to Jaafar: "Seest thou this woman, and the marks of beatings upon her? Verily I cannot keep silence, nor rest, until I know the history of this damsel and of the two hounds." But Jaafar replied:

"O my lord, these damsels have made us vow that we would not speak of that which concerned us not, lest we should hear that which would not please us!" The Caliph then turned to the mendicants and said: "Are ye of this house?" "No," they answered, "we thought that this house belonged to the man who is sitting with thee." But at this the porter exclaimed: "Verily, I have never seen this place before to-night! I wish that I had passed the night among the mounds, rather than here!" Then the men all consulted together and said: "We are seven men, and they are but three women, therefore we will force them to tell us their history." And they all agreed to this except Jaafar. "This is not right or honourable," he said, "for we are their guests, and they made a covenant with us that we should not ask concerning what we saw." Words followed words, at last it was decided that the porter should question the ladies.

The porter approached the mistress of the house and said: "O my mistress, I ask thee and conjure thee, by Allah, that thou tellest us the story of these two hounds, and why thy sister bears the scars of beatings." The lady turned to the other men, and inquired: "Did ye bid him ask this?" They answered: "Yes," excepting Jaafar, who was silent. Then the mistress of the house became filled with anger, and she tucked up her sleeve above her wrist, and struck the floor three times, and immediately a door opened and there rushed forth from it seven black slaves, each having in his hand a drawn sword. The lady said to them: "Tie behind them the hands of these men of many words. But give them a short respite, until I have inquired of them their histories, before ye behead them." And the black slaves threw the men to the ground and bound their hands behind them.

"By Allah, O my mistress," exclaimed the porter, "kill me not for the offence of others! Verily our night would have been pleasant, if it had not been for these mendicants, whose presence is enough to convert a well-peopled city into a heap of ruins! And as the poet says:

'How good it is to pardon one able to resist!
How much better to pardon one who is helpless!'"

On hearing these words the lady's anger changed to laughter, and turning to the Caliph and Jaafar she said: "Were ye not persons of high distinction, I would behead you immediately. But each of the others shall relate his story, and the cause of his coming to our abode, and then go his way in peace and safety!"

The first to advance was the porter, who said: "O my mistress, I am a porter. This cateress loaded me and brought me here. This is my story, and peace be on thee." Then said the lady: "Go in peace!" "Nay," answered the porter, "I will not go until I have heard the stories of my companions." The first mendicant then advanced and related as follows:

STORY OF THE FIRST ROYAL MENDICANT—THE LOST TOMB

KNOW, O my mistress, that the cause of my having lost my eye is this: My father was a King, and he had a brother who was also a King. It happened that I was born on the same day that the son of my uncle was born, and years and days passed away until we attained to manhood.

Now it was my custom to visit my uncle yearly, and to remain with him several months. On one of these occasions my uncle was absent, and my cousin paid me great honour. He slaughtered sheep for me, and strained the wine, and we sat down to feast. Then said my cousin: "O son of my uncle, wilt thou assist me in a great affair? I beg that thou wilt not oppose me in that which I desire to do!" and he made me swear to him with great oaths that I would aid him to attain his desire. Rising immediately he absented himself for a while, and then returned, followed by a woman veiled and magnificently dressed. He said to me: "Take this woman to the burial-ground, and wait there for me."

I could not oppose him, or refuse to comply with his request, on account of the oaths I had sworn, so I took the woman, and went with her to the burial-ground. When we had sat there a short time, my cousin came, bearing a basin of water, and a bag of plaster, and a small adze. Going to a tomb in the midst of the burial-ground, he pried apart the stones and dug up the earth with the adze, and uncovered a flat stone, under which was a vaulted staircase. He then looked towards me and said: "O son of my uncle, when I have descended into this place, replace the trap-door and the earth above it as they were before. Do thou then knead together the plaster in this bag and the water in this basin, and plaster the stones of the tomb, so that no man may know that it hath been opened. For a whole year I have been preparing this place, and no one knew of it but Allah! May Allah never deprive thy friends of thy presence! Farewell, O son of mine uncle!" And having uttered these words, he took the woman by the hand, and together they descended the stairs.

When they had disappeared, I replaced the trap-door, doing as my cousin had ordered me, until the tomb was restored to the state in which it was at first. After which I returned to the palace of mine uncle, who was still absent on a hunting excursion. I slept that night, and when morning came I repented of what I had done for my cousin, but repentance was of no avail. I went out to the burial-ground, and searched for the tomb, but could not discover it. I ceased not my search until the approach of night, but not finding the place, re-turned to the palace. I neither ate nor drank. My heart was troubled respecting my cousin, since I knew not what had become of him, and I fell into excessive grief. I passed the night sorrowful until morning, and went again to the burial-ground, where I searched among all the tombs, but I could not find the one for which I looked. My grief increased until I almost went mad, so I departed and returned to my father's country.

On my arrival at his capital, a party of men at the city-gate, sprang upon me, and bound me. I was struck with utmost astonishment and excessive fear for I was the son of the Sultan of that city, and the men who bound me were the servants of my father. I asked the cause of this conduct, and one of them who had been my servant said: "Fortune hath betrayed thy father! The troops have been false to him, and his Vizier hath killed him, and we were lying in wait to take thee." And the men took me bound before the Vizier.

Now the Vizier hated me, and the cause of his enmity

was this: as a boy I was fond of shooting with the cross-bow. It happened one day that as I was standing on the roof of my palace, a bird alighted on the roof of the palace of the Vizier who was standing there at that time. I aimed at the bird, but the bullet missed it and struck the eye of the Vizier, and knocked it out. When I had thus put out his eye he could say nothing, because my father was King of the city. This was the cause of the enmity between him and me.

I stood before the Vizier with my hands bound, and he pointed to the place where his eye had been, and said: "If thou didst this unintentionally, I will do the same to thee purposely!" And he thrust his finger into my left eye, and pulled it out. He then placed me bound in a chest, and said to the executioner, "Take this fellow, and convey him without the city, and put him to death with thy sword, and let the wild beasts devour him."

Accordingly the executioner went forth with me from the city, and having taken me from the chest, bound hand and foot, was about to bandage my eye, and kill me. Whereupon I wept and besought him to save me. He had served my father, and I had shown kindness to him, so he said: "Depart with thy life, and return not to this country, lest thou perish, and cause me to perish with thee." As soon as he had said this I kissed his hands, and fled from his presence.

I journeyed to my uncle's capital, and presenting myself before him, informed him of the death of my father, and of the manner in which I had lost my eye. Upon this he wept bitterly, saying: "Thou hast added to my trouble and grief, for thy cousin has been lost for some days, and I know not what hath happened to him!" Seeing his grief I could no longer keep silence respecting my cousin, so I informed him of all that had happened.

My uncle on hearing this news rejoiced exceedingly. "Show me the tomb," he said. "By Allah, O my uncle," I replied, "I know not where it is. I searched for it several times, but could not recognize its place." Whereupon my uncle and I went together to the burial-ground, and looking to the right and left, lo, I discovered it.

When we had removed the earth, and lifted up the trap-door, we entered the tomb. We descended fifty steps, and arriving at the bottom of the stairs, there issued a smoke from the tomb that nearly blinded our eyes, whereupon my uncle exclaimed: "There is no strength, nor power but in Allah, the High, the Great!" and we proceeded further, and found ourselves in a saloon, filled with flour and grain and different kinds of food. A curtain was suspended over a couch, my uncle lifted the curtain, and found there his son, and the woman who had descended with him, converted into black charcoal, as if they had been thrown into a pit of fire.

When my uncle saw this spectacle, he spat in his son's face and exclaimed: "This is what thou deservest, O wretch!" and struck him with his shoes. Astonished at this action, and grieved for my cousin, I said: "O my uncle, what is this that hath happened to thy son? And why are he and the damsel converted into black charcoal?" "O son of my brother," he replied, "know that this my son loved an evil enchantress, and wished to marry her, and I forbade the marriage. But the Devil got possession of him, and he made this place beneath the ground, and stocked it with the provisions thou seest here. He then took advantage of my absence and married the evil woman, and brought her here. But the fire of truth hath consumed them, and converted them into charcoal, and the punishment of the world to come will be more severe and lasting!"

We then ascended, and, having replaced the trap-door, and the earth above it, returned to our abode. Scarcely had we seated ourselves in the palace, when we heard the sound of drums and trumpets. Warriors galloped about, and the air was filled with dust, and, lo, the Vizier who had slain my father, had come with his army to assault the city unawares. The inhabitants not being able to withstand, submitted to him.

Knowing that if the Vizier should see me he would kill and destroy me, I shaved off my beard, and put on the garments of a mendicant, and came hither, to this Abode of Peace, in the hope that some one would introduce me to the Prince of the Faithful, the Caliph of the Lord of all creatures, that I might relate to him my story. I arrived in this city to-night, and as I stood perplexed, not knowing where to turn, I saw this mendicant and joined him. So we walked on together, and darkness overtook us, and Destiny directed us to thy abode.

The lady, having heard the story of the first royal mendicant, said to him: "Depart and go thy way in peace!" But he replied: "I will not depart until I have heard the stories of the others."

The second mendicant then advanced, and having kissed the ground, began his story.

STORY OF THE SECOND ROYAL MEN-
DICANT—THE LEARNED APE

I WAS not born with only one eye. I am a King and the son of a King. I studied the science of the stars, and the writings of the poets, and, under the tuition of learned professors, I made myself proficient in all the sciences. I surpassed the people of my age! My handwriting was extolled by all scribes, and my fame spread among all countries, and my history among all Kings.

The King of India, hearing of me, sent gifts and curious presents, and requested my father to allow me to visit him. My father therefore prepared for me six ships, and I embarked with my attendants. We sailed for six months, after which we came to land, and, having disembarked, we loaded ten camels with presents and commenced our journey. Soon there appeared a cloud of dust, which rose and spread until it filled the air. When it cleared we saw approaching us rapidly sixty horsemen, like fierce lions, whom we perceived to be Arab highwaymen. When they saw that we were a small company, and that we had ten loads of presents for the King of India, they galloped towards us, pointing their weapons at us. They attacked us, and slew some of the young men, and the rest fled. I also fled after receiving a severe wound, while the Arabs remained and took possession of the treasure and presents.

I proceeded not knowing whither to direct my steps, until I arrived at the summit of a mountain, where I took refuge in a cavern until the next morning. I then

resumed my journey and arrived at a flourishing city.
I entered and saw a tailor sitting in his shop. I saluted
him and he returned my salutation, and welcomed me,
and asked me the reason of my having come hither.
I acquainted him with all that had befallen me from
first to last, and he was grieved for me, and said: "O
young man, reveal not thy case to any one, for I fear
what the King of this city might do to thee, since he is
the greatest of thy father's enemies."

The tailor then placed food and drink before me, and
we ate together. I remained with him for three days.
Then as I knew no trade or occupation, by which to
earn my bread, the tailor bought for me an axe and a
rope, and sent me with a party of wood-cutters to cut
firewood in the desert. Accordingly I went forth with
them, and cut some wood, and brought back a load
upon my head, and sold it for half a piece of gold.

Thus I continued to do for the space of a year. One
day I went into the desert, according to my custom.
I came to a tree around which I dug. As I was removing the earth from its roots, the axe struck against a
ring of brass, and I cleared away the earth from it, and
found that it was fastened to a trap-door of wood. I
lifted the trap-door, and beneath it was a staircase.
I descended, and at the bottom I passed through a
door into a palace, strongly constructed, where I found
a lady as beautiful as a pearl of great price.

When the lady saw me she exclaimed: "Art thou a
man or a Genie?" I answered her: "I am a man."
"And who," she asked, "hath brought thee to this
place, in which I have lived for five and twenty years
without ever seeing a human being?" Her words
sounded sweetly to me and I related to her my story

from beginning to end. She was grieved at my case and wept and said: "I also will acquaint thee with my story."

"Know then," said the lady, "that I am the daughter of the King of India, the Lord of the Ebony Island. My father married me to the son of my uncle, and on my wedding night, the Afrite, Jarjarees, a descendant of the accursed Eblis, carried me off, and soaring with me through the air, alighted in this place, to which he conveyed ornaments, garments, linen, furniture and food and drink. Once in every ten days he visiteth me. If I desire to see him at any other time, I touch with my hand the lines inscribed on this cabinet, and as soon as I remove my hand he is before me."

After this the lady took me by the hand and conducted me through an arched door into a small and elegant apartment. Here she seated me by her side upon a mattress, and served sherbet of sugar infused with musk, and she then placed food before me, and we ate and drank together. I had never seen the like of her in my whole life, and I was filled with joy, and said to her: "Shall I take thee up from this subterranean palace? Shall I release thee from this Genie? Verily I will instantly demolish this cabinet upon which is the inscription, and let the Afrite come, that I may kill him!" The lady entreated me to refrain, but paying no attention to her words, I kicked the cabinet with violence, and immediately the lady exclaimed: "The Afrite has come! Save thyself! Ascend by the way that thou camest!"

In great fear I forgot my sandals and my axe, and ascended the stairs, and turning around to look I saw the ground open, and there arose from it an Afrite of hideous aspect, who said: "Wherefore is this disturbance? What misfortune has befallen thee?" Then looking about the palace to the right and left, he saw the sandals and the axe. "Accursed woman," he exclaimed in great rage, "these are the property of a human being, who hath visited thee! Verily, I will punish thee for thy disobedience!" So saying he began to beat her with violence, after which he cut off her head with his sword.

Not being able to endure her cries nor the sight of her death, I ascended the stairs, overpowered with fear, and arriving at the top, replaced the trap-door as it was at first, and covered it over with earth. Returning to my companion the tailor, I found him awaiting me with great anxiety caused by my long absence. I thanked him for his tender concern for me, and entered my apartment. As I sat meditating upon what had befallen me, and blaming myself for having kicked the cabinet, the tailor came to me and said: "In the shop is a foreigner who asks for thee, he has thine axe and sandals." On hearing these words I turned pale and trembled, but immediately the floor of my chamber clove asunder, and there arose from it the stranger, and, lo, he was the Afrite! He seized me, and soared with me through the sky, to such a height that I beheld the world beneath me as though it were a bowl of water. Alighting upon a mountain, he took up a little dust, and having muttered and pronounced certain words over it, sprinkled me with it, saying: "Quit this form, and take the form of an ape!" And instantly I became an ape of a hundred years of age. And the Genie flew away and left me.

When I saw myself changed to this form, I wept, but determined to be patient under the tyranny of fortune. I descended from the summit of the mountain, and after having journeyed for the space of a month, arrived at the sea shore, and I saw a vessel in the midst of the sea, with a favourable wind, approaching the land. I hid myself behind a rock on the beach, and when the ship came close by I sprang into the midst of it. But as soon as the sailors and merchants on board saw me they cried out: "Turn out this unlucky brute from the ship! Kill him with the sword!" At this tears flowed from my eyes, at the sight of which the captain took compassion on me, and said to the passengers: "O merchants, this ape hath sought my aid, and I will give it to him. He is under my protection, let no one therefore trouble him." The captain then treated me with kindness and I became his servant.

We continued our journey for fifty days with a fair wind, and cast anchor under a large city. When we had moored our vessel there came to us some mem-looks from the King of the city. They complimented the merchants on their safe arrival, saying: "Our King greeteth you, rejoicing in your safety. He hath sent to you this roll of paper, desiring that each of you shall write a line upon it, for the King's Vizier, who was a great scribe, is dead, and the King hath sworn that he will not appoint any one to his office who cannot write equally well."

Though I was in the form of an ape, I arose and snatched the paper from their hands. Fearing that I would tear it or throw it into the sea, they cried out against me, and would have killed me, but the captain said: "Suffer him to write, and if he write well I will adopt him as my son, for I never saw a more intelligent ape." So I took the pen and ink, and wrote in an epistolary hand, and in a more formal, large hand, and in two different and smaller hands, and returned the paper to the memlooks. They took it back to the King, and the hand of no one pleased him except mine. The memlooks then explained to him that I was an ape, and the King was astonished at their words. He shook with delight, and sent messengers to the ship with a mule and a dress of honour, saying: "Purchase this ape, and clothe him with this dress, and mount him upon the mule and bring him hither."

So they brought me to the King, and I kissed the ground before him three times, and the persons present were astonished at my polite manners, especially the King who presently ordered his people to retire. They did so, none remaining but the King, and a eunuch, and a young memlook and myself. The King then commanded that a repast should be brought, and they placed before him delicious viands, and the King made a sign to me that I should eat, whereupon I arose and, having kissed the ground before him seven times, sat down to eat with him. After the table was removed I washed my hands, and taking the ink-case and the pen and paper, I wrote two verses. The King looking at what I had written was filled with astonishment. He then sent for a chess-table. I advanced and arranged the pieces, and I played with him twice, and beat him, and the King was filled with wonder at my skill.

The King then said to the eunuch: "Go to thy mistress, and tell her to come and see this wonderful ape!" The eunuch went and returned with his mistress, the King's daughter, who as soon as she saw me, veiled her face, and said: "O my father, how is it that thou art pleased to send for me, and suffer a strange man to see me!" "O my daughter," answered the King, "there is no one here but the young memlook, and the eunuch who brought thee up, and this ape, with myself, thy father. From whom then dost thou veil thy face?" "This ape," she said, "is the son of a King whom the Afrite, Jarjarees, the descendant of the accursed Eblis, hath enchanted. This whom thou supposedst to be an ape, is a learned and wise man."

The King was amazed at his daughter's words, and said to her: "By what means didst thou discover that he was enchanted?" "O my father," she answered, "an old woman who was a cunning enchantress taught me the art of enchantment. I know a hundred and seventy modes of performing it, by the least of which I could transport the stones of thy city beyond Mount Kaf, which is at the end of the world, and make its site to be an abyss of the sea, and convert its inhabitants into fish in the midst of it!" "I conjure thee, then, in the name of Allah," said her father, "to restore this young man that I may make him my Vizier." "With pleasure, O my father!" replied the King's daughter, and taking a knife upon which were engraved some Hebrew names, she marked with it a circle on the floor. Within this she wrote names and talismans, and soon the palace became immersed in a fearful gloom, and, lo, the Afrite appeared before us in a most hideous shape, with hands like winnowing-forks, and legs like masts, and eyes like burning torches, so that we were terrified at him.

The Afrite instantly assumed the form of a lion, and, opening his mouth, rushed upon the lady. But she plucked a hair from her head, and muttered with her lips, and the hair became a piercing sword, with which she struck the lion, and cleft him in twain by the blow, but his head was changed into a scorpion. The lady immediately transformed herself into an enormous serpent, and crept after the scorpion. A sharp contest ensued between them, and the scorpion became an eagle, and the serpent changing into a vulture pursued the eagle.

The latter then transformed himself into a black cat, and the King's daughter became a wolf, and they fought long and fiercely together, till the cat seeing himself overcome changed himself into a large red pomegranate which fell into a pool.

The wolf pursued the pomegranate which flew into the air, and then fell upon the pavement of the palace, and broke in pieces, and the grains were scattered all about the palace. The wolf seeing this transformed himself into a cock, and picked up the grains, all except one which remained hidden by the side of the pool of the fountain. The cock began to cry and flap his wings, but when he saw the grain which had lain hid by the side of the pool, he uttered a great cry and pounced upon it, but the grain fell into the midst of the water, and became a fish, and sank into the water. The cock became a fish of a larger size and plunged in after the other.

For a while the fish were absent from our sight, but at length we heard a terrible cry, and the Afrite arose as a flame of fire, casting fire from his mouth, and fire and smoke from his eyes and his nostrils. The King's daughter also became a vast body of flame, and overtook the Afrite, and blew fire in his face. Some sparks struck us from both him and her; her sparks did us no harm, but one from him struck me in my eye and destroyed it, and a spark from him reached the face of the King, and burned his beard and mouth, and struck out his lower teeth; another spark fell on the breast of the eunuch who was burned and died immediately.

We expected destruction, and gave up all hope of preserving our lives, when we heard the King's daughter exclaim: "Allah is most great! Allah is most great! He hath conquered and aided the faithful, but hath abandoned the denier of the faith of Mohammed, the chief of mankind!" And we looked towards the Afrite, and, lo, he had become a heap of ashes.

The lady then said: "Bring me a cup of water," and it was brought to her. She pronounced over it some words, and sprinkling me with it, said: "Be restored by the virtue of the name of Truth to thy original form." And immediately I became a man as I was at first, except that my eye was destroyed.

After this she cried out: "The fire! The fire! O my father, I shall no longer live! I picked up all the grains of the pomegranate, excepting the one in which was the life of the Genie. Had I picked up that he had died instantly, but I saw it not, and suddenly he came upon me, and a fierce contest ensued between us, under the earth, and in the air, and in the water. Every time he tried a new mode, I employed against him one more potent, until he tried against me the mode of fire. Rarely does one escape against whom fire is employed. Destiny aided me so that I burned him first, but a spark from him entered my breast, and now I die, and may Allah supply my place with thee!"

And having thus said, lo, a spark ascended from her breast to her face, and she wept and exclaimed: "I testify that there is no deity but Allah, and Mohammed is His prophet!" She then became a heap of ashes.

The King on beholding his daughter in this state, plucked out the remainder of his beard and slapped his face, and rent his clothes. I also did the same, while we both wept for her. Then came the chamberlains and other great officers of the court, who finding the King with two heaps of ashes before him, were astonished. He informed them what had befallen his daughter with the Afrite, and great was their grief. The women shrieked with the female slaves, and continued their mourning seven days. The King gave orders to build, over the ashes of his daughter, a great tomb with a dome, and illuminated with candles and lamps. But the ashes of the Afrite they scattered in the wind, exposing them to the curse of Allah.

The King then fell ill, and was near unto death. His illness lasted a month, but after this he recovered his health, and, summoning me to his presence, said: "O young man, we passed our days in the enjoyment of the utmost happiness, until thou camest to us. Would that I had never seen thee nor thy ugly form! I have lost my daughter, who was worth a hundred men, and I have been burned, and have lost my teeth, my eunuch also is dead! It was not in thy power to prevent these afflictions, but they happened on thy account, therefore, O my son, go forth from my city, and depart in peace."

So I departed, O my mistress, from his presence, but before I quitted the city, I entered a public bath and shaved my beard. I traversed various regions, and passed through great cities, and bent my course to the Abode of Peace, Bagdad, in the hope of obtaining an

"BE RESTORED TO THY ORIGINAL FORM"

interview with the Prince of the Faithful, that I might relate to him all that had befallen me.

And the third mendicant then advanced and thus related his story:

THE STORY OF THE THIRD ROYAL MENDICANT—KING AGIB

O ILLUSTRIOUS lady, my story is not like those of my two companions, but more wonderful! My name is Agib. I was a King and the son of a King, and when my father died, I succeeded to his throne, and governed my subjects with justice and beneficence. I took pleasure in sea-voyages, and my capital was on the shore of an extensive sea, interspersed with fortified and garrisoned islands, which I desired for my amusement to visit. I therefore embarked with a fleet of ten ships, and took with me provisions sufficient for a whole month.

I proceeded twenty days, after which there arose against us a contrary wind, but at day-break it ceased, and the sea became calm, and we arrived at an island, where we landed and cooked some provisions and ate. We remained on the island two days. We then continued our journey, and when twenty days more had passed, we found ourselves in strange waters, unknown to the captain. And behold we perceived something looming in the distance sometimes black, and sometimes white.

When the captain perceived this strange object, he threw his turban on the deck, and plucked his beard and said to those who were with him: "Destruction awaits us! Not one will escape! Know that we have wandered out of our course and that we have no wind to carry us back from the fate that awaits us, and to-morrow we shall arrive at a mountain of black stone, called loadstone. The current is now bearing us violently towards it, and the ships will fall to pieces, and every nail in them will fly to the mountain, and adhere to it, for Allah hath given to the loadstone a secret property by virtue of which everything of iron is attracted towards it. There is upon the summit of that mountain a cupola of brass supported by ten columns. Upon the top of this cupola is a horseman of brass, having in his hand a brazen spear, and upon his neck suspended a tablet of lead, upon which are engraved mysterious names and talismans. As long as this horseman remains upon the horse, so long will every ship that approaches be destroyed, with every person on board, and all the iron contained in it will cleave to the mountain, and no one will be safe until the horseman shall have fallen from the horse.'' The captain then wept bitterly, and we felt that our destruction was sure, and every one of us bade adieu to his friend.

On the following morning we drew near to the mountain. The current carried us towards it with great violence, and when the ships were close to it, they fell asunder, and all the nails, and everything else that was of iron, flew from the ships towards the loadstone. It was near the close of day when the ships fell to pieces. Some of us were drowned and some escaped, and I know not what became of those that were saved. As for myself, I clung to a plank, and the wind and waves cast it upon the mountain.

When I had landed I found a way to the summit, resembling steps cut in the rock. So I exclaimed: "In the name of Allah," and ascended, holding fast to the notches, and arrived safely at the summit. Rejoicing greatly at my escape, I immediately entered the cupola, and performed my prayers, after which I slept. I heard in my dream a voice saying to me: "O Agib, son of Khaseeb, when thou awakest from thy sleep, dig beneath thy feet, and thou wilt find a bow of brass, and three arrows of lead, whereon are engraved talismans. Take the bow and the arrows, and shoot at the horseman that is upon the top of the cupola. When thou hast shot at the horseman, he will fall into the sea, the bow also will fall, and do thou bury it in its place. As soon as thou hast done this the sea will swell and rise until it reaches the summit of the mountain, and there will appear upon it a boat bearing a man. He will come to thee having an oar in his hand. Do thou embark with him, but utter not the name of Allah, and he will convey thee in ten days to a safe sea, where on thy arrival thou wilt find one who will take thee to thy city. All this shall be done if thou utter not the name of Allah."

Awaking from my sleep, I sprang up, and did as the voice had directed. I shot the horseman, and he fell into the sea, and the bow having fallen from my hand, I buried it. The sea then became troubled and rose to the summit of the mountain. In a little while I beheld a boat in the midst of the sea, approaching me. When the boat came to me I found in it a man of brass, with a tablet of lead upon his breast, engraved with names and talismans. Without uttering a word I embarked in the boat. The man rowed me ten successive days, after which I beheld the islands where I should soon be in safety. In the excess of my joy, I exclaimed: "In the name of Allah! There is no deity but Allah! Allah is most great!" As soon as I had said this the man of brass cast me out of the boat, and sank into the sea.

Being able to swim, I swam until night, and a great wave like a vast castle, threw me upon the land. I ascended the shore, and after I had wrung out my clothes, and spread them upon the ground to dry, I slept. In the morning I put on my clothes, and looking about me, found that I was upon a small island in the midst of the sea.

While I was reflecting upon my misfortunes, I beheld a vessel bearing a number of men. I arose immediately, and climbed into a tree, and, lo, the vessel came to the shore, and there landed from it ten black slaves, bearing axes. They proceeded to the middle of the island, and digging up the earth, uncovered and lifted up a trap-door. After which they returned to the vessel, and brought from it bread and flour and clarified butter and sheep and every needful thing. There then came from the vessel an old sheikh, enfeebled and wasted by extreme age, leading by the hand a young man of great beauty. He was like a fresh and tender twig, enchanting and captivating every heart with his elegant form. The party proceeded to the trap-door, and entering it became concealed from my eyes.

They remained beneath about two hours, after which the sheikh and the slaves came out but the youth came not with them. They replaced the earth, and embarked, and set sail. Soon after I descended from the tree, and went to the excavation. I removed the earth, and entering, saw a flight of wooden steps, which I descended. At the bottom I beheld a handsome dwelling place, furnished with silk carpets, and there was the youth, sitting upon a high mattress, with sweet-smelling flowers and fruits placed before him. On seeing me he became pale, but I saluted him and said: "Fear not, O my master! O delight of mine eye! I am a man like thyself and the son of a King. Fate hath impelled me to thee that I may cheer thee in thy solitude."

The youth when he heard me thus address him, rejoiced exceedingly at my arrival, his colour returned, and he said: "O my brother, my story is wonderful. My father is a jeweller. On the day that I was born the astrologers came to him and said: 'Thy son will live fifteen years. There is in the sea a mountain called the Mountain of Loadstone, whereon is a horseman of brass, and when the horseman shall be thrown down from his horse thy son will be slain. The person who is to slay him is he who will throw down the horseman, and his name is King Agib.'

"My father was greatly afflicted by this announcement, and when I had nearly attained the age of fifteen years, the astrologers came again, and informed him that the horseman had fallen into the sea, and that it had been thrown down by King Agib. On hearing this my father prepared for me this dwelling, and here left me to remain until the fateful period be passed, of this there now remaineth but ten days. All this he did from fear lest King Agib should kill me."

When I heard this I was filled with wonder and said within myself: "I am King Agib, and it was I who threw down the horseman, but verily I will neither kill him nor do him any injury!" Then I said to the youth: "Far from thee be both destruction and harm! Thou hast nothing to fear. I will remain with thee to serve thee, and will go forth with thee to thy father, and beg of him to send me back to my country." The youth rejoiced at my words, and I sat and conversed with him until night, when I spread his bed, and covered him, and slept near to his side. In the morning I brought him water and he washed his face, and said to me: "May Allah requite thee with every blessing! If I escape from King Agib, I will make my father reward thee abundantly." "Never," I replied, "may the day arrive that would bring thee misfortune!" I then placed before him refreshments, and after we had eaten together, we passed the day conversing with the utmost cheerfulness.

I continued to serve him for nine days, and on the tenth the youth rejoiced at finding himself in safety. "O my brother," he said, "I wish that thou wouldst in thy kindness warm for me some water, that I may wash myself and change my clothes." "With pleasure," I replied, and I arose and warmed the water, after which he entered a place concealed from my view, and, having washed himself and changed his clothes, laid himself down upon a mattress to rest after his bath.

He then said to me: "Cut up, O my brother, a water-melon, and mix its juice with some sugar." So I arose, and taking a melon brought it upon a plate, and said to him: "Knowest thou, O my master, where is the knife?" "See here it is," he answered, "upon the shelf over my head." I sprang up hastily, and took the knife from its sheath, and, as I was drawing back, my foot slipped, as Allah had decreed, and I fell upon the youth, grasping in my hand the knife, which entered his body, and he died instantly.

When I perceived that he was dead, and that I had killed him, I uttered a loud shriek, and beat my face and rent my clothes, saying: "O what a calamity! O what a calamity! O Allah, I implore thy pardon, and declare to thee my innocence of his death!"

With these reflections I ascended the steps, and having replaced the trap-door, looked over the sea, where I saw the vessel that had come before, approaching and cleaving the waves in its rapid course. So I climbed into a tree, and, concealing myself among its leaves, sat there until the vessel cast anchor, when the slaves landed with the old sheikh, the father of the youth.

They went to the place, and were surprised at finding the earth moist, and when they descended the steps, discovered the youth lying on his back, showing a face of beaming beauty, though dead, and clad in white, clean clothing, with the knife remaining in his body. They all wept at the sight, and the father fell down in a swoon, which lasted so long that the slaves thought he was dead. At length, however, he recovered, and came out with the slaves, who had wrapped the body of the youth in his clothes. They then took back all that was in the subterranean dwelling to the vessel, and departed.

I remained by day hiding myself in a tree, and at night walking about the open part of the island. Thus I continued for the space of two months, when I perceived that on the Western side of the island, the water of the sea every day retired, until the land that had been beneath it became dry. I crossed this dry tract, and arrived at an expanse of sand. I then saw in the distance what appeared to be a fire, and advancing towards it, found it to be a palace, overlaid with plates of copper, which, reflecting the rays of the sun, seemed from the distance to be fire.

When I drew near to the palace, there approached me an old sheikh, accompanied by ten young men who were each blind of one eye. As soon as they saw me they saluted me, and asked my story, which I related from first to last, and they were filled with wonder. They conducted me into the palace, where I saw ten benches, upon each of which was a mattress covered with blue stuff, and each of the young men seated himself upon one of these benches, while the sheikh took his place on a smaller one. After which they said to me: "Sit down, young man, and ask no question concerning our being blind of one eye."

We ate and drank together, and then the sheikh arose, and brought from a closet, upon his head, ten covered trays. Placing these upon the floor, he lighted ten candles, and stuck one of them upon each tray. He then removed the covers and, lo, each tray was filled with ashes mixed with pounded charcoal. The young men tucked up their sleeves above the elbows, and blackened their faces, and slapped their cheeks, exclaiming: "We were reposing at our ease, and our impertinent curiosity suffered us not to remain so!" Thus they did until morning, when the sheikh brought them some hot water, and they washed their faces, and put on other clothes.

I remained with the young men a whole month, during which every night they did the same, and my heart was troubled at their strange behaviour. At length I said to them: "I conjure you, by Allah, to remove this disquiet from my mind, and to inform me of the cause of your exclaiming: 'We were reposing at our ease, and our impertinent curiosity suffered us not to remain so.' If ye inform me not I will leave you and go my way." On hearing these words they replied: "We have concealed this affair from thee, lest thou shouldst become blind of one eye like us, and, know, O young man, if this befall thee, thou wilt be banished from our company."

But I still persisted in my request, whereupon they all arose and taking a ram, slaughtered and skinned it, and said to me: "Take this knife with thee, and get into the skin of the ram, and we will sew thee up in it, and go away. Presently a bird called a Roc will come, and taking thee up by its talons, will fly away, and set thee down upon a mountain. Cut open the skin with this knife and the bird will fly away. Thou must arise as soon as it hath gone, and journey for half a day, and thou wilt see before thee a lofty palace, encased with red gold, and set with precious stones, such as emeralds and rubies. If thou enter it thy misfortune will be as ours, for our entrance into that palace was the cause of our being blind."

They then sewed me up in the skin and entered their palace. Soon after came an enormous, white bird, which seized me, and flew away, and set me down upon the mountain. Whereupon I cut open the skin, and got out, and the bird as soon as it saw me flew away. I rose up quickly and proceeded towards a palace encased in red gold. When I entered it I beheld, at the upper end of a saloon, forty young damsels, beautiful as so many moons, and magnificently attired. As soon as they saw me they exclaimed: "Welcome! Welcome!

O our master and our lord! We have been a month expecting thee." They then seated me upon a mattress, and brought to me some refreshments, and, when I had eaten, they sat and conversed with me, full of joy and happiness.

At the approach of night, they all assembled around me, and placed before me a table of dried and fresh fruits, with other delicacies that the tongue cannot describe, and one began to sing, while another played upon the lute. And I passed an evening of such enjoyment as I had never before experienced.

Thus I continued to live in the palace of red gold for the space of a whole year. On the first day of the new year, the damsels seated themselves around me and began to weep, and they bade me adieu, clinging to my skirts. "What calamity hath befallen you?" asked I. "Know," they answered, "that we are the daughters of Kings. It is our custom every year to absent ourselves for forty days, after which we return for a year of feasting and joy. We are now about to depart, and we deliver to thee the keys of the palace, which are a hundred in number, belonging to a hundred closets. Open each of these, and amuse thyself, and eat and drink, and refresh thyself, but do not open the closet that hath a door of red gold. If thou open this, the consequence will be a separation between us and thee! Our hearts whisper to us that thou wilt not regard our warning, therefore we weep!" Upon hearing this, I swore to them that I would not open the closet, and they departed urging me to be faithful to my promise.

I remained alone in the palace, and at the approach of evening I opened the first closet. Entering I found a mansion like a paradise, with a garden containing green trees, loaded with ripe fruit, abounding with singing birds, and watered with copious streams. I wandered among the trees, scenting the fragrance of the flowers, and listening to the warbling of the birds as they sang the praises of Allah, the One, the Almighty. After admiring the mingled colours of the apple, the sweet smelling quince diffusing an odour like musk and ambergris, and the plum shining as the ruby, I retired from the garden, and having locked the door, opened that of the next closet.

Within this I beheld a spacious tract planted with numerous palm-trees, and watered by a river flowing among roses, jasmine, marjoram, eglantine, and narcissus and gilliflower, the odours of which, diffused in every direction by the wind, filled me with utmost delight. I locked again the door of the second closet and opened that of the third.

Within this I found a large saloon, paved with various coloured marbles, and with costly minerals and precious gems, and containing cages of sandal and aloes-wood, full of singing birds and other birds, upon the branches of the trees planted there. My heart was charmed and I slept there until morning.

When daylight came I opened the door of the fourth closet and within I found a great building in which were forty closets with open doors. Entering these I beheld pearls, rubies, chrysolites, emeralds and other precious jewels such as the tongue cannot describe. I was astonished at the sight and said: "Such things as these are not to be found in the treasury of any King! I am now the King of my age, and all these riches, through the goodness of Allah, are mine, together with the forty damsels!"

Thus I continued to amuse myself, opening door after door, and passing from one room to another, until thirty-nine days had elapsed, and I had opened all the doors excepting that which they had forbidden me to open. My heart was then disturbed by curiosity respecting this hundredth closet, and the Devil, in order to plunge me into misery, induced me to open it. When I had entered I perceived a fragant odour which intoxicated me so that I fell down insensible, and remained for some time in this state; but at length recovering, I fortified my heart and proceeded. I found the floor overspread with saffron, and the place illuminated with golden lamps and candles, which diffused the odours of musk and ambergris. Two large perfuming-vessels filled with aloes-wood and ambergris, and a perfume compounded with honey, spread fragrance through the whole place. And, lo, I saw a black horse, of the hue of the blackest night, before which was a manger of white crystal filled with sesame, and also another manger containing rose-water infused with musk. He was saddled and bridled, and his saddle was of red gold.

Wondering at the sight of him I said within myself: "This must be an animal of extraordinary quality!" and I led him out and mounted him, but he moved not from his place. I kicked him with my heel, but still he moved not. So I took a cane and struck him with it, and as soon as he felt the blow he uttered a sound like thunder, and, expanding a pair of wings, soared with me to an immense height through the air, and then alighted upon the roof of another palace, where he threw me from his back, and, by a violent blow with his tail upon my face, struck out my eye and left me.

In this state I descended from the roof, and below I found the ten one-eyed young men, who as soon as they beheld me exclaimed: "No welcome to thee!" "Receive me into your company," said I, but they replied: "Verily thou shalt not remain with us, so get thee hence!" I departed from them with mournful heart and weeping eye, and, Allah having decreed me a safe journey hither, I arrived at Bagdad, after I had shaved my beard and become a mendicant.

CONTINUATION OF THE STORY OI THE PORTER AND THE LADIES OF BAGDAD AND THE THREE ROYAL MENDICANTS

THE mistress of the house then liberated all the men. They accordingly departed, and when they had gone out into the street, the Caliph inquired of the mendicants whither they were going. They answered that they knew not whither to go. Whereupon the Caliph said to Jaafar: "Take them home with thee, and bring them before me to-morrow, and we will then see what we can do for them." Jaafar did as he was commanded, and the Caliph returned to his palace, but was unable to sleep during the remainder of the night.

On the following morning the Caliph sat upon his throne, and when his courtiers had presented themselves and gone away, excepting Jaafar, he said: "Bring before me the three ladies, and the two hounds, and the mendicants." So Jaafar arose and brought them, and, placing the ladies behind curtains, said to them: "Fear naught for ye are forgiven because of your kindness to us, and because ye knew us not. Know that ye are now in the presence of the Prince of the Faithful, the Caliph Haroun Er Raschid, therefore relate to him nothing but the truth." And when the ladies heard these words the eldest of them advanced and related her story.

THE STORY OF THE FIRST OF THE THREE LADIES OF BAGDAD— THE TWO HOUNDS

O PRINCE of the Faithful, my story is wonderful, for these two hounds are my sisters. After the death of my father, who left us five thousand pieces of gold, these my two sisters married. When they had resided some time with their husbands, each of the latter prepared a stock of merchandise, and received from his wife a thousand pieces of gold, and they all set forth on a journey together, leaving me here. After they had been absent four years, my sisters' husbands lost all their property, and abandoned them in a strange land, and my sisters returned to me in the garb of beggars.

When I recognized them, I exclaimed: "How is it that ye are in this condition?" and they told me all that had happened. Thereupon I sent them to the bath, and clad them in new apparel, and said to them: "O my sisters, ye are my elders, and I am young, so ye shall be to me in the place of my father and my mother!

The inheritance, which I shared with you, Allah hath blessed, partake therefore of its increase, for my affairs are prosperous, and I and ye shall fare alike!"

They remained a whole year with me during which I treated them with the utmost kindness. After this period they married again without my consent, yet I gave them dowries from my own property. They went to their husbands, who, after they had resided with them for a short time, defrauded them of all they possessed, and, setting forth on a journey, left them destitute. So my sisters again returned to me in a state of beggary. They implored my forgiveness, saying: "Be not angry with us! We promise thee that we will never again marry." I replied: "Ye are welcome, O my sisters, for I have no one dearer to me than yourselves." And I received them and treated them with every kindness, and we remained happily together for the space of a year.

After this I resolved to fit out a vessel for a mercantile voyage. Accordingly I stocked a large ship with various goods, and necessary provisions, and my sisters desiring to accompany me, I took them, and set sail. But first I divided my property in two equal portions, one of which I took with me, and the other I left behind concealed; for I thought that possibly some evil accident might happen to our ship, and if our lives were saved, we should find the concealed property of service to us.

We continued our voyage night and day, till at length the vessel lost its course, and the captain knew not whither to steer. For ten days we had a pleasant wind, and after that a strange city loomed before us. We asked the captain the name of this city but he did not know it, nor did he know the sea which we were navigating; he suggested, however, that we should land our goods and enter the city and sell and exchange there.

So we entered the port and the captain landed, and after a while returned to us saying: "Arise and go up into the city, and see what Allah hath done unto his creatures, and pray to be preserved from his anger!" So we entered the city, and found all its inhabitants changed into black stones. We were amazed at the sight, and as we walked through the market-streets, we saw the merchandise, and the gold, and the silver in their original state. We then separated, each of us attracted from his companions by the wealth and stuffs in the shops,

Alone I ascended to the citadel, and entering the King's palace, found all the vessels of gold and silver in their places, and the King himself changed into black stone and seated in the midst of his chamberlains and viceroys and viziers, and clad in apparel of astonishing richness. He was sitting upon a throne adorned with pearls and jewels, every one of the pearls shining like a star. His dress was embroidered with gold, and around him stood fifty memlooks, attired in divers silks, and having in their hands drawn swords.

Stupefied at this spectacle, I entered the saloon of the women's apartment, upon the walls of which were hung silken curtains. Here I beheld the Queen, attired in a dress embroidered with fresh pearls, and having on her head a jewelled diadem, and necklaces of different kinds upon her neck. All her clothing remained as they were at first, though she herself was changed into black stone.

Here also I found an open door. Entering it I saw a flight of seven steps, by which I ascended to an apartment paved with marble, furnished with gold-embroidered carpets, and containing a sofa of alabaster, ornamented with pearls and jewels, and covered with rich silks. My eyes were attracted by a gleam of light, and when I approached the spot whence it proceeded, I found a brilliant jewel, of the size of an ostrich egg, placed upon a small stool, diffusing a light like a candle. In this apartment I likewise observed some lighted candles, and reflecting that there must then have been some person to light them, I passed thence to another part of the palace, and continued to explore the different apartments, until the approach of night.

When I would have left the palace I could not find the door, so I returned to the place in which there were the lighted candles, and there I laid myself upon the sofa, and covering myself with a quilt, repeated some words of the Koran, and composed myself to sleep. At midnight I heard a recitation of the Koran performed by a melodious and soft voice. I arose and looking about saw a closet with an open door. I entered it and found it to be an oratory, lighted lamps were suspended in it, and upon a prayer-carpet spread upon the floor sat a young man of handsome aspect.

Wondering that he had escaped the fate of the other inhabitants of the city, I saluted him, and he raised his eyes, and returned my salutation. I then said to him: "I conjure thee by the truth of the Koran which thou art reading, that thou answer the question which I am about to ask thee." Whereupon he smiled, and replied: "Do thou first acquaint me with the cause of thine entrance into this palace, then I will answer thy question." So I told him my story and inquired of him the history of this city.

He closed the Koran and having put it in a bag of satin, seated me by his side, and he thus addressed me: "Know that this city belonged to my father, and he is the King whom thou hast seen changed into stone, and the Queen whom thou hast seen is my mother. They were all Magians worshipping fire in the place of Allah, the Almighty. They swore by the fire and the light and the shade and the heat, and the revolving orb.

" My father had no son until in his declining years he was blessed with me, whom he reared until I attained manhood. Happily for me there was in my family an old woman who was a Mohammetan. My father committed me to her care, saying: 'Take him, and rear him, and educate him, and serve him in the best manner.' The old woman received me, but took care to instruct me in the faith of Mohammet, and she made me commit to memory the whole of the Koran. After a few years the old woman died.

"The inhabitants of the city now increased in their impiety and arrogance. While they were in this state they heard an invisible and mysterious crier proclaim in a voice like thunder: 'O inhabitants of this city, abstain from the worship of fire, and worship Allah, the Almighty!' The people were struck with consternation, and flocking to my father, the King of the city, said to him: 'What is this alarming voice which hath astounded us by its terrible sound?' But he answered them: 'Let not the voice terrify you, nor let it turn you from your faith.' And their hearts inclined to his words. So they persevered in the worship of fire, and remained in their impiety for another year. Then was the voice heard a second time, and again in the next year they heard it a third time, but still they persisted in their evil ways, drawing upon themselves the abhorrence and indignation of Heaven.

"One morning shortly after daybreak all the inhabitants of this city were changed into black stones, together with their beasts and all their cattle. Not one of the inhabitants escaped excepting myself. From the day on which this catastrophe happened I have continued, as thou seest, in prayer and fasting, and reading the Koran, but I have become weary of this solitary state, having no one to cheer me with his company."

On hearing these words I said to the young man: "Wilt thou go with me to the city of Bagdad? If so, I have here a ship laden with merchandise which will carry thee thither." I continued to persuade him until he gave his consent. In the morning we arose and entering the treasuries, took away much wealth. We descended from the citadel into the city, where we met the slaves and the captain of the ship, who were searching for me. They rejoiced at seeing me, and I related to them the history of the young man, and the cause of the enchantment of the people of the city, and of what had befallen them, and they were filled with wonder. But when my two sisters saw the young man, they envied me on his account, and plotted evil against me.

We embarked again, and spread our sails and departed. We continued our voyage with a favourable wind until we drew near to the city of Balsora, the buildings of which loomed before us at the approach of evening. As soon as we had fallen asleep my sisters took up both myself and the young man and threw us into the sea. The youth being unable to swim was drowned, but I awoke and found myself in the sea, and the providence of Allah supplied me with a piece of timber, upon which I placed myself, and the waves cast me upon the shore of an island.

During the remainder of the night I walked along this island, and in the morning I saw a neck of land, bearing the marks of a man's feet, and united with the main land. The sun having risen, I dried my clothes in its rays, and proceeded along the path across the neck of land, until I drew near to the shore upon which stands the city of Balsora. And, lo, I beheld a snake approaching me, followed by a serpent which was trying to destroy it. The tongue of the snake was hanging from its mouth, because of its fatigue, and I was filled with compassion. So I took up a stone and threw it at the head of the serpent, which instantly died. The snake then extended a pair of wings, and soared aloft into the sky, leaving me in wonder at the sight.

Being fatigued I laid myself down and slept, but I woke after a little while and found a damsel seated at my feet, and gently rubbing them with her hands. I immediately sat up, feeling ashamed that she should do this for me, and said to her: "Who art thou? What dost thou want?" "How soon thou hast forgotten me!" she exclaimed. "I am she to whom thou hast just done a kindness by killing my enemy, for I am a daughter of the Genii and the serpent was a Genie at enmity with me. As soon as thou hadst rescued me I flew to the ship, from which thy sisters cast thee, and transported all that it contained to thy house. I then transformed thy sisters by enchantment into two black hounds, for I knew all that they had done to thee."

Having thus said she took me up, and placed me with the two black hounds on the roof of my house. I found all the treasures that the ship had contained in the midst of my house, nothing was lost. Then said the daughter of the Genii to me: "I swear by that which was engraved upon the seal of Solomon, that if thou do not inflict three hundred lashes on these hounds every day, I will come and transform thee in like manner." So I have continued ever since to inflict upon them these stripes, though pitying them while I do so.

The Caliph heard this story with astonishment, and then said to the second lady: " And what occasioned the stripes of which thou bearest the marks?" She answered as follows:

THE STORY OF THE SECOND OF THE THREE LADIES OF BAGDAD— THE BITTEN CHEEK

O PRINCE of the Faithful, my father at his death left considerable property, and soon after that event I married one of the wealthiest men of the age, who a year after our marriage died, and I inherited from him eighty thousand pieces of gold.

As I was sitting one day there entered my apartment an old woman, disgustingly ugly, who saluted me, and said: "I have an orphan whose marriage I am to celebrate this night. Will you not be present at her nuptial festival, as she is broken-hearted, having none to befriend her but Allah, whose name be exalted!" The old woman then wept, and being moved with pity and compassion, I assented, upon which she desired me to prepare myself, telling me that she would come at the hour of nightfall and take me. So saying she kissed my hand and departed.

I arose immediately and attired myself, and when I had completed my preparations, the old woman returned. So I put on my outer garments, and taking my female slaves with me, proceeded until we arrived at a street in which a soft wind was delightfully playing, where we saw a gateway overarched with a marble vault, forming the entrance to a palace which rose from the earth to the sky.

The old woman knocked at the door of the palace, and when it was opened, we entered a carpeted passage, illuminated by lamps and candles, and decorated with jewels and precious metals. Through this passage we passed into a magnificent saloon, furnished with mattresses covered with silk, lighted by hanging lamps and by candles, and having, at its upper end, a couch of alabaster decorated with pearls and jewels, and canopied by curtains of satin. There arose from the couch a lady beautiful as the moon, who exclaimed: "Most welcome art thou, O my sister, thou delightest me by thy company, and refreshest my heart! I have a brother who hath seen thee at a fête. He is a young man, more handsome than myself, and his heart is enchained by thy love, and he hath bribed this old woman to go to thee and obtain for me an interview. My brother desireth to marry thee this night, according to the ordinance of Allah and his apostle."

When I heard these words, and saw myself thus confined in the house so that I could not escape, I consented, and the lady rejoicing clapped her hands, and opened a door, and there entered a young man so surpassingly handsome that my heart immediately inclined to him. No sooner had he sat down than the Cadi and four witnesses entered. They saluted us, and proceeded to perform the ceremony of the marriage contract between me and the young man, which having done they departed.

We lived together in utmost happiness for the space of a year, after which I begged that he would allow me to go to the bazaar in order to purchase some stuffs for dresses. Having obtained his permission I went thither in company with the old woman, and seated myself at the shop of a young merchant with whom she was acquainted. She desired him to show me his most costly stuffs. He produced for us what we wanted, and when we handed him the money, he refused to take it saying: "It is an offering of hospitality to you for your visit this day." Whereupon I said to the old woman: "If he will not take money, return to him his stuff." But he would not receive it again, and exclaimed: "Verily I will take nothing from thee save a single kiss, which I shall value more than the entire contents of my shop!" "What will a kiss profit thee?" asked the old woman. Then turning to me she said: "O my daughter, thou hast heard what the youth hath said, no harm will befall thee if he give thee a kiss, and thou shalt take what goods thou wantest. Let him kiss thee without thy speaking, and thou shalt take back thy money." Thus she continued to persuade me, until I consented, and held the edge of my veil in such a manner as to prevent the passers-by from seeing me. Whereupon the young man put his mouth to my cheek beneath the veil, but instead of kissing me, he gave my cheek a violent bite. I fell into a swoon from the pain, and the old woman laid me on her lap till I recovered, when I found the shop closed, and the old woman uttering expressions of grief.

I returned home in a state of great uneasiness and fear. My husband came in to me and asked: "What hath befallen thee, O my mistress, during this excursion?" I answered: "I am not well." "And what is this wound," said he, "that is on thy cheek?" I answered: "When I went out to-day, to purchase some stuff for a dress, a camel loaded with fire-wood drove against me in the crowded, narrow street and tore my veil, and wounded my cheek." "To-morrow then," he exclaimed, "I will ask the governor to hang every seller of fire-wood in the city!" "Verily," said I, "burden not thyself by an injury to any one. The truth is that I was riding upon an ass, which took fright, and I fell upon the ground, and a stick lacerated my cheek." "If that be so," he replied, "I will go to-morrow to Jaafar and ask him to kill every ass-driver in this city." "Wilt thou," said I, "kill these men on my account, when this which befell me was decreed by Allah?"

Upon this my husband seized me violently, then sprang up, and uttered a loud cry. A door opened and there came forth from it seven black slaves, who dragged me, and threw me down in the middle of the apartment. Thereupon my husband ordered one of them to hold me by my shoulders and to sit upon my head, and another to sit upon my knees and to hold my feet. A third then came with a sword in his hand, and said: "O my lord, shall I strike her with the sword, and cleave her in twain, that each of these slaves may take a half and throw it into the Tigris for the fish to devour?" My husband answered: "Strike her, O Saad! Cleave her in twain!" So the slave approached me, and I now felt assured of my death, but suddenly the old woman threw herself at my husband's feet, and kissing them exclaimed: "O my son, by the care with which I nursed thee, I beg thee to pardon this damsel, for she hath committed no offence that deserveth such a punishment!" And she wept and importuned him until at length he said: "I pardon her, but must cause her to bear upon her body such marks of her offence as shall last for the remainder of her life!" So saying he commanded the slaves to strip off my vest, and, taking a quince-stick, he beat me upon my back and sides until I became insensible from the violence of the blows. He then ordered the slaves to take me away as soon as it was night, and to throw me into my house, in which I formerly resided.

The slaves accordingly executed their lord's commands, and when they had deposited me in my house, I applied myself to the healing of my wounds, but after I had cured myself my sides still bore the marks of having been beaten with canes. I continued to apply remedies for four months before I was restored. Then I repaired to view the house in which this event had happened, but I found it reduced to ruin, and the whole street pulled down, and the site of the house occupied by mounds of rubbish.

Under these circumstances I went to reside with my sister, and I found with her these two hounds. Having saluted her I informed her of all that had happened to me. She then related to me her own story, and that of her sisters, and I remained with her, and neither of us ever mentioned the subject of marriage. Afterwards we were joined by this our sister, the cateress, who every day goes out to purchase for us whatever we happen to want.

CONCLUSION OF THE STORY OF THE PORTER AND THE LADIES OF BAGDAD AND THE THREE ROYAL MENDICANTS

THE Caliph was astonished at this story, and ordered it to be recorded in a book, as history, and to be deposited in his library. He then said to the first lady: "Knowest thou where the daughter of the Genii, who enchanted thy sisters, is to be found?" "O Prince of the Faithful," answered the lady, "she gave me a lock of her hair, and said, 'When thou desirest my presence, burn a few of these hairs, and I will be with thee quickly, though I should be beyond Mount Kaf!'"

"Bring then the hair," said the Caliph. The lady produced it, and the Caliph burned a portion of it. Immediately the palace shook, and there was a sound like thunder, and, lo, the daughter of the Genii appeared before them. She was a Mohammetan, therefore she greeted the Caliph by saying: "Peace be on thee, O Caliph of Allah!" To which he replied: "On thee be peace, and the mercy of Allah and his blessings!"

The daughter of the Genii then said: "Know that

this lady rescued me from death by killing my enemy, and I, having seen what her sisters had done to her, transformed them by enchantment into two hounds. But, if now thou desire their restoration, O Prince of the Faithful, I will restore them as a favour to thee and to her." "Do so," said the Caliph, "and then we will consider the affair of this lady who hath been beaten. If she hath told the truth, I will punish him who hath oppressed her." The daughter of the Genii replied: "O Prince of the Faithful, I will guide thee to the discovery of him, who oppressed this lady, and took her property. He is thy nearest relative."

She took a cup of water, and, having pronounced a spell over it, sprinkled the faces of the two hounds, saying: "Be restored to your original forms." Whereupon the hounds became again two young damsels. Having done this the daughter of the Genii said: "O Prince of the Faithful, he who beat the lady is thy son Elemeen, who had heard of her beauty and loveliness." The Caliph was astonished, and immediately summoned before him his son Elemeen, and inquired of him the history of the lady, and the young prince related to him the entire truth.

The Caliph then sent for the Cadis and witnesses, and the first lady and her two sisters, who had been transformed into hounds, he married to the three mendicants, who were sons of Kings, and these he made chamberlains of his court. The lady who had been beaten he restored to his son Elemeen, giving her a large property, and ordering that the house should be rebuilt in a more handsome style. Lastly, the lady cateress he took as his own wife. He appointed her a separate lodging for herself, with female slaves to wait upon her. He also allotted her a regular income, and afterwards built for her a palace.

* * * * * * * * *

"And this," said Sheherazade, "is not as wonderful as the story of the Magic Horse."

Chapter III

STORY OF THE MAGIC HORSE

THERE was in ancient times, in the country of the Persians, a mighty King who had a daughter like the shining moon and a flowering garden, and a son as beautiful as the day. Now this King on a certain time held a festival, and opened his palace, and gave gifts to his lords and chamberlains and to the people of his dominion. While he was sitting upon his throne, on the second day of the festival, there came to him a sage, leading a horse of ivory and ebony. The sage advanced, kissed the ground before the King, and said to him: "O King of the age, whenever I mount this magic horse, and turn the pin in his ear, he will transport me through the air to the most distant part of the world. Accept thou this wonderful horse, and in return bestow upon me thy daughter."

The King's son hearing this advanced and said: "O my father, permit me first to mount this horse and make a trial of it?" "Do so, O my son," the King replied, "and try it as thou desirest." The Prince accordingly arose, mounted the horse, turned the pin in the horse's ear, and, lo, the horse moved, and soared with him towards the upper regions of the air, and continued its flight with lightning rapidity until it was out of sight of the people. The horse continued to ascend with terrible velocity, until the Prince became filled with alarm. But he knew no way of returning to the earth, and he repented of having mounted the horse.

He then examined the animal, and perceived on its left shoulder a button formed like the head of a cock. He turned this, and, lo, the horse began to descend, little by little, and he ceased not to descend for the whole remainder of the day, until approaching the earth, the Prince discerned strange countries and cities, and among them a wonderful city in the midst of a land beautifully verdant with trees and rivers. The name of that place was Sana.

The day had nearly departed, and the sun was set when the Prince arrived at the city. He flew around it viewing it right and left, and he said to himself: "I will pass the night here and in the morning return to my father." And he searched for a place to descend in safety, where no one might see him. Now in the midst of the city a palace rose high in air, surrounded with walls and battlements, so he turned the pin of descent, and the horse flew steadily downward to the flat roof of the palace, where the Prince dismounted, and sat upon the roof until he knew that the inmates had betaken themselves to rest.

Hunger and thirst pained him, for since he had parted from his father he had not eaten food, and he said to himself: "Verily such a place as this is not devoid of the necessities of life!" He then left the horse and finding a flight of steps, he descended by them to a court paved with marble, in the midst of the building, but he heard not any sound, nor the cheering voice of an inhabitant. So he paused in perplexity, and looked right and left not knowing whither to go.

While he stood thus, he beheld a light approaching, and he saw a party of female slaves, among them a damsel radiant like the splendid full moon. She was the daughter of the King of the city, and her father, who loved her with great affection, had built for her this palace. She came hither this night to divert herself, and she walked among her female slaves, attended by a eunuch armed with a drawn sword. They entered the court of the palace, and the female slaves spread the carpets and cushions, scattered sweet odours from perfuming vessels, and sported and rejoiced together.

While they were thus engaged, the King's son rushed upon the eunuch, struck him a blow which laid him prostrate, and, taking the sword from his hand, dispersed the female slaves to the right and left. And when the King's daughter saw his beauty and loveliness, she said: "Perhaps thou art he who yesterday demanded me in marriage of my father, and whom he rejected saying that he was of hideous aspect. Verily my father lied, for thou art a handsome person!" For the son of the King of India had requested her of her father, and he had rejected him because he was of frightful appearance, and she imagined that the Prince now before her was he who had asked her in marriage. So she came to him, embraced, and kissed him, and seated him beside her.

The eunuch recovered from the blow, and arose, and seeing the King's daughter sitting with the Prince, he was filled with consternation, for the King had charged him with the office of guarding her from misfortune and evil accident. He ran shrieking to the King, and

he rent his clothes, and threw dust upon his head.
"O King," he cried, "go to the assistance of thy daughter, for a devil of a Genie, in human form, hath gotten possession of her!"

When the King heard these words he rose hastily, and went to the palace. He entered the passage leading to the court, and stationing himself at a door, raised a curtain little by little, and beheld the Prince sitting with his daughter, conversing, and the young man was of the most comely form, with a face like the shining full moon.

The King was enraged, and he raised the curtain, and rushed in upon them with a drawn sword in his hand. The Prince sprang upon his feet, and, taking his own sword in his hand, shouted at the King with an amazing cry which terrified him, and was about to attack him with the sword, but the King perceiving that the Prince was stronger than he sheathed his weapon, and met him with courtesy. "O young man," said he, "art thou a human being or a Genie?" "How is it that thou takest me for a devil?" the Prince replied, "I am of the sons of the ancient Persian Kings, who, if they wished to take thy kingdom, would make thee to totter from thy glory and dominion, and despoil thee of thy goods!"

The King hearing these words feared him, and trembled, but answered: "If thou be of the sons of Kings, how is it that thou hast entered my palace, and without my permission visitest my daughter? I have killed the Kings and the sons of the Kings on their demanding her of me in marriage! Who will save thee from my power if I command my slaves to kill thee? Who then can deliver thee from my hand!" "Verily," answered the Prince, "I wonder at thee, and at the foolishness of thy judgment! Dost thou wish for thy daughter a better husband than myself? Hast thou seen anyone more firm of heart, and more glorious in authority and troops and guards than I am?" "No, by Allah," answered the King, "but I would that thou demand her in marriage publicly." "Thou hast said well," rejoined the Prince, "but, O King, if thy slaves and servants and troops were to assemble against me, and slay me, thou wouldst disgrace thyself! Now what I propose to thee is this, either that thou meet me in single combat, and he who killeth the other shall be worthy of the kingdom, or else, when the morning cometh, that thou send forth to me thy soldiers and thy troops. I will then convince thee that I am a Prince that the King should desire for a son-in-law!" To this last the King consented and they sat and conversed together until morning.

When day dawned, the King sent for his Vizier and commanded him to collect all his troops, and equip them with arms and mount them on horses. The Vizier summoned the chiefs of the army, and the grandees of the empire, and ordered them to mount their horses, and go forth, armed for battle, to the plain in front of the palace.

The King then arose and went to the plain, where he caused an excellent horse, equipped with handsome saddle and bridle, to be brought for the Prince, but he refused it saying: "O King, none of thy horses pleaseth me. I will mount none but the horse on which I came." "And where," asked the King, "is thy horse?" "It is on the roof of thy palace," answered the Prince. And when the King heard these words he was astonished beyond measure, and exclaimed: "Woe to thee! Verily thou liest, for how can a horse be upon the roof?"

He then gave orders to his chief officers to go to the roof and bring what they might find. They ascended and beheld the horse standing there. They approached with wonder, and found it to be of ebony and ivory. They then raised it, and carried it without stopping, until they placed it before the King, and the people gathered around it, amazed at the beauty of its make, and at the richness of its saddle and bridle.

The King likewise admired and wondered at it, and said to the Prince: "O young man, is this thy horse?" "Yes, O King," answered he, "but I will not mount it, unless the troops retire to a distance." So the King commanded the troops that were about him to retire as far as an arrow might be shot.

The Prince then seated himself firmly upon his horse, and turned the pin of ascent. Immediately his horse bestirred itself, and moved about with violent action, and its body became filled with air. Then it arose and ascended into the sky. When the King saw that the Prince had arisen and ascended aloft, he called out to his troops: "Woe to you! Take him before he can escape!" But his viziers and lieutenants replied: "O King, can anyone catch a flying bird? This is no other than a great enchanter. Allah hath saved thee from him, therefore praise Him, whose name be exalted, for thine escape!"

The King returned to his palace, and acquainted his daughter with all that which had happened, and when she heard that the Prince had flown away, she lamented greatly, and fell into a violent sickness. And when her father saw her in this state, he pressed her to his bosom, kissed her between the eyes, and endeavoured to comfort her, but her weeping and wailing increased in violence. Thus was the case of the King's daughter.

Now, as to the Prince, when he had ascended into the air, he began to reflect on the beauty of the damsel and her loveliness, and his heart was moved with love for her. When night came he returned to the city of Sana, and descended upon the roof of the palace. He left his horse, and walked down stealthily until he came to the chamber of the King's daughter. She had taken to her pillow, and around her were her female slaves and nurses. The Prince went in and saluted them, and when the damsel heard his voice, she rose up and embraced him, saying: "Thou hast rendered me desolate, and hadst thou been absent from me any longer I had perished!" "Were it not for my love for thee, O most beautiful of all damsels," answered the Prince, "I would have slain thy father, but I love him for thy sake!"

He then persuaded her with many words, to journey with him to his father, and his kingdom, and there become his wife. She consented, and the Prince rejoicing took her by the hand, and led her to the roof of the palace. He mounted his horse, and placed her behind him, turned the pin of ascent in the shoulder of the horse, and soared upward into the sky. He ceased not to journey with her in his course through the air, until he arrived at the city of his father.

He deposited the King's daughter in one of the royal gardens, in a pavilion, and placed the ebony horse before the door, and charged the damsel, saying: "Sit here until I send to thee my messenger, for I am going to my father to ask him to prepare for thee a palace and a suitable reception, so that thou mayest enter the city with all due honour."

So the Prince left her, and proceeded until he arrived at the royal palace. And when his father saw him, he rejoiced at his coming and met and welcomed him. "O my father," said the Prince, "know that I have brought the daughter of the King of Sana, and I have left her in one of the royal gardens, so that thou mayest prepare the procession of state, and go forth to meet her."

The King, delighted at this news, commanded the people of the city to decorate their shops and houses, and rode forth magnificently robed, with all his soldiers and the grandees of the empire, and all his memlooks and servants. The Prince took forth from his palace, ornaments and rich garments fit for kings, and prepared for the King's daughter a camel-litter of green, red and yellow brocade, in which he seated Indian and Greek and Abyssinian slave-girls.

He accompanied the litter to the garden, and left it without while he entered and sought the pavilion where he had left the King's daughter. He searched for her but found her not, nor did he find the horse. He slapped his face, and rent his clothes, and began to search throughout the garden, but he found not the damsel. He sought the keepers of the garden and asked: "Have ye seen anyone pass or enter the garden?" They answered: "We have not seen anyone enter this garden, except the Persian sage. He came to gather herbs." So when the Prince heard their words he knew that the Persian sage had stolen the damsel and the horse.

Now, it had happened, in accordance with destiny,

HE PLACED HER BEHIND HIM, AND SOARED UPWARD INTO THE SKY

that when the Prince had left the damsel in the pavilion, that the Persian sage entered the garden and he smelt the odour of musk and other perfumes, which sweet scent was from the garments of the King's daughter. The sage proceeded in the direction of this odour, until he came to the pavilion, where he saw the horse that he had made standing at the door, and his heart was filled with joy and gladness, for he had mourned after it greatly. He entered the pavilion, and found the damsel sitting there, resembling in her beauty the shining sun in the clear sky. As soon as he beheld her, he knew that she was of high birth, and that the Prince had brought her upon the horse, and had left her in the royal garden, while he returned to the city to prepare for her a stately procession.

When the King's daughter raised her eyes she saw the sage, and was filled with fear, for he was of most hideous and foul aspect. But he kissed the ground before her humbly and said: "O my mistress, I am the messenger of the Prince, who has sent me to remove thee to another garden. Let not the hideousness of my face affright thee, for the Prince chose to send me, on account of my frightful aspect, as he was jealous of thee."

The damsel believed the sage's words, and she arose and went with him, placing her hand in his. Then he mounted the ebony horse, and placed the damsel behind him, binding her tightly. He turned the pin of ascent and the body of the horse became filled with air, ascended into the sky, and with great rapidity bore them out of sight of the city. When the damsel saw this she was filled with anxiety. "O thou," she exclaimed, "what means it that we leave the city behind?

Why dost thou disobey thy lord?" "He is not my lord!" replied the sage. "May Allah curse him for he is base and vile! Verily he stole my horse, and made himself master of it, and now I have again obtained possession of it, and of thee too, and I will torture his heart as he has tortured mine! But be of good courage and cheerful eye for I shall be a better husband unto thee than he." When the King's daughter heard this she slapped her face, cried out, and wept violently, but the sage continued his flight until he arrived at the land of the Greeks, where he descended into a verdant meadow, with rivers and trees.

This meadow was near to a city, in which dwelt a King of great dignity, and it happened on that day he went forth to hunt, accompanied by the grandees of his empire, and passing by the meadow he saw the sage, with the ebony horse and the damsel by his side. The sage was not aware of their approach until the slaves of the King rushed upon him, and took him together with the damsel and the horse. They placed all before the King, who when he saw the evil aspect of the sage, and the beauty and loveliness of the damsel, said to her: "O my mistress, what relation art thou to this sheikh?" The sage answered him hastily: "She is my wife," but the King's daughter hearing this was indignant. "O King," she said, " I know him not! He is not my husband, but he took me away by force and stratagem." Then the King commanded his attendants to seize the sage, beat him and carry him to the city, and imprison him there, and they did so. He then took the damsel and the ebony horse to his palace. Thus did it befall the sage and the damsel.

As for the Prince, he prepared for travel, and taking

what money he required, he journeyed forth, seeking the damsel and the sage from town to town and city to city. At length he arrived at the country of the Greeks, he alighted at an inn, and overheard a party of merchants talking together. And he heard one say: "O my companions, I have met with a wonderful thing! I was in such and such a city, and the people told me a strange tale, how the King of that city went forth to hunt attended by a party of the grandees of his empire. They passed a verdant meadow, and found a man standing, and by his side a woman of great beauty and elegance, and with him a horse of ebony. The man was of hideous aspect, and the woman endowed with perfect grace, and the ebony horse was a wonderful thing!"

When the Prince heard this he approached the merchant, and questioned him with mildness and courtesy, until he learned the name of the city and the name of the King. He passed the night happy and in the morning set forth on his journey. He arrived at the city at eventide, and the gate keepers took him and put him in prison, intending in the morning to present him to the King. But the jailors when they saw how comely he was could not bear to imprison him, so they seated him with themselves and shared with him their food, until he was satisfied.

"From what country art thou?" they asked. He answered, "I am from the land of Persia." Then one of the jailors said: "We have with us in the prison a Persian, who is a great liar. He pretendeth that he is a sage. The King found him with a woman of surpassing beauty, and a wonderful ebony horse. The King took the woman, and desired to marry her, but she went mad, and he is now searching for a remedy for her malady." Now when the Prince heard this he cast about in his mind for means by which to attain the deliverance of the King's daughter.

When the jailors desired to sleep, they put him in prison, and closed the doors. The morning came, and the gate keepers took him, and presented him to the King who questioned him, and said: "What is thy name, and what thy art or trade, and what is the reason of thy coming unto this city?" "O great King," the Prince answered, "my name is Harjeh, and I come from the land of the Persians." The King rejoicing exceedingly, answered, "O excellent sage, thou hast come at a time when we need thee most!" We have in the palace a mad woman, and if thou canst cure her I will heap thee with riches and honours."

The King then conducted him to the chamber in which was the damsel. And the Prince found her beating herself, and falling down prostrate. And when she saw the youth, and heard his voice, she knew him, and uttered a great cry, and fainted away. When she was restored the Prince put his mouth to her ear, and whispered: "O my mistress, keep silent, spare thy life and mine! Be patient and firm! For we stand in need of patience and good management in order to escape from this tyrannical King."

Then the Prince arose, and went forth full of joy and happiness. "O fortunate King," said he, "I have discovered her remedy and cure. Her recovery will be effected by the means of the ebony horse, which thou foundest with her. Therefore go thou forth to the place where thou first sawest her and take with thee the ebony horse, and the damsel."

Accordingly the King sent forth the horse which he had found with the damsel and the Persian sage, and taking the damsel with him he went to the meadow. The Prince ordered that the damsel and the horse should be placed as far from the King and his attendants as the eye could reach. He then mounted the horse, and placed the damsel behind him. He pressed her to him and bound her firmly, and turned the pin of ascent, whereupon the horse rose with them into the air. The troops continued to gaze at him with wonder, until he disappeared before their eyes. And the King remained half a day expecting his return. At last in despair and grief he took his troops, and went to his city.

As for the Prince he bent his course towards the city of his father, and ceased not his journey until he descended upon the roof of his palace. He then repaired to his father and his mother, and saluted them and acquainted them with the arrival of the damsel, and they rejoiced exceedingly. They prepared the marriage festivities and the rejoicings lasted a month, after which the King broke the ebony horse, and destroyed its power so that it could fly no more.

The Prince wrote a letter to the King of Sana informing him that he had married his daughter, and that she was happy and well, and he sent it by a messenger bearing precious presents and rarities. The messenger transmitted the letter to the King of Sana, who treated him with honour and sent in return a magnificent present to his son-in-law.

Thus the Prince and the King's daughter lived happily until the King, the father of the young man, was taken from the world, and the Prince reigned after him over his dominions. He ruled his subjects with justice, and the people obeyed him. Thus the King and the King's daughter continued to live, passing a most agreeable and pleasant life until they were visited by the terminator of delights and the separator of companions.

*   *   *   *   *   *   *   *   *

And Sheherazade, having finished the story of the Magic Horse, proceeded to relate the wonderful adventures of Sindbad of the Sea.

Chapter IV

STORY OF THE SEVEN VOYAGES OF SINDBAD OF THE SEA

THERE was in the time of the Caliph, the Prince of the Faithful, Haroun Er Raschid, in the city of Bagdad, a man called Sindbad the Porter. He was a poor man and carried burdens for hire upon his head. It happened one day that he carried a heavy burden, and the day was hot, so that he was wearied by the load. In this state he passed by the house of a merchant. The ground before it was swept and sprinkled, and the air was cool, and by the side of the door was a wide bench. There came forth from the door a pleasant, gentle gale laden with an exquisite odour, so that the Porter was delighted and sat down upon the bench and listened to the melodious sounds of stringed instruments, and to joyous voices laughing and singing. He also heard the voices of black birds, nightingales, turtle doves and ring doves, warbling and praising Allah, whose name be exalted.

The Porter was moved with curiosity and delight, and he advanced to the door and looked in and saw within the house a great garden, wherein he beheld pages, slaves and servants, hurrying to and fro, and there blew upon him an odour of delicious and exquisite viands, and of delicate wine. Upon this he raised his eyes, and said: "O Allah! O Creator! Thou enrichest whom thou wilt, and whom Thou wilt Thou abasest! Thou hast bestowed wealth upon the owner of this palace, while I am wretched and weary, and spend the day carrying other people's burdens!" Scarcely had Sindbad the Porter finished lamenting, when, lo, there came forth from the door a handsome page, in magnificent apparel. He took the Porter by the hand and said to him: "Enter. Answer the summons of my master, for he calleth for thee."

The Porter left his burden with the door-keeper in the passage, and entered the house with the page. He found himself in a grand chamber, in which he beheld noblemen and great lords. A feast was spread with all kinds of flowers and sweet scents, and fresh and dried fruits, together with an abundance of delicious viands, and beverages prepared from the fruit of the choicest grape-vines. On both sides of the hall were ranged beautiful slave-girls performing upon instruments of music, and at the upper end of the chamber was a great and venerable man. He was handsome in countenance, with an aspect of gravity, dignity, and majesty.

Sindbad the Porter was confounded when he saw all this, and said to himself: "Verily this is Paradise, or the palace of the King or Sultan!" He then saluted the assembly, kissed the ground before them, after which he stood hanging his head in humility. But the master of the house requested him to seat himself, and placed before him delicious food. So Sindbad the Porter advanced and having said: "In the name of Allah, the

Compassionate, the Merciful," ate until he was satisfied, and then said: "Praise be to Allah," and washed his hands, and thanked his host.

"Thou art welcome," said the master of the house. "What is thy name, and what trade dost thou follow?" "O my master," answered the porter, "my name is Sindbad the Porter, and I carry burdens for hire." At this the master of the house smiled, and said: "Know, O porter, that my name is like thine for I am Sindbad of the Sea. I heard thy lamentation at my door, and I will now inform thee of all that happened to me, and befell me before I attained this prosperity. My story is wonderful, for I have suffered severe fatigue, and great troubles and many terrors. I have performed seven voyages, and connected with each voyage is a wonderful tale."

Thereupon Sindbad of the Sea related as follows:

SINDBAD'S FIRST VOYAGE—THE ISLAND-FISH

KNOW, O masters, that my father was a merchant, of first rank, who possessed abundant wealth and ample fortune. He died when I was a young child, leaving me wealth and buildings and fields. When I grew up, I ate and drank well, associated with young men, and wore handsome apparel. I ceased not to live in this manner until I returned to my reason, and found that my wealth had passed away.

Repenting of my prodigality, I arose and sold my apparel, and furniture, and buildings, and all that my hand possessed, and amassed three thousand pieces of silver. I remembered the saying of one of the poets:

"He who diveth in the Sea seeking for pearls,
Acquireth lordship, and good fortune!"

Accordingly I decided to perform a sea-voyage. I bought commodities and merchandise, and such other things as were required for travel. I embarked in a ship, with a company of merchants, and we traversed the seas for many days and nights. We passed by island after island, and from sea to sea, and from land to land, and in every place we bought and sold, and exchanged merchandise.

We continued our journey until we arrived at an island like one of the gardens of Paradise, and at that island the master of the ship brought us to anchor. All who were on the ship landed, and took with them fire-pots, and lighted fire in them. Some cooked, others washed, and others amused themselves. I was among those who were amusing themselves upon the shore of the sea.

Suddenly the master of the ship called out in his loudest voice: "O ye passengers! whom may Allah preserve! Come quickly into the ship. Hasten to embark! Flee for your lives! This apparent island upon which ye are, is not really an island, but it is a great fish that hath become stationary in the midst of the sea, and the sand hath accumulated upon it, and trees have grown upon it, until it looks like an island! When ye lighted the fires, it felt the heat, and put itself in motion, and now it will descend with you to the bottom of the sea!" The passengers hearing these words, hastened to the vessel, leaving their merchandise and their fire-pots and their copper cooking vessels. Some reached the ship, and others reached it not. The island moved, and descended to the bottom of the sea, with all that were upon it, and the roaring sea closed over it.

I was among those who remained behind upon the island, so I sank into the sea with the rest. But Allah, whose name be exalted, delivered me and saved me from drowning. There floated towards me a great wooden bowl, in which the passengers had been washing, and I laid hold of it, and got into it, and beat the water with my feet, like oars, while the waves sported with me, tossing me from right to left.

The master of the vessel caused her sails to be spread, and pursued his voyage regardless of those who were in the sea, and I ceased not to look at that vessel until it disappeared from sight. When night came I felt sure of destruction, but I remained safe for a day and a night, and the winds and the waves aided me until the bowl stopped under a high island, whereon were trees overhanging the sea. I laid hold upon the branch of a lofty tree, and clung to it, and climbing up by its means I landed upon the island. I found that my legs were benumbed, and saw marks upon them of the nibbling of fish, of which I had been insensible by reason of the violence of my anguish and fatigue!

I threw myself upon the island like one dead, and became unconscious, and I remained in this condition until the next day. The sun having risen, I awoke and found that my feet were swollen, and that I was reduced to a state of excessive weakness. I dragged myself along in a sitting posture, and then I crawled upon my knees. There were in the island fruits in

abundance, and springs of sweet water. I ate some of
the fruits and drank the water, and continued to live
in this manner for several days. My spirit then revived,
and my power of motion returned, and having made
myself a staff to lean upon I walked along the shore,
until there appeared a peculiar object in the distance.
I imagined that it was a wild beast or one of the beasts
of the sea, and I walked towards it, and, lo, it was a
mare of superb appearance, picketed in a part of the
island near the sea shore.

I approached her but she cried out with a great cry,
and I trembled and was about to retire, when behold
a man came forth from a hole in the earth, and called
to me, and pursued me saying: "Who art thou?
Whence hast thou come? What is the cause of thy
arrival in this place?" So I answered him: "O my
master, I am a stranger, and I was in a ship, and was
submerged in the sea with certain of the other passengers, but Allah supplied me with a wooden bowl, and
I got into it and it bore me along until it cast me upon
this island."

The man then laid hold of my hand and said: "Come
with me." I therefore went with him, and he descended
into a grotto beneath the earth, and conducting me
into a large subterranean chamber, he seated me and
brought food. I was hungry so I ate until I was satisfied, and my soul was at ease. He then asked me what
had happened to me, and I acquainted him with my
whole affair from beginning to end, and he wondered
at my story.

Then said the man: "Know that we are a party dispersed in this island, and we are the grooms of the
King Mihrage, having under our care all his horses."

And even as he spoke his companions came, each leading a mare, and seeing me with him, they inquired who I might be, and when they understood the case -they drew near and spread the table, and ate, and invited me to eat with them. After which they arose, and mounted the horses, taking me with them.

We journeyed until we arrived at the city of King Mihrage, and the grooms went in to him, and related my story. After which they presented me to him, and he welcomed me in an honourable manner, saying: "O my son, verily thou hast experienced an extraordinary preservation! Praise be to Allah for thy safety!" He then treated me with beneficence, and made me keeper of the sea-port. He invested me with a handsome and costly dress, and I became a person of high importance.

I remained in his service for a long time, and, whenever I went to the shore of the sea, I used to inquire of the merchants and sailors if they knew the direction of the city of Bagdad, but none knew it, or knew anyone who went there. I was weary at the length of my absence from home, and I longed to return thither. In this state I continued for some time, during which I amused myself with the sight of the islands belonging to King Mihrage. I saw there an island called Kasil, in which at night is heard mysterious beatings of tambourines and drums, and the people told me that it is inhabited by that strange being called Dagial, the false and one-eyed. I saw also in the sea, in which is that island, a fish two hundred cubits long, and a fish whose face is like an owl's. I likewise saw many other wonderful and strange things, such as if I related them to you, the description would be too long.

I continued to amuse myself with the sight of those islands, until I stood one day on the shore of the sea, with a staff in my hand, as was my custom, and, lo, a great vessel approached the harbour of the city. The master furled its sails, brought it to anchor, and put forth a landing plank, and the sailors brought out everything that was in the vessel to the shore. Then said I to the master: "Doth aught remain in thy vessel?" "Yes, my master," he answered, "I have goods in the hold, but their owner was drowned, and we desire to sell them, in order to convey their price to his family in the city of Bagdad, the Abode of Peace." "And what," said I, "was the name of this man, the owner of the goods?" "His name was Sindbad of the Sea," answered the master, "and he was drowned on his voyage with us."

When I heard this I looked attentively at the master, and recognized him, and I cried out with a great cry: "I am the owner of the goods! I am Sindbad of the Sea," and I told him all that had happened to me. But the master said: "Thou verily art a deceiver! Because thou heardest me say that I had goods whose owner was drowned, therefore thou desirest to take them without price! We saw Sindbad when he sank, and with him were many of the passengers, not one of whom escaped." But I related to the master all that I had done from the time that I went forth with him from the city of Bagdad, and I related to him some circumstances that had occurred between him and me, and the master and merchants were convinced of my truthfulness and recognized me.

They then gave me my goods and I found nothing missing. So I opened the bales and took forth precious and costly things and carried them as a present to the King. When he heard what had occurred he treated me with exceeding honour, giving me a large gift in return. Then I sold my bales, and purchased other goods and commodities of that city, after which I begged the King to grant me permission to depart to my country and my family. So he bade me farewell, and gave me an abundance of rich and costly things.

I embarked in the vessel, and Fortune aided us, so that we arrived in safety at the city of Balsora. There we landed, and remained a short time, and after that I repaired to the city of Bagdad, the Abode of Peace. I had an abundance of bales, and goods, and merchandise of great value, and with it I procured servants, and memlooks, and slave-girls, and black slaves, so that I had a large establishment, and I purchased houses and furniture, more than I had at first. I enjoyed the society of my friends and companions, and forgot the fatigue and difficulty and terror of travel. I occupied myself with delights and pleasures, and delicious meats and exquisite drinks, and continued to live in this manner for some time. Such were the events of my first voyage, and to-morrow if it be the will of Allah, whose name be exalted, I will relate to you the tale of the second of my seven voyages.

Sindbad of the Sea then made Sindbad the Porter sup with him, after which he presented him with a hundred pieces of gold, and the Porter thanked him, and went his way. He slept that night in his own abode, and when the morning came he performed his morning-prayers and repaired to the house of Sindbad of the Sea, who welcomed him with honour. After the rest of his companions had come, and food and drink were set before them, and they were merry, then Sindbad of the Sea began his story thus:

SINDBAD'S SECOND VOYAGE—THE VALLEY OF DIAMONDS

KNOW, O my brothers, I lived most comfortably as I told ye yesterday, until one day I felt a longing to travel again to lands of other peoples, and for the pleasure of seeing the countries and islands of the world. I decided to set forth at once, and taking a large sum of money I purchased with it goods and merchandise suitable for travel, and packed them up. Then I went to the banks of the river, and found a handsome new vessel, with sails of comely canvas, and manned by a numerous crew. So I embarked my bales in it, as did also a party of merchants and we set sail that day.

The voyage was pleasant, and we passed from sea to sea, and from island to island, and at every place where we cast anchor, we met merchants and great men, and we sold, bought and exchanged goods. Thus we continued to voyage until we arrived at a beautiful island, abounding with trees of ripe fruit, and where flowers diffused their fragrance, and birds warbled, and pure rivers flowed, but there was not an inhabitant on the whole island. The master anchored our vessel, and the merchants and other passengers landed to amuse themselves. I also landed upon the island with the rest, and sat by a spring of pure water among the trees. The zephyr was sweet, and the time was pleasant, and I fell asleep, enjoying that sweet zephyr and the fragrant gale. When I awoke, I found that the master had forgotten me, and the vessel had sailed with the passengers, and not one had remembered me, neither merchant nor sailor, so I was left alone in the island.

I had with me neither food nor drink, nor worldly goods, and I was desolate, weary of soul, and despairing of life. I began to weep and wail, and to blame myself for having undertaken the voyage and fatigue, when I was reposing at ease in my abode and country, in ample happiness, enjoying good food, and good drink, and good apparel, not being in want of anything, either of money or goods or merchandise. I repented of having gone forth from the city of Bagdad, and of having set out on a voyage over sea.

After a while I comforted myself, and arose, and walked about the island. I climbed up a lofty tree, and saw naught save sky and water, and trees and birds, and islands and sand. Looking attentively, I saw, on the island, an enormous white object, indistinctly seen in the distance. I descended from the tree, and proceeded in that direction without stopping. And, lo, it was a huge white dome, of great height and immense circumference. I drew near to it, and walked around it, but found no door, and I could not climb it because of its excessive smoothness. I made a mark at the place where I stood, and went around the dome measuring it, and, lo, it was fifty full paces!

Suddenly the sky became dark, and the sun was hidden. I imagined a cloud had passed over it, and I raised my head, and saw a bird of enormous size, bulky body, and wide wings, flying in the air, and this it was that concealed the sun, and darkened the island.

My wonder increased, and I remembered a story, which travellers and voyagers had told me long before. How in certain islands there is a bird of enormous size called the Roc, and it feedeth its young ones with elephants. I was convinced therefore that the dome was the egg of a Roc, and I wondered at the works of Allah, whose name be exalted!

While I was considering this wonder, lo, the bird alighted upon the dome, and brooding over it with its wings, stretched out its legs behind upon the ground, and slept over it. Thereupon I arose, and unwound my turban from my head, and twisted it into a rope. I fastened it tightly about my waist, and tied myself to one of the feet of the bird, saying to myself: "Perhaps this bird will convey me to a land of cities and inhabitants, and that will be better than my remaining on this island."

I passed the night sleepless, and, when the dawn came and the morning appeared, the bird rose from its egg, uttered a great cry and flew up into the sky, drawing me with it. It ascended, and soared higher and higher, then it descended gradually, until it alighted with me upon the earth. When I reached the ground, I hastily unbound myself from its foot, loosed my turban, shaking with fear as I did so, and walked away. The Roc took something from the earth in its talons, and soared aloft, and I looked at the thing and saw that it was a serpent of enormous size, which the bird had taken, and was carrying off towards the sea.

I walked about the place, and found myself in a large, deep, wide valley, and by its side a great mountain, very high, whose summit I could not see because of its excessive height, and I could not ascend it because of its steepness. Seeing this, I blamed myself for what I had done: "Would that I had remained on the island," I said, "since it is better than this deserted place! For in that island are fruits that I might have eaten, and I might have drunk from its rivers, but in this place are neither trees nor fruits nor rivers! Verily every time I escape from one calamity I fall into another that is greater and more severe!" Then I arose, and encouraging myself, walked down the valley, and, lo, its ground was composed of magnificent diamonds, a stone so hard that neither iron nor rock can have any effect upon it, nor can anyone cut it or break it except by the means of the lead-stone.

All that valley was likewise occupied by venomous serpents, of enormous size, big enough to swallow an elephant. These serpents came out of their holes in the night, and during the day they hid themselves fearing lest the Rocs should carry them off, and tear them to pieces. The day departed, and I began to search for a place in which to pass the night, fearing the serpents who were beginning to come forth. I found a cave near by with a narrow entrance, I therefore entered, and seeing a large stone I pushed it and stopped up the mouth of the cave. I said to myself I am safe in this cave, and, when daylight cometh, I will go forth, and look for some means of escape from this valley.

I prepared to repose, when looking towards the upper end of the cave I saw a huge serpent sleeping over its eggs. At this my flesh quaked, and I raised my head, and passed the night sleepless, until dawn arose and shone, then I removed the stone with which I had closed the entrance to the cave, and went forth from it, giddy from sleeplessness and hunger and fear.

I walked along the valley, and, lo, a great slaughtered animal fell before me. I looked but could see no one, so I wondered extremely, and I remembered a story which I had heard long ago from merchants and travellers; how in the mountains of diamonds are experienced great horrors, and that no one can gain access to the diamonds. To obtain these stones the merchants employ a stratagem. They take a sheep and slaughter it, and skin it, and cut up its flesh, which they throw down from the mountain to the bottom of the valley, and the meat being fresh and moist some of the diamonds stick to it. The merchants leave it until midday, when large birds descend to the valley, and taking the meat up in their talons, carry it to the top of the mountain, whereupon the merchants cry out, and frighten away the birds. They then remove the diamonds sticking to the meat, and carry them to their own country leaving the flesh for the birds and wild beasts. No one can procure the diamonds but by this stratagem.

Therefore when I beheld that slaughtered animal, and remembered this story, I arose and selected a great number of large and beautiful diamonds, which I put into my pocket, and wrapped in my turban, and within my clothes. While I was doing this behold another great slaughtered animal fell before me. I bound myself to it with my turban, and lying down on my back, placed the meat upon my bosom, and grasped it firmly. Immediately an enormous bird descended upon it, seized it with its talons, and flew up with it into the air, with me attached to it. It soared to the summit of the mountain where it alighted. Then a great and loud cry arose near by, and a piece of wood fell clattering upon the mountain, and the bird frightened flew away.

I disengaged myself from the slaughtered animal, and stood up by its side, when, lo, the merchant, who had cried out at the bird, advanced and saw me standing there. He was very much terrified, and when he saw that there were no diamonds on the meat he uttered a cry of disappointment. "Who art thou," exclaimed he, "who hath brought this misfortune upon me?" "Fear not, nor be alarmed," answered I, "for I am a human being, a merchant like thyself, and my tale is prodigious, and my story wonderful! I have with me an abundance of diamonds, and I will share them with thee to repay thee for those thou hast lost." The man thanked me for this and conversed with me, and, behold, the other merchants heard me talking with their companion, and they came and saluted me. I acquainted them with my whole story, relating to them all I had suffered upon the voyage. Then I gave the owner of the slaughtered animal to which I had attached myself, a number of the diamonds that I had brought with me from the valley. And I passed the night with the merchants, full of utmost joy at my escape from the valley of serpents.

When the next day came we arose, and journeyed over that great mountain. At length we arrived at a garden in a great and beautiful island, wherein were camphor trees, and under the shade of each a hundred men might rest. Camphor is obtained from a tree by making a perforation in the upper part. The liquid camphor is the juice of the tree, and floweth from the perforation and hardens into gum. After this operation the tree dries up and dies. In the island too is a wild beast, called a rhinoceros. It is a huge beast, with a single thick horn, in the middle of its head. It is so strong that it lifteth a great elephant upon its horn, and pastureth upon the shore without being conscious of the weight, and the elephant dieth, and its fat melted by the heat of the sun, flowing down the horn of the rhinoceros, entereth its eyes, so that it becometh blind. Then the beast lieth down upon the shore, and the Roc cometh and carrieth it off with the elephant still on its horn, and the bird feedeth his young ones with both the rhinoceros and the elephant. I saw also in that island an abundance of buffaloes, the like of which existeth not among us.

We continued our journey and soon arrived at a city, where I exchanged a part of my diamonds for merchandise and gold and silver. After which I journeyed from country to country, and from city to city, selling and buying, until I arrived at the city of Bagdad, the Abode of Peace. I entered my house, bringing with me a great quantity of diamonds and money and goods. I made presents to my family and relations, and bestowed alms and gifts, and feasted with my friends and companions, and thus I forgot all that I had suffered. This is the end of the account of what befell and happened to me during the second voyage. To-morrow, if it be the will of Allah, whose name be exalted, I will relate to you the events of the third of my seven voyages.

When Sindbad of the Sea had finished his story, all the company marvelled. They supped with him, and he presented to Sindbad the Porter a hundred pieces of gold; the latter took them and went his way wondering at the things that Sindbad of the Sea had suffered.

When morning came the Porter arose, performed his morning prayers, and repaired to the house of Sindbad of the Sea. When the rest of the party had come, and after they had eaten and drunk, and enjoyed themselves, and were merry and happy, Sindbad of the Sea began thus:

SINDBAD'S THIRD VOYAGE—THE WONDER VOYAGE

KNOW, O my brothers, that my third voyage was more wonderful than the preceding ones. When I returned from my second voyage, I resided in the city of Bagdad for a length of time, in the most perfect prosperity, delight, joy and happiness. Then my soul became desirous of travel and diversion. So I considered the matter, and decided to set forth immediately. I bought an abundance of goods suited to a sea-voyage, and packed them up, and departed to the city of Balsora. There I beheld, near the bank of the river, a great vessel, in which were many merchants and other passengers. I therefore embarked in that vessel, and we departed relying on the blessing of Allah, whose name be exalted. We proceeded from sea to sea, and from island to island, and from city to city, and at every place, we amused ourselves, and bought and sold.

One day we pursued our course in the midst of a raging sea, when, lo, the master, standing at the side of the vessel, suddenly slapped his face, furled the sails, cast the anchors, plucked his beard, rent his clothes and uttered a great cry. "Know, O passengers," exclaimed he, "that the wind hath driven us out of our course in the midst of the sea, and destiny hath cast us, through our evil fortune, towards the Mountain of Apes. No one hath ever arrived at this place, and escaped!"

Scarcely had the master spoken before a band of apes, numerous as locusts, surrounded the ship on every side. Their numbers were so excessive that we feared to kill one or strike him or drive him away, lest the others should fall upon us and destroy us. They were the most hideous of beasts, and covered with hair like black felt. They had yellow eyes, and black faces, and were of small size. They climbed up the cables and severed them with their teeth, and they severed all the ropes so that the vessel inclined with the wind, and stopped at the island. The apes then put all the merchants and passengers ashore, and taking the ship sailed away in it, leaving us upon the island, and we knew not whither they went.

We wandered about until we discovered a pavilion, with high walls, having an entrance with folding doors which were open, and the doors were made of ebony. We entered and found a wide, large court, around which were many lofty doors. Over the fire-pots hung cooking utensils, and on the floor were many bones. As we were fatigued, we sat down on a great bench, and fell asleep. Suddenly the earth trembled, and we heard a dreadful noise, and there entered the pavilion a creature of enormous size in human form. He was black, of lofty stature like a great palm-tree. He had two eyes like two flames, and tusks like the tusks of swine, and a mouth of prodigous size, and lips like the lips of a camel, hanging down upon his bosom. His ears hung down upon his shoulders, and the nails of his hands were like the claws of lions.

When we beheld him we were so filled with dread and terror that we became as dead men. The creature came to us and seized me in his hand, lifted me from the ground, and felt me and turned me over, and I was in his hand like a little mouthful. He continued to feel me as a butcher feeleth the sheep that he is about to slaughter, but he found me lean and having no flesh. He therefore put me down, and took another from among my companions, and turned him over, then let him go. In this manner he felt us, and turned us over one by one, until he came to the master of our ship, who was a fat, broad-shouldered man. He seized him as does the butcher the animal that he is about to slaughter, and having thrown him upon the ground, put his foot upon his neck and broke it.

Then he brought a long spit and thrust it through him. After which he built a fierce fire, and placed over it the spit, turning it about over the burning coals, until the master was thoroughly roasted, when he took him off the fire, and separated his joints as a man separates the joints of a chicken. He ate his flesh, and after gnawing his bones, tossed them by the side of the fire-pot. He then threw himself down, and slept upon the bench, making a fearful noise with his throat.

We wept and said: "Would that we had been drowned in the sea, or that the apes had eaten us! For it would be better than being roasted upon burning coals!" We then arose, and went forth to find a place to hide in. But we could find no hiding place, and, when night came, we returned to the pavilion by reason of our fear. We had sat there a little while, and, lo, the earth trembled beneath us, and the black creature approached us, and took us one by one, and turned us over, until one pleased him, whereupon he seized him, and killed and roasted him as he had done with the master of the ship. He then slept, making a dreadful noise with his throat, as before. When morning came he arose, and went his way.

Then said one of our company: "Verily we must contrive some stratagem to kill him, and rid the earth of such a monster!" "Hear, O my brothers," I answered, "if we must kill him, let us first make some rafts of this fire-wood, each raft to bear three men, after which we will kill him, and embark on our rafts, and proceed over the sea to whatsoever place Allah shall desire. And if we be not able to kill him, we will embark anyway, and if we be drowned we shall be preserved from being roasted over the fire!" We all agreed upon this matter, and commenced the work. We removed the pieces of fire-wood out of the pavilion, and constructed rafts, moored them to the shore, stowed upon them some provisions, after which we returned to the pavilion.

When it was evening, lo, the earth trembled beneath us, and the black came in like a biting dog! He turned us over, and felt us, one after another, and having taken one of us, did with him as he had done with the others. He ate him, and slept upon the bench, and the noise in his throat was like thunder.

We then arose, and took two iron spits, and put them in the fierce fire until they were red hot, and became like burning coals. We grasped them firmly, and went to the black, while he lay asleep snoring, and thrust

WHEN WE BEHELD HIM WE WERE FILLED WITH DREAD AND TERROR

them into his eyes, all of us pressing upon them with our united strength and force. Thus we pushed them into his eyes as he slept, and his eyes were destroyed, and he uttered a terrible cry. He arose, and began to search for us, while we fled in every direction, and he saw us not for his sight was blinded. Then he sought the door, feeling for it, and went forth crying out so that the earth trembled.

We hastened to the rafts, and scarcely had we reached them before the black returned, accompanied by a female, greater than he, and more hideous in form. As soon as we beheld the horrible female with him, we loosed the rafts, and pushed them out to sea. But each of the two blacks took masses of rock, and they cast them at us, until they had destroyed all the rafts but one, and the persons upon them were drowned. There remained of us only three, I and two others, and the raft we were on conveyed us to another island.

We landed, and walked about this island until the close of day, when night overtook us, so we slept a little. We awoke from our sleep and, lo, a serpent of enormous size, of large body and wide belly, had surrounded us. It approached one of us, and swallowed him to his shoulders, then it swallowed the rest of him, and we heard his ribs crack. After which the serpent went away. We mourned for our companion, and were in the utmost fear for ourselves, saying: "Verily every death we witness is more horrible than the preceding one!"

We arose, and walked about the island, eating and drinking of its rivers, and when night came my companion and myself found a lofty tree, so we climbed up it, and slept. When it was day, the serpent came,

looking to the right and left, and advancing to the tree
upon which we were, climbed to my companion, swallowed him to his shoulders, and then it wound itself
around the tree, and I heard his bones break. The
serpent swallowed him entire, descended from the
tree, and went its way.

I remained upon that tree the rest of the night, and
when day came I descended more dead than alive from
excessive fear and terror. I desired to cast myself into
the sea, but it was no light matter, for to live was sweet,
so I tied a wide piece of wood upon the soles of my feet
crosswise, and I tied one like it upon my left side, and a
similar one on my right side, and another on the front
of my body, and I tied a long and wide one on the top
of my head, crosswise, like that which was on the soles
of my feet. I bound them tightly, and threw myself
upon the ground. Thus I lay in the midst of the pieces
of wood, and they enclosed me like a box.

When evening arrived, the serpent approached, but
could not swallow me, as I had the pieces of wood on
every side. It went round me, then retired from me,
and returned again to me. Every time it tried to
swallow me the pieces of wood prevented it. It continued to attack me thus, from sunset until daybreak
arrived and the light appeared, then the serpent went
its way in the utmost vexation and rage.

I loosed myself from the pieces of wood in a state
like that of the dead. I arose, and walked along the
island, and looking towards the sea, beheld a ship in
the distance, in the midst of the deep. I took a great
branch of a tree, and made signs with it, calling out,
and the sailors saw me. They approached the shore,
and took me with them in the ship. They asked me my

story, and I informed them of all that had happened to me from beginning to end. They then clad me in some of their garments, and put food before me, and I ate until I was satisfied, and my soul was comforted.

We proceeded on our voyage, until we came in sight of an island, called the Isle of Selahit, where sandal-wood is abundant. The master anchored the ship, and the merchants and other passengers took forth their goods to sell and buy. Then said the master to me: "Thou art a stranger and poor, and hast suffered many horrors, and I desire to aid thee to reach thy country. Know, that there was with us a merchant, who was lost at sea, and I will commit to thee his bales of goods, that thou mayest sell them in this island, after which we will take the price to his family. If thou wilt take charge of the sale we will give thee something for thy trouble and service." For this kind and beneficent offer I was full of gratitude, and readily agreed to look after the goods.

The master ordered the porters and sailors to land the goods upon the island, and to deliver them to me. "Write upon them," said he, "the name of Sindbad of the Sea, who was left behind at the island of the Roc, and of whom no tidings have come to us." Upon this I uttered a great cry, saying: "O master, I am Sindbad of the Sea! I was not drowned," and I told him all that had happened unto me. And when the merchants and passengers heard my words, they gathered around me, some of them believed me, and others disbelieved. While we were talking, lo, one of the merchants, on hearing me mention the Valley of Diamonds, advanced and said: "Hear, O company, my words. I have already related to you the wonderful thing I saw on my travels.

I told you that when I cast my slaughtered animal into the Valley of Diamonds, that there came up with my beast a man attached to it, and ye believed me not, but accused me of lying. This is the man, and he gave me diamonds of high price, and he informed me that his name was Sindbad of the Sea, and he told me how the ship had left him in the island of the Roc."

When the master heard the words of the merchant, he looked at me a while with a searching glance, then said: "What is the mark of thy goods?" "Know," I answered, "that the mark of my goods is of such and such a kind." He therefore was convinced that I was Sindbad of the Sea, and embraced and saluted me, and congratulated me upon my safety.

I disposed of my merchandise with great gain, selling and buying at the islands, until we arrived at Balsora, where I remained a few days. Then I came to the city of Bagdad, and entered my house, and saluted my family, companions and friends. I rejoiced at my safety, and gave alms to the poor, and clad the widows and orphans. And I ceased not to live thus, eating and drinking, and making merry with my friends, and I forgot all the horrors I had suffered. Such was the most wonderful of the things that I beheld during that voyage, and to-morrow, if it be the will of Allah, whose name be exalted, I will relate to thee the story of my fourth voyage, for it is more wonderful than the stories of the preceding voyages.

Then Sindbad of the Sea gave the porter a hundred pieces of gold, and commanded the attendants to spread the table. So they spread it, and the company supped wondering at that story, and at the events described. Sindbad the Porter took the gold, and went his way, and passed the night in his house. When the morning came, and diffused its light, he arose, and performed the morning-prayers, and walked to the house of Sindbad of the Sea, who received him with joy. As soon as the rest of the company came, the servants brought forth food, and the party ate and drank and enjoyed themselves. Then Sindbad of the Sea related to them the fourth story, saying:

SINDBAD'S FOURTH VOYAGE—THE BURIAL CAVE

KNOW, O my brothers, that after I returned to the city of Bagdad, and met my friends and companions, and was enjoying the utmost pleasure, leading the most delightful life, my wicked soul suggested to me to travel again to other countries, and I felt a longing to see different races, and for selling and gains. So I resolved upon this, and purchased precious goods, suitable to a sea-voyage and, having packed up my merchandise, I went to the city of Balsora, where I embarked my bales, and joined myself to a party of the chief men of that city, and we set forth.

The vessel proceeded with us over the roaring sea, agitated with waves, but the voyage was pleasant, and we went from island to island, and from sea to sea, until a contrary wind arose. The master cast anchor, and stayed the ship in the midst of the sea, fearing that she would sink in the deep. Suddenly a great tempest arose, which rent the sails, and the merchants were submerged with their commodities and wealth. I was submerged among the rest, and swam in the sea for half a day. But Allah, whose name be exalted, enabled me to lay hold of one of the planks from the ship, and I and a party of merchants got upon it. The next day a wind arose against us, the sea became boisterous, and the waves and wind violent, and the water cast us upon an island.

We walked along the shore of the island, and found abundant herbs, so we ate some, and then passed the night on the shore. When morning came we walked until there appeared a building in the distance. When we reached its door, lo, there came forth from it a party of naked black men. Without speaking, they seized us, and carried us to their King. He commanded us to sit down, and the blacks brought us disgusting food, which my stomach revolted against, therefore I ate scarcely any, but my companions ate most ravenously. As soon as they had eaten thus their minds became stupefied, and they devoured like madmen. Then the blacks brought to them cocoa-nut-oil, and when my companions drank it their eyes became turned in their faces, and they proceeded to consume more food after the manner of wild beasts.

I was filled with fear for myself and my companions, and I observed the naked men attentively, and, lo, they were fire-worshippers, and the King of their land was a ghoul. Every one who arrived at their country, or whom they met in the valleys or roads, they caught and they brought to their King, and they fed the cap-tive with strange food, and gave him cocoa-nut-oil to drink, in consequence of which his body became en-larged, and his mind stupefied so that he became an idiot. They fed him until he became fat, when they slaughtered and roasted him, and served him as meat to their King. But as to the servants of the King, they ate the flesh of men, without roasting or otherwise cooking it. When I saw the blacks feed my companions thus, I was in utmost anguish. As for myself I became, through hunger and fear, wasted and thin, and my flesh dried on my bones. When the blacks saw me in this state they left me, and forgot all about me.

One day as I walked along the island, I saw a herdsman sitting in the distance, and he was pasturing my companions like cattle. As soon as the man beheld me he called out: "Turn back! Go along the road to the right and thou wilt soon reach the King's highway." Accordingly I turned back, and seeing a road on my right hand, I proceeded along it day and night until I came to the other side of the island.

I was tired and hungry, so I began to eat of the herbs and vegetables, and to drink of the springs, after which I arose and walked on, whenever I was hungry eating of the vegetables. In this manner I proceeded for seven days, and on the morning of the eighth day, I saw a faint object in the distance. I approached it, and, lo, it was a party of men gathering peppers. When they saw me, they surrounded me on every side, saying: "Who art thou? Whence hast thou come?" I informed them of my whole case, and of the horrors and distresses that I had suffered.

They made me sit among them until they had finished their work, and brought me good food, of which I ate. Their work being completed, they embarked with me in a ship, and went to their island and their abodes. They then took me to their King, who welcomed me and treated me with honour, and inquired of me my story. So I related to him all my experiences from the day of my going forth from the city of Bagdad, until I had come to him. The King wondered at my story, and commanded a repast to be spread. After I had eaten I arose, and leaving his presence, diverted myself with a sight of his city. It was a flourishing place, abounding with inhabitants and wealth, and with food and markets and goods and sellers and buyers.

After I had remained in the city for a few days, I saw that its great men and little, rode excellent, fine horses without saddles, whereat I wondered. On inquiry I discovered that no one in that land had ever seen a saddle, or knew of its make or use. I sought out a clever carpenter, and took wool, and leather, and felt, and caused a saddle to be made, I then sought a blacksmith, and described to him the form of stirrups, and he forged an excellent pair, to which I attached a fringe of silk.

Having done this, I fastened the saddle to one of the King's horses, attached to it the stirrups, bridled the horse, and led him forward to the King, who thanked me, and seated himself upon it, and was greatly delighted with that saddle and gave me a large present as a reward. When his Vizier saw that I had made a saddle, he desired one like it, so I made one for him. The grandees and great lords likewise desired saddles, and I made them, with the help of the carpenter and blacksmith, and for these I received large sums. Thus I collected abundant wealth, and became in high estimation with all the people.

I sat one day with the King in the utmost happiness and honour, and he said to me: "Know, O thou, that thou art honoured among us, and we cannot part with thee, nor can we suffer thee to depart from our city. Therefore I desire to marry thee to a beautiful wife, possessed of wealth and loveliness. I will lodge thee by me in a palace, so do not oppose me in this matter." I could not refuse to do as the King commanded me, so he sent immediately for the Cadi and witnesses to come, and married me forthwith to a woman of high rank and surprising beauty, possessing abundant wealth and fortune. He presented me with a great and handsome house, and gave me servants and other dependants. I loved my wife, and she loved me with great affection, and we lived together in a most delightful manner.

One day the wife of my neighbour and companion died, and I went in to console him. He was anxious, weary in soul and body, and I comforted him saying: "Mourn not for thy wife, for Allah will perhaps give thee one better than she!" But he wept bitterly and said: "O my companion, how can I marry another when I have but one more day to live! This day they will bury my wife, and they will bury me with her in the sepulchre, for it is a custom in our country, when the wife dieth to bury with her the husband alive, and when the husband dieth they bury with him the wife alive, that neither of them may enjoy life after the other."

While he was thus speaking behold the people of the city came. They prepared the body for burial, according to their custom, brought a bier and carried the woman on it, with all her apparel, ornaments and wealth. Taking the husband with them, they went forth from the city, and came to a mountain by the sea. They advanced to a certain spot, and lifted up a great stone from the mouth of a hole like a well, and threw the woman into a pit beneath the mountain. They brought the man, tied beneath his arms a rope of fibres of the palm-tree, and lowered him into the pit. They let down to him a great jug of sweet water, and seven cakes of bread. When they had let him down, he loosed himself from the rope, and they drew it up, and covered the mouth of the pit with that great stone, as it was before.

On my return to the city I went to the King, and said to him: "O King of the age, if the wife of a foreigner like myself die, do ye do with him after the manner of the country!" "Yea, verily," answered the King, "we bury him with her and do with him as thou hast seen." When I heard these words, my mind was stupefied, and I became fearful lest my wife should die before me, and they should bury me alive with her.

But a short time elapsed before my wife fell sick of a fever, and she remained ill for a few days, and died. Great numbers of people assembled to console me, and the King also came to comfort me. They washed my wife and decked her with the richest of her apparel, and ornaments of gold, and necklaces and jewels. They then placed her on the bier, and carried her to the mountain, and lifted the stone from the mouth of the pit, and cast her in. The family of my wife then advanced to bid me farewell, but I cried out that I was a foreigner, and would not submit to their custom. They laid hold upon me, and bound me by force, tying to me seven cakes of bread and a jug of sweet water, and let me down into the pit. They commanded me to loose myself from the ropes, but I would not do so, thereupon they threw down the ropes upon me, and covered the mouth of the pit with the great stone, and went their way.

I found that I was in an immense cavern beneath the mountain, and all about me lay the dead. I walked about feeling the sides of the cavern, and found that it was spacious and had many cavities in its sides, and in one of these I made a place for myself and sat down. "Alas!" said I, "would that I had not married in this country! Would that I had been drowned at sea, or had died upon the mountains! It would have been better than this evil death!" I continued in this manner blaming myself, until hunger and thirst assailed me, and I felt for the bread, and ate a little, and I drank a little water. After which I slept.

I remained in this condition for several days, eating and drinking a little at a time, fearing to exhaust the food and water. One day I awoke from my sleep and heard something make a noise in the cavern. I arose and walked toward it, and when it heard me coming it fled from me, and, lo, it was a wild beast! I followed it to the upper end of the cavern, where a light appeared like a star. I advanced and the light grew larger, so that I was convinced that it was a hole in the cavern, communicating with open country. I continued to advance and, lo, it was an aperture in the back of the mountain, which wild beasts had made, and through which they entered the cavern. I managed to force my way through the hole, and found myself on the shore of the sea, with a great mountain between me and the city from whence I came.

I praised Allah, whose name be exalted, and rejoiced exceedingly, and my heart was strengthened. I returned through the hole to the cavern, where I collected an abundance of jewels, necklaces of pearls, ornaments of gold and silver, which had been buried with the dead, and these I carried forth to the shore of the sea. Every day I entered the cavern and explored it, until I had removed all the ornaments and rarities I could find. Thus I continued to do for some time, when one day I was sitting upon the shore of the sea, and I beheld a vessel passing along through the midst of the roaring waves. So I took a white cloth and tied it to a staff, and ran along the sea shore, signalling the sailors until they saw me. They sent a boat to me and carried me to the master, who kindly embarked me and my goods in his ship. I offered him a considerable portion of my property, but he would not accept it of me, saying: "We take nothing from anyone whom we find stranded on a lonely shore, or on an island; instead we act towards him with kindness and favor for the sake of Allah, whose name be exalted."

We proceeded on our voyage from island to island, and from sea to sea, until at length we reached the city of Balsora, where I landed and remained a few days, after which I departed for Bagdad. I entered my house, saluted my family and companions, stored all my commodities, gave alms and presents, and clad widows and orphans. I then returned to my former habits of indulging in sport and merriment with my companions and brothers. Such were the most wonderful events that happened to me in the course of my fourth voyage. But, O Porter, if thou wilt sup with me to-morrow, I will inform thee what befell me during my fifth voyage, for it was more wonderful and extraordinary than the preceding voyage.

Sindbad of the Sea then presented the Porter with a

hundred pieces of gold, and the table was spread and the party supped, after which they went their ways wondering extremely. Sindbad the Porter went to his house, and passed the night in the utmost happiness and joy. When the morning came he arose, and performed his morning-prayers, and walked on until he entered the house of Sindbad of the Sea, who welcomed him, and sat with him until the rest of the companions came, after which they all ate and drank and were merry. Then Sindbad of the Sea began his narrative saying thus:

SINDBAD'S FIFTH VOYAGE—THE OLD MAN OF THE SEA

KNOW, O my brothers, that when I returned from my fourth voyage I became immersed in sport and merriment, so that I forgot all that I had suffered. Then my mind again suggested to me to travel, and to divert myself with the sight of other countries and peoples. So I arose, and bought precious goods suitable to a sea-voyage. I packed up the bales, and departed from the city of Bagdad to the city of Balsora, and walking along the river bank I saw a great, handsome, lofty ship, and it pleased me, so I purchased it. I hired a master and sailors, and bought black slaves, and embarked with my bales. There came a company of merchants who embarked with me and we set sail in the utmost joy and happiness, and pursued our voyage from island to island, and from sea to sea, buying and selling goods.

We arrived one day at a large island, deserted and

desolate, but on it was an enormous white dome, of great bulk, and, lo, it was the egg of a Roc. When the merchants had landed, to amuse themselves, not knowing that it was the egg of a Roc, they struck it with stones, so that it broke, and there poured from it a great quantity of liquid, and the young Roc appeared within the shell. The merchants pulled it out, killed it, and cut from it an abundance of meat. I was then in the ship, and knew not of it, and looking forth I saw the merchants striking the egg. I called out to them: "Do not this deed! It is a Roc's egg, and the bird will come, and demolish our ship, and destroy us!" But they would not hear my words.

Suddenly the sun was veiled, and the day grew dark, and we raised our eyes, and, lo, the wings of the Roc darkened the sky! When the bird came, and beheld its egg broken, it cried out fiercely, whereupon its mate, the female bird, came to it, and they flew in circles over the ship, uttering cries like thunder. So I called out to the master and sailors: "Push off the vessel and seek safety before we perish!" The master hastened, and the merchants having embarked, he loosed the ship, and we departed from the island. When the Rocs saw that we had put out to sea, they flew away, and soon returned, each of them having in its claws a huge mass of stone from a mountain. The male bird threw upon us the stone he had brought, but the master steered away the ship, and the stone missed it and fell into the sea. Then the mate of the male Roc threw upon us the stone she had brought, and it fell upon the stern of the ship and crushed it, and the vessel sunk with all that was in it.

I strove to save myself, and Allah, whose name be

exalted, placed within my reach a plank from the ship, so I caught hold of it, and got upon it, and the wind and the waves helped me forward and cast me on the shore of an island. I landed, exhausted with hunger and fatigue, and threw myself down, and remained thus for some time. At last I arose, and walked along the island, and saw that it resembled a garden of Paradise. There was an abundance of trees and fruits and flowers. So I ate of the fruits until I was satisfied, and I drank of the flowing rivers. Then I lay down, and slept.

In the morning I arose, and walked among the trees, and I beheld an old man sitting beside a stream, and he was clad from the waist down in a covering made of the leaves of trees. I approached, and saluted him, but he returned the salutation by a sign, without speaking. "O sheikh," said I, "what is the reason of thy sitting in this place?" He shook his head and sighed, and made a sign as though to say: "Carry me upon thy back, and transport me across this stream."

I said to myself: "I will act kindly to this old man, and perhaps I shall obtain a reward in Heaven!" So I stooped, and took him upon my shoulders, and carried him over the stream to the place he had indicated. When I said, "Descend in peace," he did not descend from my shoulders. He had wound his legs round my neck, and I looked at them, and saw that they were black and rough like the hide of a buffalo. I was frightened and tried to throw him from my shoulders, but he pressed his feet on my neck, and squeezed my throat, so that the world became black before my face, and I fell upon the ground in a fit. He then raised his legs, and beat me upon my back and shoulders, and caused me such violent pain that I was forced to rise.

He still kept his seat upon my shoulders, and, when I became fatigued with bearing him, he made a sign that I should go among the trees, to the best of the fruit. If I disobeyed him, he inflicted upon me with his feet blows more violent than those of whips, and he directed me with his hand to every place where he desired to go, and to that place I went with him. If I loitered or went leisurely, he beat me, and I was a captive to him. He descended not from my shoulders by night nor by day, and when he desired to sleep, he would wind his legs about my neck, and sleep a little, and then he would beat me until I arose.

Thus I remained for some time, until one day I carried the old man to a place in the island where I found an abundance of dried pumpkins. I took a large one, and cleansed it. I then went to a grape-vine, and filled the pumpkin with the juice of the grapes. I stopped up the aperture, and put the juice in the sun and left it for some days until it became pure wine. Every day I used to drink of it to help me endure the fatigue. So seeing me one day drinking, the old man made a sign with his hand for me to hand him the pumpkin, and fearing greatly I handed it to him immediately. Whereupon he drank all the wine that remained, and threw the pumpkin upon the ground. He then became intoxicated, and began to sway from side to side upon my shoulders. When I knew that he was drunk, I put my hand to his feet and loosed them from my neck, and I stooped with him, and sat down, and threw him upon the ground. Fearing lest he should rise from his intoxication, and torment me, I took a great mass of stone and struck him upon the head until he was dead.

After that I walked about the island, with a happy

THE OLD MAN OF THE SEA

mind, and came to the place where I was at first, on the shore of the sea, and, lo, a vessel approached from the midst of the roaring waves, and it ceased not its course until it anchored at the island. The passengers landed, and when they saw me, they approached, and inquired the cause of my coming to that place. I therefore acquainted them with all that had befallen me. Whereat they wondered extremely and said: "This old man who rode upon thy shoulders is called the Old Man of the Sea, and no one was ever beneath his limbs and escaped from him excepting thee."

They then brought me food, and I ate until I was satisfied, and they gave me clothes which I put on, covering myself decently. After this they took me with them to their ship, and proceeded night and day, until destiny drove us to a city of lofty buildings, overlooking the sea. That city is called the City of Apes.

I landed to divert myself, and the ship set sail without my knowledge. I repented of having landed, and while I sat weeping and mourning, a man of the city approached me. "O my master," said he, "art thou a stranger in this country?" "Yes," I replied, "I am a stranger and a poor man! I was in a ship which anchored here, and I landed from it to divert myself, and the ship sailed without me." "Arise," said he, " and embark with us in this boat, for if thou remain in the city during the night, the apes will destroy thee." So I immediately embarked with the people, and they pushed the boat off from the land, and passed the night on the water. Such hath always been their custom every night, for if anyone remaineth in the city, the apes come down from the mountains and destroy him. In the daytime the apes leave the city, and eat the fruits of the gardens, and sleep in the mountains, until evening, when they return to the city.

The next day, a person of the party with whom I had passed the night, said to me: "Hast thou any trade or art whereby thou mayest earn thy bread?" "No, my brother," I answered, "I am acquainted with no art, nor do I know how to make anything." Upon this the man brought me a cotton bag, and said to me: "Take this bag, and fill it with pebbles." He then led me out of the city, and I picked up small pebbles, with which I filled my bag. And, lo, a party of men came forth from the gates, and my companion said to them: "This is a stranger, so take him with you, and teach him your mode of earning your livelihood, perhaps he may in this way gain means of providing himself with food and drink, and ye will obtain a reward and recompense from Allah, whose name be exalted!"

The men welcomed me, and took me with them, each one having a bag like mine, full of pebbles. We walked until we arrived at a wide valley, wherein were lofty trees, which no one could climb. In that valley were many apes, and when they saw us they fled, and ascended the trees. Then the men began to pelt the apes with stones from their bags, and the apes plucked off the fruit of the trees, and threw them at the men. I looked at the fruit which they threw down, and, lo, they were cocoa-nuts.

I chose a tree in which were many apes, and proceeded to pelt them with stones, and they broke off the nuts from the tree, and threw them at me. So I collected a great quantity, and when the men returned home I carried off as many nuts as I could. Entering the city I went to the man, my companion, and gave him all the cocoa-nuts I had collected and thanked him for his kindness. "Take these," he said, "and sell them and make use of the price." I did as he told me, and continued every day to go forth with the men, and do as they did. I collected a great quantity of good cocoa-nuts, which I sold, and for which I received a large sum of money. I bought everything I saw that pleased me, and my time was pleasant, and my good fortune increased.

One day I was standing by the sea-side, and, lo, a vessel arrived at the city, and cast anchor by the shore. In it were merchants, who proceeded to exchange their goods for cocoa-nuts and other things. So I bade farewell to my companion, and embarked in that vessel with my cocoa-nuts and the other merchandise I had collected; after which we set sail the same day. We continued our course from island to island, and from sea to sea, and at every island where we cast anchor, I sold cocoa-nuts and received for them large sums.

We passed by an island in which are cinnamon and pepper, and there I exchanged cocoa-nuts for a great quantity of each. We passed also the island of Asirat, wherein is aloes-wood, and after that we passed by another island, the extent of which is five days' journey, and in it is the Sanfi aloes-wood, which is superior to that of the island of Asirat, but the inhabitants of this island love depravity, and the drinking of wines, and know not how to pray. After that we came to the pearl-fisheries, where I gave the divers some cocoa-nuts, and said: "Dive for my luck!" Accordingly they dived in the bay, and brought up a great number of large and valuable pearls, so I took them, and we proceeded on our way relying upon the blessing of Allah, whose name be exalted!

We continued our voyage until we arrived at the city of Balsora, where I landed, and stayed a short time. I went thence to the city of Bagdad, and entered my house and saluted my family and friends. I stored all my goods and commodities, clothed the widows and orphans, made presents to my family, my companions, and my friends. Allah had compensated me with four times as much as I had lost, and I forgot all the fatigue and terror I had suffered, and resumed my feasting and merrymaking. Such were the most wonderful things that happened to me in the course of my fifth voyage, but sup ye, and to-morrow come again, and I will relate to you the events of my sixth voyage, for it is more wonderful than this.

Then the attendants spread the table, and the party supped. When they had finished, Sindbad of the Sea presented Sindbad the Porter, with one hundred pieces of gold. He took them and departed, wondering at this affair. He passed the night in his abode, and when morning came, he arose and performed his morning-prayers, after which he walked to the house of Sindbad of the Sea, who welcomed him, and conversed with him until the rest of his companions had come. The servants spread the table, and the party ate, drank, and were merry. Then Sindbad of the Sea began to relate to them the story of the sixth voyage, saying:

SINDBAD'S SIXTH VOYAGE—THE TREASURE WRECKS

KNOW, O my brothers and my friends and my companions, that when I returned from my fifth voyage, I forgot what I had suffered, by reason of sport and merriment, and enjoyment. I continued thus until one day I saw a party of merchants bearing marks of travel, then I remembered the days of my travel, and my soul longed again to see other countries. So I determined to set forth. I bought precious and sumptuous goods, suitable for a sea-voyage, packed my bales, and went from the city of Bagdad, to the city of Balsora. There I beheld a large vessel, in which were merchants with their precious goods. I therefore embarked my bales in this ship, and we departed in safety from Balsora. We continued our voyage from place to place, and from city to city, selling and buying, and diverting ourselves with viewing different countries, and Fortune and the voyage were pleasant to us.

We were proceeding one day, and, lo, the master of the ship called out in grief and rage, threw down his turban, slapped his face, plucked his beard, and fell in the hold of the ship. The merchants and other passengers gathered about him, saying: "O master, what is the matter?" "Know, O company," he answered, "that we have wandered from our course, and have entered an unknown sea! If Allah help us not to escape, we shall perish!"

Then the master arose, and ascended the mast, and tried to loose the sails, but the wind became violent, and drove back the ship, and her rudder broke **near a** lofty mountain. The waves threw the vessel upon rocks and it broke to pieces, its planks were scattered, and the merchants fell into the sea. Some of them were drowned, and some were thrown upon the mountain.

I was of the number of those who landed upon this mountain. We crossed it and on the other side found a wide shore, whereon were treasures thrown up by the sea from ships that had been wrecked. My reason was confounded by the abundance of commodities and wealth cast up on the shore. And I beheld there a river of sweet water, flowing forth from beneath the nearest part of the mountain, and entering at the furthest part of it; and in the bed of this stream were various kinds of jewels, jacinths and large pearls suitable for Kings. They were like gravel in the channel of the river, which flowed through the fields, and all the bottom of the stream glittered by reason of ornaments of gold and silver.

In that land there is an abundance of aloes-wood, and there gusheth from the ground a spring of crude ambergris, which floweth like wax, and spreadeth upon the sea shore. The monsters of the deep come up from the sea and swallow the ambergris, and descend into the sea. When it becometh hot in their stomachs, they eject it and it riseth and congealeth on the surface of the water, and the waves cast it upon the shore, so travellers and merchants gather and sell it. As to the ambergris which is not swallowed but remaineth near the spring, it floweth over the side of the fountain, and congealeth upon the ground, and when the sun shineth upon it, it melteth, and it filleth the land with an odour like musk.

We continued to wander about the island, and collected from the wreckage of the ship a small quantity of food, which we used sparingly, eating of it every day or two days, only one meal. At last our stock became exhausted, and my companions died one by one. Each one who died, we washed, shrouded and buried in the clothes and linen, which the sea cast up. Thus it happened until all my companions had died, and left me alone upon the shore. Then I wept and said: "Would that I had died before my companions!" and I blamed myself for leaving my country and my people, after all that I had suffered during my former voyages.

Then thought I: "This river must have a beginning and an end, and it must have a place of egress into an inhabited country. I will construct for myself a raft, and I will depart on it, and if I find safety, I am safe, and if not it will be better to die in the river than in this place!" Accordingly I arose, and collected pieces of aloes-wood, and bound them together with ropes from the ships that had been wrecked. I brought some planks from the shore, and fastened them upon those pieces of wood. I made the raft to suit the width of the river, and bound it well and firmly. I piled it high with jewels and ornaments of gold and silver, and with the pearls that were like gravel, and with some of the crude ambergris. I then launched the raft upon the river, and made for it two pieces of wood like oars.

And so I departed on the raft following the current towards the mountain, and entered a tunnel through which the river ran. There was intense darkness within, and the raft continued to carry me along to a narrow place beneath the mountain, where my head rubbed the roof of the tunnel. I was unable to turn about, and I blamed myself for the situation, saying: "If this place becomes narrower, the raft will scarcely pass through, and it cannot return, so I shall perish miserably!" I threw myself down upon my face on the raft, and continued to proceed not knowing night from day, by reason of the darkness in which I was, and my terror and fear lest I should perish. In this state I continued my course along the river, which sometimes widened and at other times contracted, but the intensity of the darkness wearied me so that I was overcome with slumber, and the current ceased not to bear me along while I slept.

At length I awoke, and found myself in the light, and opening my eyes beheld wide fields on either side of the river, and the raft tied to the shore of an island, and around me a company of Indians and Abyssinians. When they saw that I had awakened they spoke to me in their language, but I knew not what they said, and imagined that it was a dream, and that this occurred in sleep. Then a man from among them advanced, and said to me in the Arabic language: "Peace be on thee, O our brother! Who art thou? Whence hast thou come? And what was the cause of thy coming to this place? We are people of the sown lands and the fields, and we came to irrigate our lands, and we found thee asleep upon thy raft. We tied it here, waiting for thee to arise at thy leisure. Now tell us what is the cause of thy coming unto this place."

"O my master," I replied, "I entreat thee to bring to me some food, for I am hungry, and after that ask of me concerning what thou wilt!" Thereupon he hastened, and brought food, and I ate until I was

satiated, and was at ease, and my fear subsided, and
my soul returned to me, and I praised Allah, whose
name be exalted! I then acquainted the people with
all that had happened to me from beginning to end,
and with what I had experienced upon the river.

They took me with them, and conveyed with me the
raft, together with all that was upon it of riches and
goods, and jewels and minerals, and ornaments of
gold and silver, and they led me to their King who was
the King of India, and acquainted him with my story.
He wondered at this exceedingly, and welcomed me
with great honours, and congratulated me on my safety.
Then I arose and took a quantity of jewels, and aloes-
wood and ambergris, and presented them to the King.
He accepted it all, treated me with the greatest honour,
and lodged me in a place in his abode. I associated with
the lords and grandees of his empire, who paid me
high respect, and I quitted not the abode of the King.

The capital of that country lies between a lofty
mountain and a deep valley. This mountain is seen at a
distance of three days, and it containeth varieties of
jacinths, and minerals, and trees of all sorts of spices.
Its surface is covered with emery, wherewith jewels are
cut into shape. In its rivers are diamonds, and pearls
are in its valleys. I ascended to the summit of the
mountain, and viewed its wonders, which are not to be
described!

I remained in this country for some time, then begged
of the King that I might return to my own land. He
gave me permission after great pressing, and bestowed
upon me abundant gifts from his treasury. He also
gave me a present and a sealed letter, saying: "Convey
these to the Caliph Haroun Er Raschid, and give him

many salutations from us." The letter was on yellow parchment, and the writing was ultramarine. The words that he wrote to the Caliph were these:

"Peace be on thee, from the King of India, before whom are a thousand elephants, and on the battlements of whose palace are a thousand jewels.

"To proceed: we have sent to thee a trifling present, accept it then from us. Thou art to us a brother and sincere friend, and the affection for you that is in our hearts is great; therefore favour us by a reply. The present is not suited to thy dignity; but we beg thee, O brother, to accept it graciously. And peace be on thee!"

And the present was a ruby cup, a span high, the inside of which was set with precious pearls; and a bed covered with the spotted skin of the serpent that swalloweth an elephant; and a hundred thousand mithkals of Indian aloes-wood; and a slave-girl like the shining full moon.

So I embarked, and departed thence, and we continued our voyage from island to island, and from country to country, until we arrived at Bagdad, whereupon I entered my house and met my family and my brethren, after which I took the present of the King of India, to the Caliph the Prince of the Faithful, Haroun Er Raschid. On entering his presence I kissed his hand, and placed before him the ruby cup, the serpent's skin, and the other things, all of which pleased the Caliph greatly, and he read the letter, and showed me utmost honour, and said: "O Sindbad, is that true which this King hath stated in his letter?" And I kissed the ground and answered: "O my lord, I witnessed in his kingdom much more than he hath mentioned. On the day of his public appearance a throne is set for the King upon a huge elephant, eleven cubits high, and he sitteth upon it, with his chief officers and pages and guests standing in two ranks, on his right and on his left. At his head standeth a man holding a golden javelin in his hand, and behind him a man in whose hand is a mace of gold, at the top of which is an emerald of the thickness of a thumb. And when the King mounteth he is accompanied by a thousand horsemen clad in gold and silk. Moreover by reason of the King's justice and good government, there is no need of a Cadi in his city, and all the people of his country know the truth from falsity."

And the Caliph wondered at my words, and conferred favours upon me and commanded me to depart to my abode. I did so and continued to live in the same pleasant manner as at present. I forgot the arduous troubles that I had experienced, and betook myself to eating and drinking, and pleasures and joy.

And when Sindbad of the Sea had finished his story, every one present wondered at the events that had happened to him. He then ordered his treasurer to give to Sindbad the Porter a hundred pieces of gold, and commanded him to depart, and to return the next day with the boon-companions, to hear the seventh story. So the Porter went away happy to his abode, and on the morrow he was present with the rest of the company, and they sat and enjoyed themselves, eating and drinking in enjoyment until the end of the day, when Sindbad of the Sea made a sign to them that they should hear his seventh story, and said:

SINDBAD'S SEVENTH VOYAGE—THE ELEPHANT HUNT

AFTER my sixth voyage I determined to go to sea no more, and my time was spent in joy and pleasures. But one day, some one knocked on the door of my house, and the door-keeper opened, and a page entered, and summoned me to the Caliph. I immediately went with him, and kissed the ground before the Prince of the Faithful, who said: "O Sindbad, I have an affair for thee to perform. I desire that thou go to the King of India, and convey to him our letter and our present."

I trembled thereat, and replied, "O my lord, I have a horror of voyaging, and when it is mentioned to me my limbs tremble! And this is because of the terrors and troubles I have experienced! Moreover, I have bound myself by an oath not to go forth from Bagdad." Then I informed the Caliph of all that had befallen me from first to last, and he wondered exceedingly thereat and said: "Verily, O Sindbad, it hath not been heard from times of old that such events have befallen anyone as have befallen thee! But for our sake thou wilt go forth this time, and convey our letter and our present to the King of India." So I replied: "I hear and obey," being unable to oppose this command.

I went from Bagdad to the sea, and embarked in a ship, and we proceeded nights and days, by the aid of Allah, whose name be exalted, until we arrived at the capital of India. As soon as I entered the city, I took the present and the letter, and went in with them to the

King, and kissed the ground before him. "A friendly welcome to thee, O Sindbad," said he. "We have longed to see thee, and praise be to Allah, who hath shown us thy face a second time!" Then he took me by the hand, and seated me by his side, and treated me with familiar kindness. "O my lord," I said, "I have brought thee a present and a letter from the Caliph Haroun Er Raschid." I then offered to him the letter, and the present which consisted of a horse worth ten thousand pieces of gold, with a saddle adorned with gold set with jewels; and a book; and a sumptuous dress; and a hundred different kinds of white cloths and silks of Egypt; and Greek carpets; and a wonderful, extraordinary cup of crystal; and also the table of Solomon, the son of David, on whom be peace!

And the contents of the letter were as follows:

> "Peace from the King Er Raschid, strengthened by Allah (who hath given to him and to his ancestors the rank of nobles and wide spread glory), on the fortunate Sultan!
>
> "To proceed: thy letter hath reached us, and we rejoiced thereat. And we send thee the book entitled 'The Delight of the Intelligent, and the Rare Present for Friends;' together with varieties of royal rarities. Therefore do us the honour to accept them, and peace be on thee!"

Then the King bestowed upon me abundant gifts and treated me with the utmost honour. After some days I begged his permission to depart, but he permitted me not save after great pressing. Thereupon I took leave of him, and went forth from his city, and set out on my journey, without any desire for travel or commerce.

We continued our voyage until we had passed many islands. When we were halfway over the sea, we were surrounded by a number of boats, and in them were men like devils, clad in coats of mail, and having in their hands swords, daggers and bows. They smote us, and wounded and killed some, while others they took captive, and having seized the ship, they conveyed us to an island, where they sold us as slaves.

A rich man purchased me, and took me to his house, fed me and gave me to drink, and clad and treated me in a friendly manner. So my soul was tranquillized, and I rested a little. One day my master said to me: "Dost thou know any art or trade?" I answered him: "O my lord, I am a merchant. I know nothing but traffic." "But dost thou know," he asked, "the art of shooting with the bow and arrow?" "Yes," I answered, "I know that." Thereupon he brought me a bow and arrows, and mounted me behind him upon an elephant. He departed from the city at the close of night, and conveyed me to a grove of large trees, where selecting a lofty, firm tree, he made me climb it, and gave me the bow and arrows, saying: "Sit here, and when the elephants come in the daytime, shoot at them with the arrows. If thou kill one, come and inform me." He then left me and departed.

I was terrified and frightened. I remained concealed in the tree until the sun rose, when the elephants came forth wandering through the grove. I discharged my arrows until I shot one, and then I went to my master and informed him of this. He was delighted with me, and treated me with honour and removed the slain elephant. In this way I continued every day shooting one, and my master coming and removing it, until one day I was sitting in the tree, concealed, when suddenly elephants innumerable came towards me roaring and growling so that the earth trembled beneath them. They surrounded the tree in which I was sitting, and a huge elephant, enormously great, wound his trunk around it, pulled it up by the roots, and cast it upon the ground.

I fell down senseless among the elephants, and the great one approached me, wound his trunk around me, raised me on his back, and went away with me, the other elephants following. He carried me a long distance, then threw me from his back, and departed, the other elephants accompanying him. When my terror had subsided, I looked about, and found myself among the bones of elephants, and the ground was covered with ivory tusks. I knew then that this was the burial place of the elephants, and that the great one had brought me here on account of the tusks.

I arose, and journeyed a night and a day, until I arrived at the house of my master, who saw that I was pale from fright and hunger. "Verily thou hast pained my heart," said he, "for I went, and found the tree torn up, and I imagined that the elephants had destroyed thee. Tell me what happened to thee." So I informed him of all that had occurred, and he took me upon his elephant, and together we journeyed to the burial place. When my master beheld those numerous ivory tusks, he rejoiced greatly, and carried away as many as he desired, and we returned to his house.

He treated me with increased favour, and said: "O my son, thou hast directed me to a means of very great gain! May Allah recompense thee well! Thou art freed for the sake of Allah, whose name be exalted!

Those elephants used to destroy many of us, but Allah hath preserved thee from them." "O my master," I replied, "may Allah bless thee! And I request, O my master, that thou give me permission to depart to mine own country." "Verily," answered he, "thou shalt return to thy home. We have a fair at which merchants come to purchase ivory. The time of the fair is now near. When the merchants arrive I will send thee with them, and they will convey thee to thy country."

Some days after this the merchants came as he had said, and bought, and sold, and exchanged. So I arose, and my master sent me with them. He paid the money for my passage, and gave me a large quantity of goods. We embarked and pursued our voyage from island to island, until we had crossed the sea, and landed on the shore. I sold my goods at an excellent rate, and bought rarities and sumptuous merchandise. I likewise bought for myself a beast to ride, and we went forth, and crossed the deserts, from country to country, until I arrived at Bagdad.

I then went in to the Caliph, and having saluted him, I informed him of all that had befallen me, whereupon he rejoiced at my safety, and thanked Allah, whose name be exalted! And he caused my story to be written in letters of gold. I then entered my house, and met my family and my brethren. And this is the end of the history of the events that happened to me during my seven voyages, and praise be to Allah, the One, the Creator, the Maker!

CONCLUSION OF THE STORY OF THE SEVEN VOYAGES OF SINDBAD OF THE SEA

AND when Sindbad of the Sea had finished his story, he ordered his servant to give Sindbad the Porter a hundred pieces of gold, saying: "How now, brother? Hast thou heard the like of these afflictions and calamities, and distresses? Have such troubles as these befallen anyone else, hath anyone suffered such hardships as I have suffered? Know then that my present pleasures are a compensation for the toil and humiliation I have endured."

And Sindbad the Porter advanced, and kissed the hands of Sindbad of the Sea, and said to him: "O my lord, thou hast undergone great horrors, and hast deserved these abundant blessings! Continue then, my lord, in joy and security! May Allah remove from thee the evils of fortune, and bless thy days forever!" And upon this Sindbad of the Sea bestowed favours on the Porter, and made him his boon companion, and he quitted him not by day nor by night, as long as they both lived.

* * * * * * * * *

And Sheherazade, having finished the relation of the seven wonderful voyages of Sindbad of the Sea, began next to relate the story of the enchanted City of Brass.

Chapter V

THE STORY OF THE CITY OF BRASS—
THE BOTTLED GENII

THERE was in olden time, in Damascus of Syria, a King named Abdelmelik. He was sitting one day among the kings and sultans of his empire, when they began to relate to each other the stories of ancient peoples. They called to mind the stories of our lord Solomon, the son of David (on both of whom be peace), and of his authority and dominion over mankind and the Genii, and over the birds and wild beasts and other things, and how Solomon used to imprison the disobedient Genii, Marids, and Devils in bottles of brass, and pour molten lead over them, and seal them with his signet.

Then Talib, the son of Sahl, related how there was once a man who embarked with others in a ship, and how during the black darkness of the night a wind arose, and carried them to the coasts of a strange land. And when the sun arose there came forth from caves people of black complexion, with naked bodies like wild beasts. They had a King of their own race, and he came attended by his people, and saluted the ship's company, saying: "No harm shall befall you." He then invited the people of the ship to a banquet of the flesh of birds and wild beasts.

When the feast was over the people of the ship went down to enjoy themselves upon the shore of the sea. And they found a fisherman who was casting his net, and when he drew it up, lo, in it was a bottle of brass, stopped with lead, which was sealed with the signet of Solomon the son of David, on both of whom be peace! The fisherman broke the seal, and there came forth from the bottle a blue smoke, that reached the clouds of Heaven, and a terrible voice was heard crying: "Repentance, repentance, O Prophet of Allah!" Then the smoke became a being of terrific aspect, and of dreadful make, whose head reached as high as a mountain, and he disappeared before their eyes. When the people of the ship saw this their hearts melted within them for fear. And the King of that land said to them: "Know that this is one of the disobedient Genii, whom Solomon the son of David imprisoned in bottles, and he poured lead over them, and threw them into the sea. Often when the fishermen cast their nets they bring up these bottles, and, when the seals are broken, there come forth Genii who think that Solomon is still living, whereupon they cry out: 'Repentance, repentance, O Prophet of Allah!'"

When Talib had finished his tale the King Abdelmelik wondered greatly. "Verily," said he, "I desire to see some of these bottles!" "O Prince of the Faithful," answered Talib, "thou art able to do so. Write orders to the Emir Mousa to journey from the Western country to this sea we have mentioned, and to bring to thee some of the bottles."

And King Abdelmelik approved of his advice, and

said: "O Talib, thou hast spoken the truth in what thou hast said, and I desire that thou shalt be my messenger to Mousa, the son of Nuseir, and thou shalt be equipped for thy journey with all wealth and dignity, and I will watch over thy family during thy absence. Therefore go in dependence on the blessing of Allah, and his aid!" And the King ordered his Vizier to write a letter to Mousa, his viceroy in the Western country, commanding him to journey in search of the bottles of Solomon, and to leave his son to govern the Western country in his stead, and to take with him guides and troops. And he sealed the letter and gave it to Talib, the son of Sahl, commanding him to hasten, and he gave him riches and riders and footmen to help him on his way.

So Talib set forth, and journeyed to the Western country. And when the Emir Mousa knew of Talib's approach, he went forth, and met him and welcomed him with joy, and Talib handed to him the letter. So the Emir took it and read it, and put it upon his head, saying: "I hear and obey the command of the Prince of the Faithful."

And Mousa summoned his great men, and asked their advice respecting the matter. "O Emir," they answered, "if thou desirest one who will guide thee to that place, have recourse to the sheikh Abdelsamad, for he is a knowing man, and hath travelled much, and he is acquainted with the deserts and the wastes and the seas, and with their inhabitants and wonders."

Accordingly the Emir sent for the sheikh, who came before him, and, lo, he was a very old man, decrepit from age and experience. The Emir Mousa saluted him, and said: "O sheikh, our lord the Prince of the

THE SHEIKH ABDELSAMAD

Faithful, Abdelmelik, hath commanded us thus and thus, and I possess little knowledge of the land, and it hath been told me that thou art acquainted with the country and its routes. Art thou willing to help accomplish the affair of the Prince of the Faithful?"

"Know, O Emir," the sheikh replied, "it is a journey of two years. On the way are difficulties and horrors, and extraordinary and wonderful things. But Allah will assuredly make this affair easy for us, through the blessing attendant upon thee, O viceroy of the Prince of the Faithful!" Then said the Emir Mousa: "It is well, let us depart immediately." And he made his son Haroun viceroy in his place, and departed together with Talib, and the sheikh Abdelsamad, and accompanied by troops of footmen and riders.

They proceeded night and day without stopping until they arrived at a silent palace. "Enter," the sheikh Abdelsamad said, "and be admonished by the fate of its inhabitants!" They advanced and found the door open, and entering they saw a great hall, the ceilings and walls of which were decorated with gold and silver. They went through the palace, and, lo, it was devoid of inhabitants, its courts were desolate, and its apartments deserted. In the midst of the building was a chamber covered by a lofty dome, rising high in the air. The chamber had eight doors of sandal-wood, with nails of gold, ornamented with stars of silver and set with precious jewels. Around about this chamber were four hundred tombs, and in the centre was a tomb of terrible appearance, whereupon was a tablet of iron, inscribed with words.

The sheikh Abdelsamad drew near to the tomb, and read the inscription, and, lo, on it was written:

"In the name of Allah, the Mighty, the Powerful! O thou, who arrivest at this place, be admonished by our misfortunes and calamities. Be not deceived by the world and its beauties, for it is a flatterer, a cheat, and a traitor! For I possessed four thousand bay horses; and I married a thousand damsels of the daughters of Kings; and I was blessed with a thousand children; and I lived a thousand years; and I amassed riches such as the Kings of the earth could not procure! I imagined that my enjoyments would continue for ever, but Allah decreed otherwise and the thunder of Truth fell upon us, and there died of us every day two, until a great company had perished. I had an army of a thousand thousand hardy men, having spears and coats of mail, and sharp swords, and I said: 'O companies of soldiers, can ye prevent that which hath befallen us from Allah the Almighty? Bring to me my wealth, a thousand hundredweight of red gold, the like quantity of white silver, and varieties of pearls and jewels. Perhaps by the means of these riches ye may purchase for me one more day of life!' And they brought the riches to me, and said: 'Alas, who can contend against the decrees of Allah!' So they resigned themselves to their fate, and perished, and I submitted to Allah with patience, until he took my soul. And if thou ask my name, I am Kosh the son of Sheddard, the son of Ad the Greater."

And the Emir Mousa wept when he heard this inscription, for he sorrowed for the fate of these people, and he passed on to another apartment of the palace, where he saw a table upon four legs of alabaster, whereupon was inscribed:

"Upon this table have eaten a thousand one-eyed Kings
Also a thousand Kings each sound in both eyes."

The Emir read all this. Then he went forth from the palace and took with him naught save the table.

And the party proceeded, with the sheikh Abdelsamad before them showing the way, until after the first day had passed, and the second and the third. They then came to a high hill, and, lo, upon it was a horseman of brass, holding in his hand a spear. On it was inscribed:

"If thou wouldst know the way to the City of Brass
Rub the hand of the horseman, and he will point thither!"

And when the Emir Mousa had rubbed the hand of the horseman, the figure turned and pointed with his spear towards another direction from that in which they were travelling, so the party turned and journeyed thither.

THE AFRITE OF THE BLACK STONE PILLAR

AS they were proceeding one day they came to a pillar of black stone, wherein was a being sunk to his armpits, and he had two huge wings, and four arms—two human arms and two like the forelegs of a lion with claws. He had hair upon his head like tails of horses, and two eyes like burning coals, and he had a third eye in his forehead, like the eye of the lynx, from which came sparks of fire. He was tall and black, and was continually crying out: "Extolled be the perfection of Allah, who hath appointed me this affliction and torture, until the day of Resurrection!"

When the people of Emir Mousa beheld this being their reason fled, and they retreated in flight. But the Emir said to the sheikh: "What is this?" "I know not what it is," he answered. "Draw near to him," the Emir said, "and learn his history." So the sheikh drew near, and said to the creature: "O thou, what is thy name, and what is thy nature, and what hath placed thee here in this manner?" And the being answered and said: "I am an Afrite of the disobedient Genii and my name is Dahish the son of Elamash. Verily my story is wonderful! It is this:

There belonged to one of the sons of Eblis, an idol of red carnelian, and I was made its guardian. And there used to worship it one of the Kings of the sea. He was a King of illustrious dignity and great glory, and he had among his troops a million evil warrior Genii who smote with swords before him. These Genii, were under my command.

Now this King had a daughter, who was endowed with beauty and loveliness, and elegance and perfection, and I described her to Solomon, on whom be peace. So he sent to her father saying: "Marry me to thy daughter, and break thy red carnelian idol, and bear witness that there is no other deity but Allah, and that Solomon is his Prophet. If thou refusest to do this, I will come to thee with forces that shall fill thy land, and leave thee like yesterday that hath passed!"

The King was insolent to the messenger of Solomon, and magnified himself and was proud. Then said he to his Viziers: "What say ye respecting the affair of Solomon the son of David? For he hath sent demand‑ing my daughter, and commanding me to break my red carnelian idol, and to adopt his faith." "O great

King," answered his Viziers, "can Solomon do unto thee any injury, when thou art in the midst of this vast sea? If he come unto thee, he cannot prevail against thee, since the hordes of the Genii will fight on thy side. But do thou now consult thy red carnelian idol, and hear his reply."

Upon this the King went immediately to his idol, and after he had offered a sacrifice and slain victims, he fell down prostrate before it, and wept. And I Dahish, the son of Elamash, entered into the body of that idol and spake to the King saying: "Fear not. If Solomon wishes to wage war against thee, go forth, and I will snatch his soul from him!" And when the King heard these words, his heart strengthened, and he determined to wage war with Solomon the son of David—on whom be peace! Accordingly he inflicted a painful beating on the messenger and returned a shameful answer, saying: "Dost thou threaten me with false words? Either come thou to me, or I will go to thee!"

When the Prophet of Allah, Solomon, heard these words, his fury rose, and he prepared his forces, consisting of obedient Genii, and men, and wild beasts and birds and reptiles. He made ready his weapons, and he mounted with his forces, upon his magic carpet, with the birds flying over his head, and the wild beast marching beneath the carpet, and he flew until he alighted upon his enemy's coast, and surrounded his island, having filled the land with the forces.

And Solomon sent to our King saying: "Behold, I have arrived, therefore submit thyself to my authority, and break thy red carnelian idol, and marry me to thy daughter, and testify that there is no deity but Allah, and that Solomon is his Prophet." But our King answered the messenger: "There is no way for my doing this thing that he requireth of me, therefore inform him that I am coming forth unto him." Accordingly the messenger returned to Solomon and gave him the reply.

Our King then sent to the people of his country and collected troops of a million disobedient Genii, to these he added Marids and Devils that were in the islands of the sea and on the tops of mountains. After this he made ready his forces, and opened his armouries, and distributed weapons.

As to the Prophet of Allah, Solomon, on whom be peace, he disposed his troops, commanding the wild beasts to form themselves into two divisions, on the right of the people, and on their left, and commanding the birds to be upon the islands. And the wild beasts and birds replied: "We hear and obey, O Prophet of Allah!" Then Solomon the Prophet of Allah set for himself a couch of alabaster, adorned with jewels, and plated with plates of red gold. He placed his Vizier Asaph, and the Kings of mankind on the right side, and his Vizier Dimiriat, and the Kings of the obedient Genii on his left, and the vipers and serpents before him.

And after this the two armies met upon a wide tract, and contended together. I refrained my troops of Marids and Devils from attacking Solomon and his army, saying: "Keep your places in the battlefield, while I go forth and challenge Dimiriat." I did so and, lo, the King of the obedient Genii came forth like a great mountain, his smoke ascending, and he approached, and smote me with a flaming fire. He cried out at me with a prodigious cry, so that I imagined the heavens had fallen and closed over me, and the mountains shook at his voice. Then he commanded his companions and they charged upon us all together. We also charged upon them and we cried out one to another. The fires rose, and the smoke ascended, the hearts of the combatants were almost cleft asunder, and the battle raged. The birds fought in the air, and the wild beasts in the dust. And my companions and troops were overcome, and my tribes were routed, and defeat befell our King, and we became unto Solomon a spoil.

And I contended with Dimiriat until I grew weak, and he vanquished me. And he rushed upon me and took me prisoner and led me bound before Solomon. The King treated me in a most evil manner, he caused this pillar to be brought, and put me in it, and sealed me with his signet, after which he chained me, and Dimiriat conveyed me to this place, and this pillar is my prison until the day of Resurrection."

Now when the Afrite had finished his story, the party wondered at the terrible nature of his form. And the sheikh Abdelsamad said to the Afrite: "Are there in this place any of the disobedient Genii confined in bottles of brass, from the time of Solomon on whom be peace?" "Yes," answered the Afrite, "in the sea of Kakar, where are a people who are descendants of Noah, whose country the deluge reached not." "And where," said the sheikh, "is the City of Brass?" The Afrite answered, "It is near!"

THE ENCHANTED CITY

SO the party left him, and proceeded until there appeared in the distance a great, black object, near which were what seemed to be two fires. "O sheikh," said the Emir Mousa, "what is this we see?" "Be rejoiced," the sheikh answered, "for this is the City of Brass, and thus is it described in the Book of Hidden Treasures. Its wall is of black stones, and it hath two towers of brass, which seem to the beholder like two fires."

And they approached the City of Brass, and, lo, it was lofty, strongly fortified, rising high in the air, impenetrable. The height of its wall was eighty cubits, and it had five and twenty invisible gates. The party stopped before the wall, and endeavoured to discover one of its gates but they could not.

"And how," said the Emir, "can we contrive to enter this city, and divert ourselves with its wonders?" He then ordered one of his young men to mount a camel and ride round the city, in the hope that he might discover a gate. So one of the youths mounted, and proceeded round the city for two days and nights, and on the third day came in sight of his companions. "O Emir," he said, "I found no gates, and the lowest part of the whole wall is here where ye have alighted."

Then the Emir Mousa took Talib, the son of Sahl, and the sheikh Abdelsamad, and they ascended a mountain opposite the city, and overlooking it, and they saw a city than which eyes had not beheld a greater! Its pavilions were lofty, and its domes were shining, its rivers were running, and its trees were fruitful. It was a city of impenetrable gates, empty and still, without the voice of people. The owls hooted in its gardens, the birds skimmed above it in circles, and the ravens croaked in its streets. The Emir, sorrowing for its lost inhabitants, descended from the mountain and returned to his troops.

They passed the day devising means of entering the city. At last Talib, the son of Sahl, said: "Let us make a ladder and mount upon it, and perhaps we shall gain access to the gate from within." So the Emir called the carpenters and blacksmiths, and ordered them to make a ladder covered with plates of iron. They did so, and set it up, and fixed it against the wall. Then said the Emir to his young men: "Which of you will ascend this ladder, and mount upon the wall, and walk along it, and contrive some means of descending into the city?" And one of them answered: "I will ascend, O Emir, and descend and open the gate." "Mount," said the Emir, "and Allah bless thee!"

Accordingly the man ascended the ladder until he reached the top. He looked over the wall into the city, and clapped his hands, and cried out: "Thou art beautiful!" Then he cast himself down into the city, and his flesh became mashed with his bones. Then said one of the party: "Perhaps another may be more steady than he." So a second ascended, and a third, and a fourth, and a fifth, and they ceased not to ascend by that ladder to the top of the wall, one after another, until twelve men had ascended, and like the first they cast themselves down into the city, and their flesh was mashed with their bones.

Then the sheikh Abdelsamad arose and having encouraged himself, saying: "In the name of Allah, the Compassionate, the Merciful!" he ascended the ladder, repeating the praises of Allah, whose name be exalted, until he reached the top, when he clapped his hands, and fixed his eyes on the city. He then laughed immoderately and called out in a loud voice: "O Emir, no harm shall befall thee and thy troop! For Allah, to whom be ascribed glory and might, hath averted from me the artifice of the Devil!" "O sheikh," called the Emir, "what hast thou seen?" "When I reached the top of the wall," answered the sheikh, "I beheld ten damsels as beautiful as moons, and they stretched out their hands to me as though they would say: 'Come to us.' And it seemed to me that beneath me was a sea of water, and I desired to cast myself down as our companions did, but I beheld them dead, and I withheld myself from the temptation, and recited a part of the Koran, and the damsels departed from me, therefore I cast not myself down. This is no doubt an enchantment contrived to keep out those wishing to enter the city."

The sheikh Abdelsamad then walked along the wall until he came to the two towers of brass, and between them were two gates of gold, without locks upon them, or any sign of the means of opening them. And looking attentively he saw in the middle of one of the gates a figure of a horseman of brass, having one hand extended as though he were pointing with it, and on it was an inscription, which the sheikh read, and, lo, it contained these words:

"In the middle of the front of the horseman's body is a pin. Turn it twelve times, and then the gate will open!"

So the sheikh examined the horseman, and found the pin, strong, firm and well fixed. He turned it twelve times, and the gate opened immediately, with a noise like thunder.

The sheikh descended, and all the troops hastened to enter the city. But the Emir Mousa cried out to them saying: "O people, if all of us enter, and harm come to us within this city, we shall all perish, therefore half shall enter, and half remain behind." So the Emir and half the troop then entered, and found within the gates, handsome benches, on which were people dead, and over their heads were elegant shields, and keen swords, and strung bows, and notched arrows. They saw also the gate-keepers, and servants, and lieutenants, lying upon beds of silk, all of them dead. And the party saw their companions lying dead, so they buried them.

They then entered the market of the city, and beheld lofty buildings, and the shops open, full of all kinds of goods and wealth. They passed on to the silk-market in which were silks and brocades interwoven with red gold and white silver, and the owners were dead, lying upon skins, and appearing as though they would speak. Leaving these they went on to the market of jewels and pearls and jacinths, and they left it and passed on to the market of the money-changers, whom they found dead, with varieties of silks beneath them, and their shops filled with gold and silver. They next visited the market of the perfumers, and, lo, their shops were filled with varieties of perfumes, bags of musk, and ambergris, and aloes-wood and camphor and other things.

And when they went forth from the market of the

perfumers, they found near unto it a silent palace, and they entered, and found banners unfurled, and drawn swords and strung bows, and shields hung up by chains of gold and silver, and helmets gilded with red gold. And in the passages of that palace were benches of ivory, ornamented with plates of brilliant gold, and with silk.

They passed hence into the interior of the palace. There the Emir Mousa beheld a great hall and opening out of the hall were four large and lofty chambers, decorated with gold and silver, and with various colours. In the midst of the hall was a great fountain of alabaster over which was a canopy of brocade, and in the four chambers were decorated fountains, and pools of water in basins lined with marble, and canals of water flowed from the pools along the floors of those chambers, the four streams meeting in a large basin in the midst of the great hall.

They entered the first chamber, and they found it filled with gold, and white silver, and pearls and jacinths and other precious jewels. They found in it also chests of red and yellow and white brocades. And they went thence to the second chamber, and opened a closet in it and, lo, it was filled with arms and weapons of war, and in the third chamber they found closets filled with weapons inlaid with varieties of gold, silver and jewels. And passing thence they found in the fourth chamber vessels of gold and silver, and saucers of crystal, and cups set with brilliant pearls, and cups of carnelian, and other utensils for food and drink. So they began to take what suited them of these things, and each of the soldiers carried off what he could.

In the large hall they saw a door of teak-wood inlaid

with ivory, and adorned with plates of brilliant gold. Over it hung a silken curtain, worked with various kinds of embroidery, and upon the door were locks of white silver. The sheikh approached the locks, and opened them by his knowledge and skill. The party entered a passage paved with marble, upon the walls of which were silken hangings, whereon were figured wild beasts and birds, all worked with red gold and white silver, and their eyes were of pearls and jacinths.

Next they entered a saloon built of polished marble, adorned with jewels. And they found in the centre of that saloon a dome-shaped chamber constructed of stones gilded with red gold, and within the chamber was a structure of alabaster, with lattice windows adorned with oblong pearls, and within the alabaster structure was a pavilion of brocade, raised upon columns of red gold, and within the pavilion was a fountain, decorated with birds, the feet of which were of emeralds. By the brink of the fountain was placed a couch adorned with pearls, jewels and jacinths, whereon was a damsel as beautiful as the shining sun. Eyes have not beheld one more beautiful! Upon her was a garment of brilliant pearls, on her head was a crown of red gold, on her neck was a necklace of refulgent gems, and upon her forehead were two jewels the light of which was like that of the sun. The couch upon which the damsel was had steps, and on the steps were two slaves, one of them white, and the other black, and in the hand of one was a weapon of steel, and in the hand of the other a jewelled sword. And upon a tablet of gold was read this inscription:

"In the name of Allah, the Compassionate, the Merciful! I am Tadmor, the daughter of the King of the Amalekites. I possessed what none of the Kings possessed, and ruled with justice, and now I rest in eternal sleep. Whoever thou art who arrivest at our city, take of the wealth what thou canst, but touch not anything that is upon my body. Fear Allah and seize naught of it! I cause this to be a charge that I give thee in confidence. And peace be on thee!"

The Emir Mousa was confounded when he read this and looked at the damsel, and he wondered at her loveliness, and the redness of her cheeks and the blackness of her hair. Then said he to his companions: "Bring the sacks, and fill them with part of these riches and these vessels and rarities and jewels." Thereupon Talib said: "O Emir, shall we leave this damsel with the things that are upon her? They are things which have no equal!" But the Emir replied: "Heardest thou not that which the damsel hath given in charge? Moreover she hath given it as a charge offered in confidence, and we are not people of treachery!" "On account of these words wilt thou leave these riches and these jewels?" said Talib. "What should the damsel do with these things? With a garment of cotton might she be covered. We are more worthy of these things than she."

Then Talib, the son of Sahl, approached the steps of the damsel's couch and ascended them until he reached the spot between the two slaves when, lo, one of these smote him on the back, and the other smote him with a sword, and struck off his head, and Talib fell down dead. So the Emir Mousa seeing the fate which had overcome Talib, the covetous, said: "May Allah not show mercy on thy resting place!" So saying he gave orders for the entry of the troops and the soldiers who loaded the camels with part of those riches, rareties and gold; after which the Emir commanded them to leave the city and to close the gate as it was before, and they did so.

They then proceeded along the sea-coast until they came in sight of a high mountain overlooking the sea. In it were many caves, and in these was a people of the blacks clad all in skins. And when they saw the troops they fled to the caves. The Emir and the troops alighted, and the tents were pitched, and the riches were put down, and the party had not rested long when the King of the blacks came down from the mountain and drew near to them. When he came to the Emir Mousa he saluted him, and asked: "Are ye of mankind or of the Genii?" "We are of mankind," the Emir answered. "We are subjects of King Abdelmelik, and we have come on account of the bottles of brass which are here in your sea, and wherein are the Devils imprisoned from the time of Solomon, the son of David, on both of whom be peace! Our King hath commanded us to bring him some bottles that he may see the Genii." The King of the blacks replied: "Most willingly."

He then feasted the Emir Mousa with fish and ordered the divers to bring up from the sea some of the bottles of Solomon, and they brought up twelve bottles wherewith the Emir was delighted. He presented the King of the blacks with many presents and gave him large gifts. In like manner the King of the blacks gave to the Emir Mousa a present of wonders of the sea in the form of human beings.

Then they bade the King of the blacks farewell, and they journeyed back until they came to the land of Syria, and went in to the Prince of the Faithful, to whom they recounted all that they had seen and done. And the King Abdelmelik said: "Would that I had been with you, that I might have beheld all these wonders!" He then took the bottles of Solomon and opened them one after another and the Genii came forth from them crying: "Repentance, repentance, O Prophet of Allah! We will not return to the like conduct ever!" And at this the King marvelled greatly. He then caused the riches to be brought, and divided among the troops, and he said: "Allah hath not bestowed upon anyone the like of glory and power which he bestowed upon Solomon, the son of David, on both of whom be peace!"

This is the end of that which hath come down to us of the history of the City of Brass, entire. And Allah is all-knowing.

*   *   *   *   *   *   *   *   *

"And this," said Sheherazade, "is not nearly as wonderful as the adventures of Hassan of Balsora."

Chapter VI

STORY OF THE ADVENTURES OF HASSAN OF BALSORA — THE FIRE WORSHIPPER

THERE was in ancient times a certain merchant residing in Balsora, and that merchant had two sons and great wealth. And it happened, as Allah decreed, that the merchant died, so his two sons prepared him for the grave, and buried him. After which they divided the wealth between them equally, and each took his portion and opened a shop. One was a dealer in copper wares and the other was a goldsmith. The name of the young goldsmith was Hassan.

Now, while Hassan the goldsmith was sitting in his shop one day, lo, a Persian walked along the market street and approaching the shop accosted him saying: "O my son, thou art a comely young man. I have not a son and I know a wonderful art, numbers of people have asked me to teach it them and I would not. But my soul inclineth to thee, so that I would teach thee, and drive poverty from thy door, then thou shalt not need any more to labour with the hammer and the charcoal and the fire." "O my master," answered

Hassan, "when wilt thou teach me this wonderful art?" The Persian replied: "To-morrow I will come to thee and will make for thee, of copper, pure gold in thy presence."

Upon this Hassan rejoiced and he bade farewell to the Persian, and went to his mother. He entered, and saluted her, and ate with her, and told her all that had happened. But his mother said: "O my son, beware of listening to Persians for they are great deceivers, who know the art of alchemy and trick people, and take their wealth, and despoil them." But he replied: "O my mother, we are poor people, we have nothing to covet that anyone should trick us. The Persian who came to me is a dignified sheikh and a virtuous man, and Allah hath inclined him towards me." Thereupon his mother kept silence in her anger.

When the morning came Hassan rose, took the keys, and opened the shop, and, lo, the Persian approached him. So he rose and desired to kiss his hand but the Persian refused and would not permit his doing that. "O Hassan," he said, "prepare the crucible and place the bellows." He therefore did as the Persian ordered him, and lighted the charcoal, after which the Persian said to him: "O my son, hast thou any copper?" And Hassan brought forth from a press a broken copper plate. Then the Persian ordered him to take the shears and to cut the plate into small pieces, and he did as he told him. He cut it into small pieces, and threw it into the crucible, and blew upon it with the bellows until it became liquid. The Persian put his hand to his turban and took forth a folded paper. He opened it and sprinkled some of its contents into the crucible and the copper in the crucible became a lump of gold.

So when Hassan beheld this he was overcome by joy. He took the lump and turned it over, and he took the file and filed it, and saw it to be of pure gold of the very best quality. Then he bent over the hand of the Persian to kiss it, and the Persian said to him: "Take this lump to the market and sell it, and take its price quickly, without speaking." Accordingly Hassan went down to the market and gave the lump to the broker, who took it and rubbed it on the touchstone and found it to be of pure gold, and he bought it for fifteen thousand pieces of silver. And Hassan went home and related to his mother all that he had done, and she kept silence in her anger.

Now on the next day, as Hassan was sitting in his shop, he looked and, lo, the Persian approached and entered. "O my son," he said, "dost thou desire to make gold this day? If so, let us repair to thy house and I will teach thee there." So Hassan arose, closed his shop and went with the Persian. He entered his house, and found his mother and informed her that the Persian stood at the door. So she put in order a chamber, and spread the carpets and cushions, and departed to a neighbour's house.

Then Hassan taking the Persian by the hand, drew him into the chamber, and placed food and drink before him saying: "Eat, O my master, that the bond of bread and salt may be established between us. May Allah, whose name be exalted, execute vengeance upon him who is unfaithful to the bond of bread and salt!" "Thou hast spoken the truth, O my son," answered the Persian, "who knoweth the true value of the bond of bread and salt?" and he ate with Hassan until they were satisfied. The Persian then took secretly forth a packet from his turban, unfolded it and wrapped its contents in a piece of sweetmeat. "O Hassan," said he, "thou art now my son, and hast become dearer to me than my soul or my wealth, and I have a daughter to whom I will marry thee," and he handed to him the piece of sweetmeat. Hassan took it, kissed his hand, and put the sweetmeat into his mouth not knowing what was secretly decreed to befall him. He swallowed the piece and immediately lost his senses and his head sank down to his feet. When the Persian saw Hassan in this state he rejoiced exceedingly. Rising to his feet he said to him: "Thou hast fallen into the snare, O young wretch! O dog of the Arabs! For many years have I been searching for thee until I have now gotten thee, O Hassan!"

He then tied Hassan's hands behind his back, and bound his feet to his hands. After which he took a chest, emptied it of the things that were in it, put Hassan into it, and locked it upon him. He emptied also another chest and put into it all the wealth that was in Hassan's abode. Then he went forth running to the market, and brought a porter, who carried off the two chests to the river bank, where was waiting a moored ship. That vessel was fitted out for the Persian, and her master was expecting him, so when her crew saw the Persian, they came and carried the two chests, and put them on board the ship. The master then cried out to the sailors: "Pull up the anchor, and loose the sails!" And the ship proceeded with a fair wind.—Such was the case with the Persian and Hassan.

But as to the mother of Hassan, when she came to the house, and beheld no one in it, nor found the chests

nor the wealth, she knew her son was lost and that
Fate had overtaken him. She slapped her face, and
rent her garments, and cried out, and wailed. And
she ceased not to weep during the hours of the night
and the periods of the day, and she built in the midst
of the house a tomb, on which she inscribed the name of
Hassan, with the date of his loss. She quitted not the
tomb, but sat by it night and day.

Now, to return to Hassan and the Persian. The
Persian was a Magian, a wicked, vile alchemist. The
name of that accursed wretch was Bahram the Magian.
He used every year to take a Mohammetan youth, and
to slaughter him over a hidden treasure. And having
now treacherously stolen Hassan the goldsmith he proceeded with him that day and night.

At sunrise the next morning, Bahram the Magian
ordered his black slaves to bring to him the chest in
which was Hassan. They brought the chest and
opened it and took him forth. The Magian then poured
some vinegar into his nostrils, and blew a powder
into his nose, whereupon Hassan sneezed and opening
his eyes, looked right and left, and found himself on
shipboard in the midst of the sea, with the Persian
sitting by him. He knew then that the cursed one had
done it, and that he had fallen into the calamity against
which his mother had cautioned him. So Hassan
pronounced the words: "There is no strength nor power
but in Allah, the High, the Great! Verily unto Allah
we belong, and verily unto him we return! O Allah,
act graciously with me and make me to endure with
patience thine affliction. O Lord of all creatures!"
Then looking towards the Persian he spoke to him with
soft words, and said to him: "O my father, what are

these deeds? Where is thy respect for the bond of bread and salt, and the oath thou swarest to me?" "O dog," answered the Persian, "doth such a one as myself know any obligation imposed by bread and salt? I have slain a thousand youths like thee, save one youth, and thou shalt complete the thousand."

Then Barham the Magian rose and ordered Hassan's bonds to be loosed, saying: "By the fire and the light and the shade and the heat I did not imagine that thou wouldest fall so easily into my net! But the fire strengthened me against thee, and aided me to seize thee, and now I will make thee a sacrifice to it!" So Hassan replied: "Thou hast been unfaithful to the bond of bread and salt!" Upon this the Magian raised his hand, and gave him a blow, and he fell and bit the deck with his teeth, and fainted, the tears running down his cheeks.

The Magian then ordered his slaves to light for him a fire, saying: "This is the fire that emitteth light and sparks, and it is what I worship. If thou wilt worship it as I do, I will give thee half my wealth and marry thee to my daughter." But Hassan cried out: "Woe to thee! Thou art surely an infidel Magian, and wor-shippest the fire instead of Allah, the Almighty King, the Creator of the night and the day!" Thereupon the accursed Magian was enraged, and arose, and prostrated himself to the fire, and ordered his slaves to throw Hassan down upon his face. So they threw him down and the Magian proceeded to beat him with a whip of plaited thongs. Then he ordered the slaves to bring Hassan food and drink, and they brought it, but he could not eat or drink. The Magian proceeded to torture him night and day during the voyage.

And they pursued their voyage over the sea for the period of three months, during which time the Magian continued to torture Hassan. At the end of the three months Allah, whose name be exalted, sent against the ship a wind, and the sea became black, and tossed the ship. And the master of the ship, and the sailors were terrified and said: "Surely Allah sends this storm because for three months the young man has been tortured by this Magian!" Then they rose against the Magian to slay him, but he spoke to them softly, persuading them, and he loosed Hassan from his bonds, pulled off from him his tattered garments and clad him in fresh raiment. And he made his peace with him saying: "O my son, be not offended with me, for I did these deeds to test thy patience! I am going to the Mountain of the Clouds, on which is an elixir which I use in my alchemy, and I swear to thee by the fire and the light that I will not harm thee in any way." So the heart of Hassan was comforted, and he rejoiced, and ate, and drank, and slept, and was content. Then the sailors rejoiced at Hassan's release, and the winds were stilled, and the darkness was withdrawn, and the voyage became pleasant.

They continued their voyage for three months more, and, at the end of that time, the vessel cast anchor on a long coast, beyond which was a desert interminable. The pebbles of that coast were white and yellow and blue and black and of every other colour. And the Magian arose, and took Hassan, and descended from the ship. They walked together until they were far from the ship and could no longer see the ship's crew. Whereupon the Magian seated himself and took from his pocket a drum of copper and a drumstick covered with silk, worked with gold, inscribed with talismans. He beat the drum, and instantly there appeared a dust from the further part of the desert. The dust dispersed, and, lo, there came toward them three she-camels. The Magian mounted one of them and Hassan mounted one, and they put their provisions on the third, and they proceeded for seven days. On the eighth day they beheld a cupola erected on four columns of red gold. They alighted from the she-camels, entered the cupola and ate, drank, and rested. Hassan happened to look about him, and he saw in the distance a lofty palace. "What is that, O my uncle?" he asked. The Magian answered: "That is the palace of mine enemy, and it is the abode of Genii, ghouls, and Devils." Then he beat the drum, and the she-camels approached and the two mounted and journeyed on until they arrived at a great and lofty mountain called the Mountain of Clouds.

Then Bahram the Magian alighted from his camel, and ordered Hassan to alight also. The Magian opened a leathern bag, and took forth from it a mill and a quantity of wheat. He ground the wheat in the mill, after which he kneaded the flour, and made of it three round cakes. He lighted a fire, and baked the cakes. He then took a camel, slaughtered it, and stripped off its skin. Then said he to Hassan: "Enter this skin and I will sew it up over thee. The Rocs will come, and carry thee off, and fly with thee to the summit of this mountain. Take this knife with thee, and when the birds set thee down on the mountain top, cut open the skin, and look down from the mountain, and I will tell thee what to do."

Then Bahram the Magian gave Hassan the three

cakes and a leathern bottle of water, and he put him
in the skin, and sewed him up. And the Rocs came, and
carried him off, and flew with him to the summit of the
mountain, and there put him down. So Hassan cut
open the skin, and came forth, and spoke to the Magian
who on hearing his words rejoiced, and danced by
reason of the violence of his joy. And he called to
Hassan: "Behind thee thou wilt see many rotten bones,
and beside them much wood. Make of the wood six
bundles, and throw them down to me, for this wood I
use in my alchemy." So Hassan threw down six bundles. And when the Magian saw that those bundles
had come down to him, he cried out: "O young wretch,
thou hast now accomplished all I desired! Remain
upon this mountain and perish, or cast thyself down to
the ground and perish there." Then the Magian
departed.

Now Hassan found himself alone on the summit of the
steep and lofty mountain, and he was filled with grief
and despair. He looked to the right and left and walked
along the summit until he came to the other side of
the mountain, and at its foot he saw a blue sea, agitated
with foamy waves, and every wave like a great mountain. He recited a portion of the Koran, and prayed
to Allah for deliverance, and then cast himself into the
sea. And, as Allah decreed, the waves bore Hassan
along safely, and cast him up on the shore.

He then arose, and walked along searching for something to eat. And he walked for a while, and, lo, he saw
a great palace rising high in the air, and it was the same
which Bahram the Magian had said belonged to his
enemy, and was the abode of Genii, ghouls, and Devils.
Hassan approached, and entered the palace, and saw

a bench in the entrance-passage, and on the bench sat two damsels like moons, with a chess-table before them, and they were playing. And one of the damsels raised her head when she saw him. "O my sister," she cried out with joy, "here is a human being, and I imagine he is the youth whom Bahram the Magian brought this year!" And Hassan cast himself down before the damsels. "O my mistresses," he entreated, "I am indeed that poor man!" Then said the younger damsel to her sister: "Bear witness, O my sister, that I take this young man for my brother by a covenant and compact before Allah. I will die for his death, and live for his life, rejoice for his joy, and mourn for his mourning." And the youngest damsel arose, and embraced Hassan, and kissed him, and taking him by the hand led him into the palace. She pulled off his tattered clothes, and brought him a suit of royal apparel, with which she clad him. She prepared for him viands of every kind and served him, and both she and her sister sat and ate with him.

Then said the damsels to Hassan: "Relate to us thine adventure with that wicked dog, the enchanter." And he related to them all that had befallen him. Then said to him the youngest damsel: "I will now relate to thee in return our whole story, so thou mayest know what manner of damsels we are."

"Know, O my brother," said the youngest damsel, "that we are of the daughters of the Kings. Our father is one of the Kings of the Genii, of great dignity, and he hath troops and guards and servants. Allah, whose name be exalted, blessed him with seven daughters, but our father was filled with such folly, jealousy and pride, that he would marry us to no one, therefore he

had us conveyed to this palace which is named the
Palace of the Mountain of Clouds. It is separated from
the rest of the world, and none can gain access to it,
neither of mankind nor of the Genii. Around it are
trees, and fruits, and rivers and running water sweeter
than honey and colder than snow. We have five sisters
who have gone to hunt in the desert, for in it are wild
beasts that cannot be numbered."

And even as the damsel spoke the five sisters returned from the chase, and the youngest damsel acquainted them with the case of Hassan. Whereupon
the damsels rejoiced and congratulated him on his
safety. And he remained with them a year, passing the
most pleasant life. And he used to go forth with them
to the chase, and slaughter the game. He amused and
diverted himself with the damsels in that decorated
palace, and in the gardens and among the flowers,
while the damsels treated him with courtesy and
cheered him so that his sadness ceased.

Now, in the following year Bahram the Magian, the
accursed, came again, having with him a comely young
man, a Mohammetan, resembling the moon in its beauty,
shackled, and tortured in the most cruel manner; and
he alighted with him beneath the Palace of the Mountain of Clouds. Hassan was sitting by the river,
beneath the trees when he beheld the Magian. In
great anger he struck his hands together and said to
the damsels: "O my sisters, aid me to slay this accursed
wretch! He hath now fallen into your hands, and with
him is a young Mohammetan, a captive, whom he is
torturing with painful torture." And the damsels
replied: "We hear and obey Allah and thee, O Hassan."
And they equipped themselves with armour and slung

on the swords. They brought to him a courser richly caparisoned, and they armed him with beautiful weapons.

Having done this, they proceeded all together, and they found that the Magian had slaughtered a camel, and skinned it, and was tormenting the young man, saying to him: "Enter this skin!" So Hassan came behind him, and cried out: "Withhold thy hand, O accursed! O enemy of Allah! O dog! O perfidious wretch! O thou who worshippest fire, and swearest by the shade and the heat!" The Magian looked around, and seeing Hassan, said to him: "O my son, how didst thou escape?" Hassan answered: "Allah delivered me! Thou hast been unfaithful to the bond of bread and salt, therefore hath Allah thrown thee into my power." And Hassan advanced and quickly smote him upon the shoulders, so that the sword came forth glittering from his vitals. And Bahram the Magian fell down dead.

Then Hassan took the leathern bag, opened it, and drew forth the drum and drumstick. He beat the drum, whereupon the camels came to him like lightning. He loosed the young man from his bonds, mounted him upon a camel, gave him the remaining food and water, and said to him: "Return thou in peace to thy home." And the young man departed rejoicing. Then the damsels, when they had seen Hassan smite the neck of the Magian, came around him admiring his courage, and thanking him for what he had done. And he and the damsels returned to the Palace of the Mountain of Clouds.

THE BIRD–DAMSELS

HASSAN continued to reside with the dan. passing a most pleasant life, and he forgot h. mother. One morning there arose a great dust from the further part of the desert, and the sky was darkened. So the damsels said to him: "Arise, Hassan, enter thy private chamber, and conceal thyself or, if thou wilt, enter the garden, and hide thyself among the trees and grape-vines, and no harm shall befall thee." And he arose and went in and concealed himself in his private chamber.

After a while the dust dispersed, and there approached numerous troops like the roaring sea, sent from the King the father of the damsels. When the troops arrived, the damsels entertained them for three days, after which the commander of the troops said: "We have come from the King your father to summon you to him. One of the Kings celebrateth a marriage-festivity, and your father desireth that ye should be present that ye may divert yourselves." The damsels arose and went in to Hassan, and told him of the summons, and they said to him: "Verily this place is thy place, and our house is thy house. Be of good heart and cheerful eye, and fear not nor grieve, for no one can come nigh unto thee in this place; therefore be of tranquil heart and joyful mind, until we come to thee again. These keys of our private chambers we leave with thee; but, O our brother, we beg thee by the bond of brotherhood that thou open not yonder door." Then they bade him farewell, and departed with the troops.

So Hassan remained in the palace alone. And he was solitary and sad, and he mourned for the damsels. He used to go alone to hunt in the desert, and bring back the game, and slaughter it, and eat alone. His gloominess and loneliness became excessive. So he arose, and went through the palace, and opened the private chambers, and he saw in them riches such as ravished his mind. And the fire of curiosity burned in his heart, and made him long to open the secret door, which the damsels had forbidden him to go near. And he said to himself: "I will arise, and open this door, and see what is within, though within be death!"

Accordingly he took the key, and opened the door, and saw therein a flight of steps, vaulted with stones of onyx. He ascended the steps to the roof of the palace, and he looked down from one side of the palace upon a strange country beneath, where were sown fields, gardens, and trees and flowers, and where wandered wild beasts, while birds warbled and proclaimed the perfection of Allah, the One, the Omnipotent. And he gazed from the other side of the palace upon a roaring sea, with foaming waves.

Now in the centre of the roof of the palace Hassan saw a pavilion supported by four columns, and built of bricks of gold, silver, jacinth and emerald. In the midst of that pavilion was a pool of water, over which was a trellis of sandal-wood and aloes-wood, ornamented with bars of red gold and oblong emeralds, and adorned with jewels and pearls, every bead of which was as large as a pigeon's egg. By the side of the pool was a couch of aloes-wood, adorned with large pearls and with jewels. And around the pavilion birds warbled, proclaiming the perfection of Allah, whose name be exalted. So Hassan was amazed when he beheld it, and he sat in the pavilion, looking at what was around it.

And while he sat wondering at the beauty of the pavilion, and at the lustre of the large pearls, lo, he beheld ten birds approach from the direction of the desert, coming to that pavilion and pool. So Hassan concealed himself, fearing lest they would see him, and fly away. The birds alighted on a great and beautiful tree which grew near the pavilion. And he saw among them a stately bird, the handsomest of them all. The ten birds seated themselves, and each proceeded to rend open its skin with its talons, and, lo, there came forth from the feathers, ten damsels more beautiful than the moon. They all descended into the pool, and washed, and played, and jested together. And, as Hassan gazed on the most beautiful damsel of them all, who had been the handsomest bird, he lost his reason, and his heart became entangled in the snare of her love. And he continued to gaze on the loveliness of the chief damsel, sighing and weeping, for she had hair blacker than night, a mouth like the seal of Solomon, eyes like those of gazelles, cheeks like anemonies, lips like coral, and a figure like a willow-branch. And while he stood gazing, behold the damsels came up out of the pool, and each put on her dress of feathers and became a bird again, and they all flew away together.

And Hassan despaired at the disappearance of the damsel, and he descended to the lower part of the palace and dragged himself to his own chamber, where he lay upon his side, sick, without eating or drinking, and thus he remained for two days. Now, while he was in this state of violent grief, lo, a dust arose from the desert, and but a little while elapsed when the troops of the damsels alighted, and encompassed the palace. **The** seven damsels also alighted, and entered the palace, and took off their arms and weapons of war, except the youngest damsel his sister, for when she saw not Hassan she searched for him. She found him in his chamber languid and wasted, his complexion was sallow and his eyes were sunk in his face because of the little food and drink he had taken. When his sister saw him in this state she sorrowed, and questioned him as to what had befallen. So he told her all that had happened to him. And she wept with pity and compassion, and bade him refrain from confiding his secret to the other damsels, lest they should slay him on account of his having opened the secret door, and she said to him: "O my brother, be of good heart and cheerful eye, for I will expose myself to peril for thee and will contrive a stratagem to help thee to gain that which thou desirest." So Hassan was comforted, and arose, and greeted the damsels.

Now at the end of a month the damsels mounted, and taking with them provisions for twenty days, went forth to hunt, but the youngest damsel remained in the palace with Hassan. When the sisters were far from the palace, the youngest damsel said to Hassan: "Arise, and show me the place where thou sawest the flying damsel." So he arose, opened the secret door, and went with her to the roof of the palace, where he showed her the pavilion and the pool. Then said his sister: "Know, O my brother, that this damsel is the daughter of the King of all the Genii. Her father hath dominion over men and Genii, enchanters and diviners, tribes and guards, and regions and cities in great numbers, and hath vast riches. He hath an army of damsels who smite with swords and thrust with spears, five and twenty thousand in number. He hath seven daughters to whom he hath assigned a vast kingdom, encompassed by a great river, so that no one can gain access to the place, neither man nor Genie. And over this kingdom he hath set to rule his eldest daughter, the chief of her sisters, and she it is whom thou lovest. The damsels who were with her are the favourite ladies of her empire, and the feathered skins in which they fly are the work of the enchanters of the Genii. Now if thou desirest to marry this damsel thou must do all that I tell thee. On the first day of every month the Queen and her damsels come here to the pool to bathe. Sit thou in a place so thou shalt see them, but they shall not see thee. When they take off their dresses, seize thou the dress of feathers belonging to the chief damsel. When she imploreth thee with tender words, give not back her dress, or she will slay thee and fly away. But do thou grasp her by the hair, and drag her to thee, and lift her up, and carrying her descend to thine apartment. Take care of the dress of feathers, for as long as thou possessest that she is in thy power, and cannot fly away to her own country." So when Hassan heard these words of his sister he was comforted and he returned with her to the lower part of the palace and waited with patience for the first day of the following month.

Now, on the first day of the new moon Hassan opened the secret door, and ascended the steps to the roof of the palace. He hid himself near the pavilion and, lo, he saw ten birds approach like lightning. The birds alighted, opened their dresses and the damsels descended into the pool, where they played and sported together. And Hassan seized the feather dress of the

chief damsel and hid it. When the damsels came forth
from the pool, each put on her dress of feathers except
his beloved, she found hers not. Upon this she cried
out, and slapped her face, and tore her clothes. And
when the others knew her dress was lost they wept,
and cried out, then flew away and left her. Then
Hassan heard the chief damsel implore: "O thou, who
hast taken my dress I beg thee restore it to me!" But
he rose from his place, and ran forward, and rushed upon
her, and laid hold of her. Then lifting her he descended with her to the lower part of the palace, and
placed her in his private chamber. He locked the
door upon her, and went to his sister, and told her how
he had gotten possession of the chief damsel, and had
brought her down to his private chamber, and said he:
"She is now sitting weeping and biting her hands."

His sister, when she heard his words, arose, and going
into the private chamber, saw the King's daughter
weeping and mourning. She kissed the ground before
her, and saluted her and the chief damsel said: "Who
are ye that do such evil deeds to the daughter of the
King? Thou knowest that my father is a great King,
and that the Kings of all the Genii fear his awful
power, and that he hath under his authority enchanters,
sages, diviners, Devils and Marids without number.
How is it right for you, O daughter of the Genii, to
lodge a human being in your palace, and to acquaint
him with our customs? If ye did not so, how could
this man have gained access to us?" So the sister of
Hassan answered her: "O daughter of the King, verily
this human being is kindly and noble, and he loveth
you." And she related to the chief damsel all that
Hassan had done.

Then the sister of Hassan arose, and brought a sumptuous dress in which she clad the chief damsel. She also brought to her some food and drink, and ate with her, and comforted her heart, and appeased her terror. She ceased not to caress her with gentleness and kindness until she was content.

The sister of Hassan then went forth to him and said: "Arise, go in to her, and kiss her hands and feet." He therefore entered, and kissed her between the eyes, and said: "O mistress of beauties, and life of souls, be tranquil in heart. I desire to marry thee, and to journey to my country, and I will reside with thee in the city of Bagdad. I will purchase for thee female slaves and male slaves, and I have a mother, the best of women, who will be thy servant."

But while he was addressing her, lo, the damsels, the mistresses of the palace, returned from the chase. They alighted from their horses and entered the palace. They brought with them an abundance of gazelles, and wild oxen and hares, and lions and hyenas, and other beasts. Hassan advanced to meet the eldest damsel and kissed her hand, and the youngest damsel his sister said: "O my sisters, he hath caught a bird of the air and he desireth ye to aid him to make her his wife." And the eldest damsel said to Hassan: "Tell thy tale and conceal naught of it." So he related all that had happened. And she said: "Show her to us." So he conducted them to the private chamber in which was the King's daughter. When they saw her they kissed the ground before her, wondering at her beauty and her elegance. And they consented to the marriage, and drew up the contract, after which they celebrated the marriage festivities in a manner befitting the daughter of Kings. And for forty days the festivities continued with pleasure, happiness, delight and joy, and the damsels presented Hassan and his bride with many gifts and rarities.

Now, after forty days Hassan was sleeping, and he saw his mother mourning for him. So he woke from his sleep weeping and lamenting, the tears running down his cheeks like rain. In the morning he arose and calling the damsels acquainted them with his dream and implored them to hasten his departure. The damsels were moved with pity for his state, and they arose, and prepared the provisions. They adorned his bride with ornaments and costly apparel, and gave to him rarities without number. After that they beat the drum, and the she-camels came to them from every quarter. They mounted the damsel and Hassan, and put upon the camels five and twenty chests full of gold and fifty of silver. And they bade him farewell with tears and embraces.

Hassan proceeded night and day, traversing with his wife the deserts and wastes and the valleys and rugged tracts, during midday-heat and early dawn, and Allah decreed them safety. So they were safe, and arrived at the city of Balsora, and they ceased not to pursue their way until they made their camels kneel at the door of his house. He dismissed the camels and advanced to the door to open it, and he heard his mother weeping with a soft voice. And Hassan wept when he heard his mother weeping and lamenting, and he knocked at the door with alarming violence. So his mother said: "Who is at the door?" And he replied: "Open." Whereupon she opened the door and looked at him and fell down in a faint. He caressed her until she recovered, when he embraced her, and she embraced him and kissed him.

He conveyed his goods and property into the house, while the damsel looked at him and his mother. He told his mother all that had happened to him with the Persian and with his sisters in the Palace of the Mountain of Clouds. And when his mother heard his story she wondered, and gazing on the damsel she was stupefied by her beauty and loveliness. She seated herself beside the damsel to comfort and welcome her.

Then said his mother to Hassan: "O my son, with this wealth we cannot live in this city, for the people know that we are poor, and they will accuse us of practising alchemy. Therefore let us arise and go to the city of Bagdad, the Abode of Peace, that we may reside under the protection of the Caliph Haroun Er Raschid."

When Hassan heard these words he approved them. He arose immediately, sold his house, and summoned the she-camels, and put upon them all his riches and goods, together with his wife and his mother. He set forth and journeyed until he reached the city of Bagdad. He bought in that city a house ample and handsome for a hundred thousand pieces of gold. To this he removed his furniture, rarities, and chests of gold and silver. And he resided in ease with his wife for the space of three years during which he was blesssed by her with two boys, named Nasir and Mansour.

Now, at the end of three years, Hassan remembered his sisters, the damsels of the Palace of the Mountain of Clouds, and he longed to see them. He went forth to the markets of the city and bought ornaments and costly stuffs, and dried fruits, the like of which his sisters had never seen nor known. And returning to his house he called his mother and said unto her: "Know, O my mother, I go on a long journey. In this closet, buried in the earth, is a chest in which is a dress of feathers belonging to my wife. Be careful lest she find it and take it and fly away with the children. Know also that she is the daughter of the King of the Genii. She is the mistress of her people, and the dearest thing that her father hath. Allow her not to go forth from the door, or to look from a window, or from over a wall, for if anything should befall her I shall slay myself on her account." And his wife heard his words to his mother, and they knew it not.

Hassan arose, went forth from the city and beat the drum and immediately the she-camels came to him. He laded twenty with rarities, after which he bade farewell to his wife and children. He then mounted and journeyed to his sisters. He pursued his journey night and day, traversing the valleys and the mountains, and the plains and the rugged tracts, for the space of ten days, and on the eleventh he arrived at the palace and went in to his sisters. And when they saw him they rejoiced at his arrival, and welcomed him exceedingly. He remained with them, entertained and treated with honour, for three months, and he passed his time in joy and happiness and in hunting.

Now, after Hassan had set forth on his journey, it happened one day that his wife longed to visit the public bath. So she entreated his mother, and gave her no rest until she arose, and prepared the things required and took the damsel and her two children, and went to the bath. When they entered all the women looked at the damsel, wondering at her beauty.

Now, it happened there came to the bath that day one of the slave-girls of the Prince of the Faithful, the Caliph Haroun Er Raschid, called Tofeh, the lute-player. She sat confounded at the sight of the damsel, who had made an end of washing, and had come forth, and had put on her clothes, when she appeared still more beautiful. The damsel then went forth to her abode.

Tofeh, the lute-player, the slave-girl of the Caliph, arose and went forth with the damsel until she knew her house. She then returned to the palace of the Caliph. She went in to the Lady Zobeide, and kissed the ground before her, and said: "O my mistress, I have been to the bath, where I saw a wonder! A damsel having with her two young children like two moons. None hath beheld the like of her nor doth there exist the like of her in the whole world! I fear, O my mistress, that the Prince of the Faithful may hear of her and that he will disobey the law, and slay her husband, and marry her." "Is this damsel endowed with such beauty and loveliness!" said the Lady Zobeide. "Verily I must see her, and if she be not as thou hast described, I will give orders to strike off thy head, O thou wicked woman!"

So the Lady Zobeide summoned Mesrour, and bade him bring quickly the damsel and the two children. And Mesrour replied: "I hear and obey." He went forth, and proceeded to the house of Hassan, and he took the wife and mother of Hassan, together with the two children, and brought them to the Lady Zobeide.

The damsel had her face covered, and the Lady Zobeide commanded her to remove her veil. She did so, and displayed a face of dazzling beauty, and the

Lady Zobeide was amazed, and pressed the damsel to her bosom, and seated her with herself upon the couch. And she gave orders to bring a suit of the most magnificent apparel and a necklace of the most precious jewels, and she decked the damsel with them, saying: "O mistress of beauties! Thou hast filled mine eye with delight! What hast thou among thy treasures?" "I have a dress of feathers," the damsel answered. "If I were to put it on, thou wouldst see a thing of wonderful make!" "And where," said the Lady Zobeide, "is this thy dress?" "It is in the possession of the mother of my husband," she answered," it is in a chest buried in a closet in my husband's house, his mother hath the key."

At this the Lady Zobeide cried out to Hassan's mother, and took the key from her. She then called Mesrour, and bade him proceed immediately to the house of Hassan, to enter the cupboard, dig up the chest, break it open, and to bring to her the dress of feathers. Mesrour took the key, and did all that the Lady Zobeide commanded, and, wrapping the dress of feathers in a napkin, he brought it to her.

She gave it to the damsel, who rising with delight, took her children in her bosom, and, wrapping herself in the dress of feathers, became a bird. She expanded her wings, and flew with her children through the window saying: "O mother of Hassan, when thy son cometh, and sorrow and despair oppress him, bid him come to me in the Islands of Wak Wak." And she flew away with her children, and sought her country. And the mother of Hassan returned to her home, and would not be comforted.

THE ISLANDS OF WAK WAK

NOW, as to Hassan, at the end of three months he bade farewell to the damsels his sisters, and setting forth he journeyed night and day and arrived at the city of Bagdad, the Abode of Peace. He entered his house, and found his mother weeping and groaning, so that she could not speak. He went about the house searching for his wife and children, and found not any trace of them. Then he looked into the closet, and found it open, and the chest also open, and the dress gone. So he knew that his wife had got possession of the dress of feathers, and taken it, and flown away, taking her children with her. He returned to his mother, and she told him all that had come to pass, and how the damsel had taken the children in her bosom, and wrapped the dress of feathers about her, and, as she flew away, had said: "O mother of Hassan, when thy son cometh, and sorrow and despair oppress him, bid him come to me in the Islands of Wak Wak."

When Hassan heard the words of his mother he uttered a great cry, and fell down in a faint, and, when he revived, he went about the house weeping and wailing for the period of five days, during which he tasted not food nor drink. His mother attempted to console him, but he would listen to naught she said, and he continued to mourn for the space of a whole month.

When a month had passed, it occurred to Hassan that his sisters, the seven damsels, might aid him to regain his wife. So he summoned the she-camels, loaded fifty with rarities and costly stuffs. He bade farewell to his mother, mounted, and pursued his way until he arrived at the palace of the damsels by the Mountain of Clouds. He went in and presented them with his gifts, and acquainted them with all that had befallen during his absence from home, and they betook themselves to soothing him, and exhorting him to have patience, and to praying for his reunion with his wife.

Now the eldest sister had an uncle, and his name was Abdelcadus, and she could summon him by means of a certain incense cast upon the fire. So the damsel said to her youngest sister: "Arise, strike the steel upon the flint, and bring me the box of incense." The youngest damsel arose joyfully, and brought the box of incense. The eldest damsel took it, and threw a small quantity of the incense upon the fire, calling on the name of her uncle. The fumes of the incense had not ceased before a dust appeared from the further part of the desert. Then the dust dispersed, and there appeared beneath it a sheikh riding upon an elephant, which was crying out beneath him. He approached the palace, and alighted from the elephant, and the damsels met, and embraced him, and kissed his hands, and saluted him.

And Abdelcadus said: "I was just now sitting with the wife of your uncle, and I smelled the incense, so I came to thee upon this elephant. What dost thou desire, O daughter of my brother?" Then the eldest damsel related to him all the story of Hassan of Balsora, and how his wife had bid him come to her in the Islands of Wak Wak. Upon this Abdelcadus shook his head, and hung his head towards the ground, and began to make marks upon the ground with the end of his finger. Then he shook his head again, and said to Hassan:

"O my son, thou art in great peril, for thou canst not gain access to the Islands of Wak Wak, even if the Flying Genii and the wandering stars assist thee, since between thee and those islands are seven valleys and seven seas and seven mountains of vast magnitude."

Now, when Hassan heard the words of the sheikh Abdelcadus he wept until he fainted, and the damsels sat around him weeping. So when the sheikh saw them in this state of grief and mourning, he pitied them, and said to Hassan: "If it be the will of Allah, whose name be exalted, thine affair will be accomplished, therefore, O my son, arise, and brace up thy nerves, and follow me."

The sheikh Abdelcadus then called the elephant and mounted him, putting Hassan behind him, and proceeded with him for the space of three days and three nights, like blinding lightning, until he came to a vast blue mountain, in the side of which was a cavern which had a door of iron. The sheikh put down Hassan, dismounted, and dismissed the elephant. He advanced to the door of the cavern, and knocked. The door opened, and there came forth a black slave, resembling an Afrite, and having in his right hand a sword, and in the other, a shield of steel. When he saw the sheikh Abdelcadus he threw down the sword and shield, and kissed the sheikh's hand. Then Abdelcadus took the hand of Hassan, and entered with him, and the slave shut the door behind them. Hassan found himself in a large and wide cave from which led a vaulted passage. They proceeded down the passage for a mile, until they came to two great doors of cast brass. The sheikh Abdelcadus opened one of the doors, entered and closed it. He remained absent an hour. He then came forth having with him a horse saddled and bridled, which when he went along flew, and when he flew the dust overtook him not. The sheikh led him forward to Hassan and said: "Mount." And the sheikh opened the other door and, lo, beyond was an extensive desert. So Hassan mounted the horse and the two passed through the door into the desert.

Then said the sheikh to Hassan: "O my son, take this letter. Proceed upon this horse to the place to which he will convey thee. When he stops at a door of a cavern like this, descend from his back, put his rein upon the pommel, and dismiss him, and he will enter the cavern, but enter not thou with him. Stay at the door of the cavern for five days, and be not weary. On the sixth day there will come forth a black sheikh, clad in black apparel, and with a beard white and long descending to his waist. When thou seest him, kiss his hands, and lay hold of his skirt, and weep before him, that he may have pity on thee. He will ask thee what thou desirest. Give him this letter, and, if he will, he can aid thee and if he will not, his young men will slay thee. This sheikh's name is Aboulruish, the son of Balkis, the daughter of the accursed Eblis. He is my sheikh and my teacher, and all mankind and the Genii humble themselves to him. Go in reliance upon the blessing of Allah."

Hassan therefore departed, giving rein to the horse, which fled with him more rapidly than lightning. He sped along on the horse for ten days until he beheld a huge object, blacker than night. When he drew near to it his horse neighed, and instantly he was surrounded by horses numerous as the drops of rain, and they began to rub against Hassan's horse. So Hassan feared them,

and was terrified. He proceeded with the horses pressing around him, until he arrived at the cavern which
the sheikh Abdelcadus had described to him. The
horse stopped at its entrance, and Hassan alighted
from him, and put his rein upon his saddle. The horse
then entered the cavern, but Hassan stayed at the
entrance as the sheikh Abdelcadus had ordered him.

He continued at the entrance of the cavern five days
and nights, sleepless and mournful. And on the sixth
day, lo, the sheikh Aboulruish came forth. He was black,
and clad in black apparel, and when Hassan saw him
he threw himself upon him, and rubbed his cheeks
upon his feet, and taking his foot he placed it upon
his head, and wept before him. And the sheikh said
to him: "What is thine affair, O my son?" And Hassan
handed the letter to the sheikh, who received it, and
entered the cavern without returning him a reply.

And Hassan remained at the entrance of the cavern
for five days more. And on the sixth day, lo, the sheikh
Aboulruish came forth clad in white apparel. He took
Hassan by the hand, and led him into the cavern, and
proceeded with him for half a day, after which they
arrived at an arched doorway, with a door of steel,
which the sheikh opened, and he and Hassan entered a
passage vaulted over with variegated stones and decorated with gold. They went down the passage until
they came to a great and spacious saloon, in the midst
of which was a garden full of all kinds of trees, flowers
and fruits; and birds warbled on the trees proclaiming
the perfection of Allah, the Omnipotent King.

In the saloon were four platforms, and on each
platform a chair, and a fountain, and at each corner of
each fountain was a lion of gold. Upon each chair was

seated a sheikh with a great number of books before him, and perfuming-vessels of gold containing fire and incense. And before each of these sheikhs were students reading to him the books.

The sheikh Aboulruish made a sign to the four sheikhs that they should dismiss the students. So they dismissed them, and the four sheikhs arose, and seated themselves before the sheikh Aboulruish, who related to them all the story of Hassan of Balsora. Then the four sheikhs said to Aboulruish: "O sheikh of the sheikhs, this young man is to be pitied, and perhaps thou wilt assist him to deliver his wife and his children. Wilt thou not act kindly towards him for the sake of thy brother the sheikh Abdelcadus?" The sheikh Aboulruish answered: "O my brothers, verily this is a perilous affair. Ye know that the Islands of Wak Wak are difficult of access, and that no one ever arrived at them without exposing himself to peril, and ye know the strength of their inhabitants and their guards. Verily this young man is a pitiable person, and he knoweth not what he is undertaking, but we will assist him as far as possible."

Thereupon the sheikh Aboulruish wrote a letter, and sealed it, and gave it to Hassan. He likewise gave him a small bag of leather, containing incense and instruments for striking fire, and said to him: "Take care of this bag. When thou fallest into a difficulty burn a little of the incense and call on my name, and I will be present with thee to deliver from the difficulty." The sheikh Aboulruish then summoned an Afrite of the Flying Genii, who immediately came. The sheikh put his mouth to the ear of the Afrite, and said to him some words, whereat the Afrite shook his head. Then said the sheikh to Hassan: "O my son, arise, mount upon the shoulders of this Afrite, Dahnash the Flyer, but when he hath taken thee up to Heaven, and thou hearest the praises of the Angels in the sky, utter not thou any words of praise, for if thou do thou wilt perish, and so will he. To-morrow he will put thee down, a little before daybreak, upon a white, clean land like camphor. When he hath put thee there, walk on ten days, until thou arrivest at the gate of a city. On thy arrival enter, and ask for its king. Salute him, kiss his hand, and give him this letter." So Hassan answered: "I hear and obey." He arose, and mounted upon the shoulders of the Afrite, and the four sheikhs arose, and prayed for his safety.

Now, when Dahnash the Afrite had taken Hassan upon his shoulders, he rose with him to the clouds of Heaven, until he heard the praises of the Angels in Heaven, and when the dawn came he put him down upon a land white like camphor, and left him, and departed. So when Hassan saw he was upon the earth, he went on night and day for ten days, until he arrived at the gate of the city of King Hasoun, King of the Land of Camphor and the Castle of Crystal. He inquired for the King and went in unto him and kissed the ground before him, and kissed the letter, and handed it to him.

The King took the letter, and read it, and shook his head and said: "O Hassan, thou hast come unto me desiring to enter the Islands of Wak Wak, as the sheikh of the sheikhs hath said. And for the sake of the sheikh of the sheikhs Aboulruish, I cannot send thee back to him without thy having accomplished thine affair. Know, O my son, I will send thee to the Islands of Wak Wak, but in thy way are many dangers, and thirsty deserts abounding with fearful spots. Be patient, however, and naught but good will happen, for I will employ a stratagem and cause thee to attain thy will, if it be the will of Allah, whose name be exalted! Soon there will come a ship to us from the Islands of Wak Wak. I will embark thee in it. When the ship moors at the Islands of Wak Wak do thou land. Thou wilt see many settees in all quarters of the shore. Do thou choose one of them, and sit beneath it, and move not. At night an army of women will come, and surround the merchandise. Stretch forth thy hand, and lay hold upon the owner of the settee beneath which thou hast placed thyself, and beg protection. If she protect thee, thou wilt accomplish thine affair, and gain access to thy wife and thy children. But, if she protect thee not, mourn for thyself, and despair of life, and be sure of thy destruction!"

The King then commanded Hassan to retire to the mansion of entertainment, and ordered his attendants to carry to him all that he required of food and drink and apparel, fit for Kings. And after a month had passed a ship came from the Islands of Wak Wak. Whereupon the King summoned Hassan before him, prepared for him what he required for the journey, and conferred upon him great favours. Then he called the master of that ship, and said to him: "Take this young man secretly with thee into the ship. Convey him to the Islands of Wak Wak, and leave him there, and bring him not back." And the master said: "I hear and obey." So he took Hassan, and put him into a chest, and embarked him in a boat; and took him to the ship when the people were occupied in removing the goods.

After that the ship departed and pursued its course for ten days, and on the eleventh day it reached the shore. The master landed Hassan from the ship, and when he went up on the shore he saw there settees, the number of which none knoweth but Allah! And he walked on until he came to a settee more beautiful than the rest and he hid himself beneath it.

And when night approached there came a crowd of women soldiers, like scattered locusts, advancing on foot, with their swords in their hands, and they were enveloped in coats of mail, and on seeing the ship's goods, they busied themselves with them. And after that they sat to take rest, and one of them seated herself upon the settee beneath which was Hassan. He therefore laid hold of the edge of her skirt, and throwing himself down began to kiss her hands and her feet, weeping. So she said to him: "O thou, arise and stand up before anyone see thee and slay thee." And Hassan came forth from beneath the settee, and rose upon his feet, kissed her hands, and said to her: "O my mistress, I throw myself upon thy protection. Have mercy upon me, who am parted from my wife and my children." When the woman heard his words she had compassion upon him and her heart was moved with pity for him, and she knew that he had not exposed himself to peril, and come to this place save for a great affair. "O my son," said she, "be of good heart and cheerful eye, comfort thy heart and thy soul, and return to thy place, and hide thyself beneath the settee until to-morrow night, and Allah will do as He desireth. Then she bade him farewell, and Hassan entered beneath the settee as before. The army passed the night until morning, having lighted candles made of aloes-wood and ambergris. And when daylight came the army occupied itself with the ship's goods until night approached, while Hassan remained beneath the settee with weeping eye and mourning heart.

Now, when night came the woman soldier, whose protection he had begged, approached him, and handed to him a coat of mail and a sword and a gilt girdle and a lance; after which she departed from him, fearing the troops. Hassan arose, clad himself in the armour, and went forth and mixed with the troops, and at break of day went with them to their camp. He entered the tent of one of the soldiers, and, lo, it was that of his companion, whose protection he had begged. When she entered, she threw down her arms, and pulled off the coat of mail and the veil, and Hassan found her to be blue-eyed with a large nose. She was a calamity among calamities, of the most hideous form, with a face marked with smallpox, and hairless eyebrows, and broken teeth, and puffed cheeks, and grey hair, and a mouth running with saliva. Her hair was falling off, and she was like a speckled, black and white serpent. And she was the chief of the troops, and the person of authority among them, and their leader.

Now, when she looked at Hassan, she asked him respecting his case, and wondered at his arrival. And Hassan related to her all that had happened to him from beginning to end. The woman wondered at his tale, and said: "Comfort thy heart and comfort thy soul. Now that thou hast come unto me, no harm shall befall thee, nor will I suffer any one of all who are in the Islands of Wak Wak to do thee any injury, and I will aid thee to attain thy desire, if it be the will of Allah, whose name be exalted! Know, O my son, that thy wife is in the seventh island of the Islands of Wak Wak, and the distance between us and it is seven months' journey, night and day. For we proceed hence until we arrive at a land called the Land of Birds, and by reason of the vehemence of the cries of the birds, and the flapping of their wings, we shall hear nothing else. Then we pass forth from it to a land called the Land of the Wild Beasts, and by reason of the vehemence of the cries of the beasts of prey and the hyenas, and other wild beasts, and the howling of the wolves and the roaring of the lions, we shall hear nothing else. We then pass forth from it to a land called the Land of the Genii, where by the reason of the vehemence of the cries of the Genii, and the rising of the flames, and the flying about of the sparks, and the smoke from their mouths, and the harsh sounds from their throats, and their insolence, they will obstruct our way, and our ears will be deafened, and our eyes will be covered with darkness, so that we shall neither hear nor see, nor will any of us be able to look behind him, for by so doing he would perish. After which there will be a vast mountain and a running river, which extend to the Islands of Wak Wak. On the banks of this river is a tree called Wak Wak, whose branches resemble the heads of the sons of Adam. When the sun riseth those heads all cry out: 'Wak Wak! Extolled be the perfection of the King, the Excellent Creator!' In like manner also when the sun setteth those heads cry out the same words. A queen ruleth over the land and under her authority are the tribes of the Genii, Marids, and Devils, also innumerable enchanters. Now, if thou fear, I will transport thee in a vessel, and convey thee to thine own country, but, if it be agreeable to thy heart to remain with us, I will not prevent thee." **Then** said Hassan: "O my mistress, I will not quit thee until I meet with my wife, or my life shall be lost."

The old woman, whose name was Shawahi, gave orders to beat the drum for departure, and the army proceeded, Hassan in company with the old woman. They ceased not to journey until they arrived at the first of the seven islands, which was the Island of Birds. They entered it and, in consequence of the vehemence of the cries, Hassan's head ached and his mind was bewildered, his eyes were blinded and his ears stopped and he feared violently and made sure of death. But they passed forth from the Land of Birds and entered the Land of Wild Beasts, where the roaring and the raging of the hyenas, wolves and lions and other beasts of prey made Hassan to quake with horror. Then they passed forth to the land of smoke and flying sparks and flames, the Land of the Genii. And when Hassan beheld it he feared, and repented of having entered it. And they escaped from the Land of the Genii, and arrived at the river, and alighting beneath a vast and lofty mountain, they pitched their tents upon the river bank. The old woman placed for Hassan a couch of alabaster, set with fine pearls, and with jewels and bars of red gold, by the side of the river. They ate, and drank, and slept in security, for they had arrived at their own country.

The next morning Shawahi said to Hassan: "O my son, describe to me thy wife, for I know every damsel in the Islands of Wak Wak, as I am the leader of the damsels and their commander, and, if thou describe her to me, I shall know her, and will contrive means for thy taking her." Accordingly he described her. Thereupon the old woman hung down her head towards the ground, then she raised it and exclaimed: "Verily I am afflicted, O Hassan! Would that I had not known thee! Thy wife is the daughter of the supreme King, his eldest daughter who ruleth over all the Islands of Wak Wak. It is impossible for thee to ever gain access to her. Return, O my son, and cast not thyself into destruction, and me with thee!" And she feared for herself and for him.

But Hassan wept, and pleaded with her until he touched her heart, and the old woman pitied him, and had compassion on him, and said kindly: "Let thy soul be happy, and thine eye cheerful, and let thy mind be free from anxiety. For with the help of Allah I will expose my soul to peril with thee, until thou shalt attain thy desire, or my death shall overtake me!"

The old woman conducted Hassan into the city, and hid him. When she saw him burning with desire to meet with his wife and his children, she arose, and repaired to the palace of the Queen Nour Elhada, and went in to her, and kissed the ground before her. Now Shawahi was in favour because she had reared all the daughters of the King, and was held in honour by them, and was dear unto the King. So when she went in the Queen rose, and embraced her, and seated her by her side, and asked her respecting her journey.

So the old woman acquainted the Queen with the story of Hassan from beginning to end. She trembled like the reed in the day of the stormy wind, until she fell down before the daughter of the King imploring her to aid Hassan and to give him access to his wife and his children. When the Queen heard her words she was violently enraged and said: "O ill-omened old woman, hath thy wickedness occasioned thee to bring a man to the Islands of Wak Wak! By the head of the King, were it not for the claim thou hast upon me, I would slay thee and him this instant, in the most abominable manner! Go forth and bring him immediately, that I may see him."

The old woman went forth confounded, and she went to Hassan, and said to him: "Arise, answer the summons of the Queen, O thou, whose last day hath drawn near." So he arose, and went with her, and presented himself before Queen Nour Elhada, and he saw her with a veil over her face. And she questioned him, and he told her all that had befallen him, and implored her to have compassion on him, and to restore to him his wife and children; then he wept and lamented. Then said the Queen Nour Elhada: "I have compassion on thee and pity thee, and I will display to thee every damsel in the city and in my islands, and, if thou know thy wife, I will deliver her to thee, but, if thou know her not, I will slay thee, and crucify thee on the door of the house of the old woman."

The Queen therefore introduced the damsels to Hassan, a hundred after a hundred, until there remained not a damsel in the city whom she did not display to him. But he saw not his wife among them. Then was the Queen enraged, and about to slay Hassan, but Shawahi advanced to the Queen, and kissed the ground before her and said: "O Queen, hasten not to punish him, for the poor man is a stranger. He hath entered our country, and eaten our food, so it is expedient that we give him his due. Now there remaineth not any of the women to display excepting thee, therefore show him thy face."

At this the Queen smiled, and uncovered her face, and when Hassan saw it he uttered a great cry and exclaimed: "Verily this Queen is either my wife or she is more like her than any other person!" And the Queen laughed until she fell backwards. "Verily," said she, "this stranger is mad, or disordered in mind!" Then turning to Hassan she asked: "What is there in thy wife that resembleth me?" "O my mistress," he answered, "all that thou hast of beauty and loveliness, and elegance and sweetness of speech, resembleth her!" The Queen then looking towards Shawahi said: "O my mother, take him back to his place immediately, and return to me, speedily."

So the old woman went forth, and took Hassan to her house. She then returned to the Queen with speed. And the Queen ordered her to arm herself, and to take with her a thousand brave horsemen, and to go to the abode of her younger sister Menar Elsena, the daughter of the supreme King, and bid her clothe her two sons in two coats of mail, and send them to their aunt the Queen. "And, O my mother," said Queen Nour Elhada, "conceal the matter from Hassan, and when thou hast received the two children, say to my sister that I invite her to visit me, and to come at her leisure."

So the old woman set forth, and did all that Queen Nour Elhada commanded, and brought to her the two children. And when the Queen saw them she embraced them, and pressed them to her bosom, then looking toward the old woman she said: "Bring now Hassan." Then turning to her chamberlain and twenty memlooks, "Go with this old woman," she said, "and bring the young man who is in her house, with speed."

So the old woman went forth, dragged along by the

chamberlain and memlooks. Her complexion had turned sallow, and the muscles of her side quivered. She entered her abode and said: "Arise, and answer the summons of this wicked, sinful, oppressive, tyrannical woman!" So Hassan arose, broken-spirited, with mourning heart, fearing, and saying: "O Allah of peace, preserve me!" He repaired with the twenty memlooks and the chamberlain and the old woman, and went in to the Queen. His sons Nasir and Mansour were sitting in her lap and she was playing with them. When his eye fell upon them he knew them, and uttered a great cry, and the two children knew him, and climbing from the lap of the Queen they exclaimed: "O our father!" and Hassan embraced his children.

Now when the Queen knew that the little ones were the children of Hassan, and that her sister Menar Elsena was his wife, she was enraged with a violent rage. She cried out to her memlooks to drag Hassan forth on his face, and to throw him out, and they did so.

Now, as to his wife, Menar Elsena, she began her journey on the second day after that on which the old woman set forth with the children. When she arrived at the city of Queen Nour Elhada, she ascended to the palace, and went in to her, and she heard her children crying out: "O our father!" So the tears flowed from her eyes, and she wept, and pressed her children to her bosom. But when the Queen saw that she pressed her children to her bosom she said: "O wicked woman, whose children are these? Hast thou married without the knowledge of thy father? Wherefore didst thou quit thy husband and take thy children? Thou hast concealed thy children from us, but we knew it, and now thy shameful secret has been exposed."

The Queen ordered her guards to lay hold upon Menar Elsena. So they seized her, and bound her hands behind her, and shackled her with shackles of iron, and inflicted upon her a painful beating. Then the Queen caused a ladder of wood to be brought to her, and extended her sister upon it, and ordered the servants to bind her on her back on the ladder, and they stretched forth her arms, and tied them with cords, uncovered her head, and wound her hair upon the ladder. Then the Queen ordered the pages to bring her a palm-stick, so they brought it, and she arose, and tucked up her sleeves, and fell to beating Menar Elsena from her head to her feet, then she called for a plaited whip, such as elephants are beaten with, and she fell to beating her with that until she fainted. Now when the old woman, Shawahi, saw this that the Queen did, she went forth fleeing from before her, weeping and cursing. But the Queen cried out to her servants to lay hold on the old woman and to drag her along on her face, and turn her out. Accordingly they dragged her, and turned her out.

As to Hassan, he arose with firmness, and walked along the bank of the river, and turned his face towards the desert. As he was proceeding he came to a lonely and perilous place, and, lo, on the ground was a rod of brass, engraved with talismans, and by the side of the rod was a cap of leather whereon were worked in steel names and characters of seals, and with the rod and cap was a parchment on which was inscribed: "Now as to the cap its secret property is this, that whosoever putteth it on his head he will become invisible. And as to the rod, this is its secret property, that whosoever possesseth it he hath authority over seven tribes of the

Genii, and all of them will serve this rod. When he who possesseth it smiteth the ground its Kings will humble themselves to him, and all the Genii will be at his service."

So Hassan rejoiced and he returned and entered the city wearing the cap, and having the rod in his hand, and none of the people saw him. He entered the palace, and ascended to the place where was Shawahi, and he went in still wearing the cap, and she saw him not. And he drew near to a shelf which was over her head, and on which were vessels of glass and china, and he shook it with his hand so that the things that were upon it fell to the floor. "I conjure thee, O devil," Shawahi cried out, "by the characters on the seal of Solomon, the son of David, (on both of whom be peace), that thou speak to me!" "I am not a devil," Hassan replied, "I am Hassan the distracted, the perplexed!" and he pulled off his cap, and the old woman knew him.

Hassan showed her the rod and the cap, and the old woman rejoiced exceedingly. "O my son," said she, "now thou canst gain possession of thy wife and thy children. I can no longer abide in the abode of this wicked woman, so I am about to depart to the cavern of the enchanters, to live with them until I die. But do thou, O my son, put on the cap and take the rod in thy hand and rescue thy wife and thy children."

Hassan then bade her farewell, and putting on the cap and taking the rod, he entered the place in which was his wife. He saw her extended on the ladder with her hair bound to it, and with a weeping eye and a mournful heart. Her children were beneath the ladder playing, and when Hassan saw the torment and abasement and contempt she was suffering he wept, and removed his cap, whereupon the children saw him and cried out: "O our father!" And when his wife saw him she uttered a loud cry. "How camest thou here?" she exclaimed, "hast thou descended from the sky, or risen from the earth?" And her eyes filled with tears. "O my mistress," Hassan replied, "and mistress of every queen, I have exposed my life to peril and come hither, and either I will die or I will deliver thee from the trouble in which thou art and I and thou and my children will journey to my country in spite of this wicked woman, thy sister. I came to deliver thee by the means of this rod and by the means of this cap." And he related to her the properties of the cap and the rod.

Then Hassan waited until night approached. He loosed his wife, and kissed her head, pressed her to his bosom, and kissed her between the eyes. He then took up the elder child, and she took up the younger child, and they went forth from the palace. Allah let down the veil of his protection over them so they arrived in safety at the outside of the palace. They stopped at the outer door, but found it locked. And while they were despairing of escape, they heard a voice on the other side of the door saying: "I am Shawahi, I will open the door to thee if thou wilt swear to take me with thee, and not leave me with this wicked woman!" So they swore as she desired and she opened the door, and they went forth, and found her riding upon a red earthen jar, upon the neck of which was a rope of the fibres of the palm-tree, and it was turning about beneath her, and moving with great speed.

She rode before them, and said to them: "Follow me,

and be not terrified, for I know forty modes of enchantment, by the least of which I could make this city a roaring sea agitated with waves, and enchant every damsel in it so that she would become a fish, but I was unable to do anything because of my fear of the King, the father of Nour Elhada. However I will show you the wonders of my enchantment. Follow me, relying upon the blessing of Allah, whose name be exalted!" So Hassan and his wife rejoiced and felt sure of escape.

THE SEVEN KINGS OF THE GENII

THEY went forth from the city, and Hassan, taking the rod in his hand, struck with it the ground. And, lo, the earth clove asunder, and there came forth from it seven Afrites, each of them having his feet on the earth and his head in the clouds. They kissed the ground before Hassan three times, and said with one voice: "At thy service, O our master, and ruler over us, what dost thou command? If thou desirest we will dry up for thee the seas, and remove for thee the mountains. Know we are seven Kings, and each King of us ruleth over seven tribes of the Genii, and the Devils and the Marids, including Flyers and Divers, and dwellers in the mountains and the deserts and the wastes, and the inhabitants of the sea. Order us to do as thou wilt, for we are the servants and slaves of the rod."

Then said Hassan: "Show me your company and your troops and your guards." "O our master," they replied, "if we should show thee our company we would fear for thee and for those with thee, for we have numerous troops, of various forms and makes and faces and bodies. Some of us are heads without bodies, and bodies without heads, and among us are some like wild beasts and animals of prey. But, what dost thou desire of us now?" "I desire," said Hassan, "that ye carry me and my wife and this virtuous woman immediately to Bagdad." When they heard these words they hung their heads, "O master and ruler over us," they replied, "Solomon the son of David (on both of whom be peace) made us swear that we would not carry any of the sons of Adam upon our backs, but we will immediately saddle for thee horses of the Genii, which will convey thee to thy country, thee and those that are with thee. The distance between us and Bagdad is a seven years' journey to the ordinary horseman. But the sheikh Abdelcadus, who mounted thee upon the elephant, traversed with thee in ten days a space of three years' journey, and the Afrite Dahnash traversed with thee in a night and day, the space of three years' journey. And from Bagdad to the palace of the damsels is a year's journey. So these make up the seven years. But our horses will arrive with thee at Bagdad in less than a year, after thou shalt have endured difficulties, troubles and horrors, and traversed thirsty valleys, and dismal wastes, and deserts and dangerous places. Perhaps the people of these islands, the enchanters and sorcerers, will overcome us and take thee from us. But be thou resolute, and fear not, for we are at thy service until thou arrivest at thine own country." And Hassan thanked them and said: "Hasten with the horses!" And they replied: "We hear and obey."

They then struck the ground with their feet, and **it** clove asunder, and they descended into the earth. And after a while, lo, they came up bringing with them three horses saddled and bridled. On the front of each saddle was a pair of saddle-bags, containing food and a leather bottle of water. Hassan mounted a courser, taking a child before him, and his wife mounted the second courser, and took a child before her. Then Shawahi, the old woman, alighted from her red earthen jar and mounted the third courser.

So they departed and travelled all that night and the next day, until they arrived at a mountain. And, lo, they beheld a phantom-like form, resembling a pillar, and it was lofty, like smoke ascending to the sky. When they drew near to that black object they found it to be an Afrite, whose head was like a huge dome, and his dog-teeth were like hooks, and his nostrils like ewers, and his ears like shields, and his mouth like a cavern, and his hands like winnowing-forks, and his legs like masts, his head was amid the clouds and his feet were upon the earth.

And the Afrite bowed himself before Hassan, and kissed the ground and said: "O Hassan, fear me not for I am chief of the inhabitants of this land, and this is the first island of Wak Wak. I am a Mohammetan and I will be thy guide until thou goest forth from these islands, and I will not appear save at night." Accordingly the Afrite went before them, and their hearts became happy, and they rejoiced exceedingly, and felt sure of escape.

They ceased not to traverse the valleys and the wastes for the space of a whole month. On the thirty-first day there arose a dust, and the day was darkened by it. So when Hassan beheld it he became pale with fear. And they heard alarming noises, and the old woman said to Hassan: "O my son, these are the troops of the Islands of Wak Wak. Strike the earth with the rod!" Whereupon he did so, and the seven Kings came up, and saluted him, and said to him: "Fear not nor grieve. Ascend with thy wife and thy children, and her who is with thee, upon the mountain, and leave us with these troops. We know ye are in the right and they are in the wrong, and Allah will defend us against them." Hassan and his wife and his children and the old woman alighted, and ascended the side of the mountain.

The seven Kings called forth their troops from the earth, and the Queen Nour Elhada approached, with troops disposed on the right and left, and the chiefs went around them and ranged them company by company. The two armies met, and the two hosts dashed against each other, and the fires raged, and the heroes advanced boldly, and the cowards fled, and the Genii cast forth from their mouths burning sparks, and the fires of war raged among them. They ceased not to fight, and contend until the troops of Wak Wak were defeated, and the Queen Nour Elhada taken captive, together with the grandees of her kingdom and her chief officers.

When the morning came the seven Kings presented themselves before Hassan, and set for him a couch of alabaster ornamented with fine pearls and jewels, and he seated himself upon it. They also set by it another couch for the Lady Menar Elsena, and that couch was of ivory overlaid with brilliant gold. And they set another couch for the old woman Shawahi. They then brought forward the prisoners, among them the Queen

Nour Elhada, who had her hands bound behind her, and her feet shackled. When Shawahi saw her she said: "O wicked, tyrannical woman! Thou shalt be tied to the tails of horses, and driven to the sea, that thy skin may be lacerated!" Thereupon Hassan gave orders to slay all the captives, and the old woman cried out: "Slay ye them! Let not one of them remain!"

But, when the Lady Menar Elsena saw her sister in this state, shackled and in captivity, she wept for her, and implored Hassan to save her alive. "Her torture of thee was abominable," he replied, "but whatever thou desirest do it." Thereupon the Lady Menar Elsena gave orders to loose all the prisoners, and they loosed them for the sake of her sister, and they loosed her sister also, after which Menar Elsena advanced to her and embraced her, and made a reconciliation between her and the old woman, and their hearts were comforted. They then passed the night conversing together till morning. When the sun arose, they bade each other farewell. Hassan and his wife journeyed to the right and Queen Nour Elhada together with Shawahi journeyed to the left, and all went to their own countries.

Hassan ceased not to proceed with his wife and his children for the space of a whole month, after which they came in sight of a city around which were fruits and rivers. When they arrived at the trees, they alighted from the backs of their horses, and sat down to rest, and, lo, many horses advanced towards them. When Hassan saw them he arose to his feet, and met them, and, behold, they were King Hasoun, the Lord of the Land of Camphor and the Castle of Crystal, and his attendants. Hassan advanced to the King, and

kissed his hands, and saluted him. The King alighted
from the back of his courser, and seated himself with
Hassan upon furniture spread beneath the trees.
Hassan acquainted him with all these events, and the
King wondered at them. "O my son," he said, "no
one ever obtained access to the Islands of Wak Wak,
and returned from them, excepting thee, and thy case
is wonderful! But praise be to Allah for thy safety!"
Then the King arose, and took Hassan and his wife
and his children to the mansion of entertainment. They
remained with the King three days eating, and drinking, and enjoying sport and mirth.

Hassan then begged King Hasoun that he might
journey to his country, and he gave him permission.
So he mounted with his wife and children, and the King
mounted with them, and they proceeded ten days, and
when the King desired to return he bade Hassan farewell, and Hassan continued his journey.

And they journeyed on for the space of another
month, when they came to a great cavern, the ground of
which was of brass. And, lo, the sheikh Aboulruish
came forth from the entrance of the cavern. And Hassan saw him, and alighted from his courser, and kissed
his hands, and the sheikh rejoiced at his coming,
and conducted him into the cavern. Hassan proceeded
to tell the sheikh all that had happened to him in the
Islands of Wak Wak.

Now while they were talking some one knocked on the
door of the cavern. The sheikh Aboulruish opened
the door, and he found that the sheikh Abdelcadus
had come riding upon the elephant. The sheikh
Aboulruish advanced, and saluted, and embraced him,
then said to Hassan: "Relate to the sheikh Abdelcadus

all that hath happened to thee, O Hassan." So Hassan proceeded to relate to the sheikh all that had happened to him from the first to the last, until he came to the story of the rod and cap, whereupon he presented the cap to the sheikh Aboulruish and said unto the sheikh Abdelcadus: "Accompany me to my country, and I will give thee the rod." And the two sheikhs rejoiced thereat exceedingly, and prepared for Hassan riches and treasures that cannot be described.

Hassan remained with them three days, then he mounted his beast, and his wife mounted another. The sheikh Abdelcadus whistled, and, lo, the huge elephant advanced trotting from the further part of the desert. The sheikh Abdelcadus took him, and mounted, and proceeded with Hassan, his wife and his children. They pursued their journey traversing the land in its length and breadth, until, lo, the green cupola and the pool, and the green palace, and the Mountain of Clouds appeared to them in the distance.

They drew near to the palace, and alighted, and behold the damsels of the palace came forth to meet them. They saluted their uncle, and they embraced Hassan, and it was to them as a festival-day. Then Hassan gave the rod to Abdelcadus, who mounted, and returned to his abode.

Hassan remained with the damsels ten days eating, drinking, and in joy and happiness, and after the ten days he made ready for his journey. His youngest sister arose, and prepared for him wealth and rarities that cannot be described. He bade the damsels farewell, and mounted, with his wife and his children, and departed from the Palace of the Mountain of Clouds. He proceeded over a desert tract for the space of two months and ten days, until he arrived at the city of Bagdad, the Abode of Peace. And he came to his house and knocked, and his mother opened the door. When she saw Hassan she embraced him, and wept, and cried out saying: "Praise be to Allah, O my son, for thy safety, and for that of thy wife and thy children!"

When the morning came Hassan put on a suit of the most beautiful stuff, and went forth to the market. He bought male black slaves, and female slaves, and stuffs and precious ornaments and apparel, and furniture and costly vessels, of which the like existed not in the possession of Kings. He bought also houses and gardens, and other things. He resided with his children and his wife and his mother, eating, drinking, and delighting. And they ceased not to pass a most comfortable life, until they were visited by the exterminator of delights and the separator of companions.

* * * * * * * * *

"This story is indeed wonderful," said Sheherazade, "but it is not more wonderful than what befell Caliph the fisherman and the beautiful Koutelkuloub, the slave-girl of the Caliph Haroun Er Raschid," and Sheherazade related as follows:

Chapter VII

THE STORY OF CALIPH THE FISHER-MAN—THE LUCK APES

THERE was in ancient times, in the city of Bagdad, a poor fisherman named Caliph. Early one morning he took his net, and went with it to the River Tigris. When he arrived at the river he spread his net, and cast it the first, and the second time, but nothing came up in it. He ceased not to cast until he had done so ten times, but nothing whatever came up. So his heart was heavy, and he sat upon the bank, hanging down his head toward the ground. Then after saying a prayer he thought to himself: "I will cast the net this time also and rely on the goodness of Allah!"

Accordingly he advanced, and cast his net as far as he could into the river, and he folded his cord, and waited a while. Then he drew the net, and found it heavy. He managed it gently, and drew it until it came up on the bank, and, lo, in it was a one-eyed, lame ape who had about his waist a piece of ragged stuff.

When Caliph saw him he cried out with horror and amazement. He seized the ape, and bound him with a rope, and tied him to a tree, and began to beat him with a whip. But the ape cried out with a human tongue:

"O Caliph, beat me not, for I am thy luck ape! Leave me tied to this tree, and go to the river, and cast thy net, relying upon Allah."

When Caliph heard the words of the ape he wondered, but he advanced to the river, and cast the net, and slackened the cord, and waited. He drew, and found the net heavier than the first time, and he ceased not to draw until it came up on the bank. And, lo, in it was another ape, but this ape was red, and around his waist was a blue garment.

Then said Caliph to the red ape: "Verily this is a day of wonders! This day is a day of apes! And who art thou, O thou unlucky one?"

"Dost thou not know me, O Caliph?" answered the second ape, "I am the Good Luck Ape of Abussaadat, the money-changer. I bring to him in the morning five pieces of gold, and again five pieces of gold in the evening."

When Caliph heard this he looked angrily at the first ape. "See," he said, "O thou unlucky, how generous are the apes of other people! Thou camest to me this morning, lame and one-eyed, with thine unlucky face, and I became a pauper, a bankrupt, hungry!" He then took the whip, and whirled it round in the air three times, and was about to beat his luck ape, but the ape of Abussaadat called out: "Leave him, O Caliph, and come to me and I will make thee rich. Take thy net and cast it into the river, and whatever cometh up, bring it to me."

So Caliph took his net, recited a prayer, and cast his net into the river, and waited a while. And he drew, and, lo, in the net there was a large fish, with a great head. Its tail was like a ladle, and its eyes were big like two pieces of gold. And when Caliph saw it he rejoiced for he had not caught the like of it in all his life. He took the fish, wondering at it, and brought it to the ape of Abussaadat, the money-changer.

The ape said to him: "O Caliph, bring some green grass, and put half of it into a basket, and put the fish upon it, and cover it with the other half. Then place the basket upon thy shoulder, and go into the city of Bagdad until thou enterest the market of the money-changers. Thou wilt find at the upper end of the market the shop of Abussaadat, the sheikh of the money-changers, and thou wilt see him sitting upon a mattress, with a pillow behind him, and before him two chests, one of gold and the other of silver, and with him his memlooks and black slaves and pages. Advance to him. Put thy basket down before him and say: 'O Abussaadat, I went forth to-day to fish, and cast the net in thy name, and Allah sent this fish.' Thereupon he will say: 'Hast thou shown it to anyone beside me?' and do thou answer, 'No.' Then he will take the fish and give thee a piece of gold for it, but do thou return it to him. And he will give thee two pieces of gold, but return them to him. So he will say to thee: 'Tell me what thou desirest.' Then shalt thou tell him that thou wilt not sell the fish save for two sayings, and bid him rise upon his feet, and proclaim these words: 'Bear witness, O ye who are present in the market, that I have exchanged my ape for the ape of Caliph the fisherman, and have exchanged for his lot my lot, and for his fortune my good fortune.' And," continued the ape, "If Abussaadat pronounce these two sayings, then every day will I present myself to thee in the morning and evening, and will bestow on thee every day ten pieces of gold, while this lame, one-eyed ape will present himself in the morning to Abussaadat, and will inflict him every day with a debt which he will be obliged to pay, until he is reduced to poverty, and is possessed of nothing. Now unbind thou this lame ape and let us both go into the water." And Caliph the fisherman replied: "O King of Apes, I hear and obey." And he loosed the apes and they descended into the water.

He then took the fish, washed it, and put beneath it some green grass in a basket, covered it also with grass, and, placing it on his shoulder, proceeded singing:

"Commit thine affairs to Allah, and thou wilt be safe;
  Act kindly throughout thy life, and thou wilt not repent;
  Associate not with the suspected, for thou wouldst be sus-
    pected;
  Keep thy tongue from reviling, for thou wouldst be reviled."

He ceased not to walk until he entered the city of Bagdad, and until he came to the market of the money-changers, as the ape had directed him.

And he found Abussaadat, the sheikh of the money-changers, sitting at the upper end of the market. And, lo, all came to pass even as the ape had said, and Abussaadat rose to his feet and proclaimed the two sayings, and took the fish, and Caliph departed rejoicing.

So Caliph the fisherman left the money market, and taking his basket and net, went to the River Tigris and cast the net. Then he drew it and found it heavy, and when he pulled it forth, lo, it was full of fish of all kinds. And there came to him a strange woman, having a plate, and she bought a fish for a piece of gold. And there came to him a strange eunuch also, who bought of him for a piece of gold. Thus it happened until he had sold ten fish for ten pieces of gold. And he ceased not to sell every day ten fish for ten pieces of gold until the end of ten days, so that he amassed a hundred pieces of gold.

Now on the eleventh morning when Caliph arose from sleep, he thought upon the hundred pieces of gold and said to himself: "If I leave them in the house robbers will steal them, and if I put them in a belt some one will see them and will lie in wait to slay me." So he arose and sewed a pocket in the upper border of his vest, and tying the hundred pieces of gold in a purse, he put them in the pocket.

He then took his net, his basket and his staff and went to the River Tigris, and cast his net. He drew and nothing came up in it. He removed to another place and cast again and nothing came up for him. He ceased not to remove from place to place, casting the net on the way, but still there came not up for him aught. So he said to himself: "I will cast but this once, in the name of Allah." So he cast with all his force, and with the violence of rage, and the purse in which was the hundred pieces of gold, flew from his bosom, fell into the river, and was carried away by the force of the current.

When Caliph saw this he threw down his net, stripped off his clothes, and leaving them upon the bank descended into the river, and dived for the purse, and he dived, and came up about a hundred times, until he became weak, but he found not that purse. And he returned to the bank and sought his clothes but they had disappeared. And filled with despair he unfolded his net and wrapped himself in it, and, taking his staff in his hand, and the basket upon his shoulder, he went trotting along like a stray camel, running to the right and left, and backwards and forwards, with dishevelled hair and dust-coloured, like a disobedient Genie let loose from Solomon's prison.—Such was the case of Caliph the fisherman.

CALIPH THE PIPER

NOW the Caliph Haroun Er Raschid was sitting one day in his chamber when there came to him a jeweller having with him a female slave who was endowed with beauty and loveliness and fine stature. She was versed in the sciences and arts, and composed verses, and played on all kinds of musical instruments, and her name was Koutelkuloub. And the Caliph gave orders to pay the jeweller ten thousand pieces of gold as the price of that slave-girl.

Then the Caliph's heart became engrossed by Koutelkuloub, so that he forgot the Lady Zobeide, and neglected the affairs of his realm. This conduct was grievous to the lords of the empire, and they complained thereof to the Vizier Jaafar. So the Vizier waited until the time of Friday-prayers, when he entered the mosque and met the Prince of the Faithful, and related to him many stories of extraordinary love, in order that he might draw forth a statement of his feelings.

Then said the Caliph: "O Jaafar, my heart is entangled in the snare of love, and I know not what is to be done!" "Know, O Prince of the Faithful," the Vizier Jaafar replied, "that the best of the Kings and the sons of the Kings glory in hunting and sports, if thou doest likewise thou wilt probably forget this slave-girl, Koutelkuloub." "Excellent is thy advice, O Jaafar," said the Caliph, "let us go forth immediately to hunt."

So, when the Friday-prayers were over, they both went forth from the mosque and mounted, and went to hunt, accompanied by the troops. And when they came to the desert the heat was oppressive, so Er Raschid said: "O Jaafar, I am violently thirsty." "Behold, O Prince of the Faithful," answered Jaafar, "I see a distant object on a high mound. It is either the keeper of a garden, or the keeper of a ground for melons and cucumbers. In either case he must have water there. I will go to him and bring thee some." But Er Raschid replied: "My mule is more swift than thine. I will go and drink and return. Stay thou here with the troops."

So the Caliph urged his mule, which went like the wind, and bore him in the twinkling of an eye to the distant object, which he found to be no other than Caliph the fisherman, with his naked body wrapped in the net, and his eyes red like burning lamps. His form was horrible, his figure bending, and with dishevelled hair and dust-coloured, he resembled an Afrite, or a lion.

Er Raschid saluted him and Caliph the fisherman returned his greeting with rage, his breath would have kindled fires. And Er Raschid said to him: "O man, hast thou by thee any water?" And Caliph replied: "O thou, art thou blind or mad? Go to the River Tigris, for it is behind this mound." So Er Raschid went round behind the mound and descended to the

River Tigris, and drank and watered his mule. Then he went up and returning to Caliph the fisherman said to him: "Wherefore, O man, art thou standing here, and what is thine occupation?" "Verily this question," Caliph replied, "is more foolish than thy question respecting water. Dost thou not see the net and the basket on my shoulder?" Then said Er Raschid: "It seemeth that thou art a fisherman, but where are thy garments?" Now when Caliph the fisherman heard Er Raschid mention his garments he imagined that this was the man who had taken his clothes from the banks of the river. So he descended from the top of the mound, more swiftly than blinding lightning, and seizing the bridle of the mule of the Caliph, said: "O man, give me my things, and desist from sport and jesting, or I'll beat thee with this staff." Now, when the Caliph saw the staff in the hands of Caliph the fisherman, he thought: "I cannot endure from this pauper half a blow with this staff!" and as he wore a long vest of embroidered satin, he pulled it off and said to the fisherman: "O man, take this vest instead of thy clothes." Caliph the fisherman therefore took it, and turned it over, and said: "Verily my clothes are worth ten such things as this variegated cloak!" He then put the vest on, and, seeing it was too long for him, he took his knife, and cut off one-third so that the garment reached but just below his knees.

Now Er Raschid had large cheeks and a small mouth, wherefore Caliph the fisherman thought him a singer or a piper. He then looked towards Er Raschid and said: "By Allah, I conjure thee, O piper, that thou tell me the amount of thy wages that thou receivest every month from thy master, for the art of piping." "My

wages," replied the Caliph, "are ten pieces of gold."
"O, poor man," said the fisherman, "the sum of ten
pieces of gold I gain every day! Wilt thou be my servant? If so I will teach thee the art of fishing, and share
my gain with thee, and I will protect thee from thy
master with this staff." And Er Raschid answered him:
"I consent to that."

So Caliph the fisherman caused the Caliph Haroun
Er Raschid to descend from the back of his mule. He
made him to tie his mule, to tuck up his skirts into
his girdle, and to hold the net, and cast it into the River
Tigris. And Er Raschid did all as the fisherman told
him. He cast the net into the river, and pulled it, but
could not draw it up. Caliph came to him and pulled
it with him; but together they could not draw it up.
So the fisherman said: "O ill-omened piper, if I took
thy cloak instead of my clothes the first time, this
time I will take thine ass, if I see my net mangled, and
I will beat thee until thou shalt be in an abominable
condition!" Er Raschid replied: "Let thee and me
again pull together." And the two together pulled the
net and when they had drawn it up with difficulty,
they looked and, lo, it was full of all kinds of fish. Then
said Caliph to Er Raschid, "O piper, verily thou art an
ugly fellow, but after a while thou wilt become an excellent fisherman. Now mount thine ass and go to the
market, and bring two great baskets, and I will take
care of the fish until thou come again. Hasten and delay not." And the Caliph replied: "I hear and obey."

Er Raschid left him, and left the fish, and urged on
his mule, being in a state of utmost joy. He ceased
not to laugh at what had happened to him until he
came to Jaafar. When Jaafar saw him, he kissed the

ground before him and said: "O Prince of the Faithful, what was the cause of thy delay, what happened to thee?" "An extraordinary event," the Caliph answered, "a mirth-exciting, wonderful thing hath happened to me!" and he repeated the story of Caliph the fisherman, and of his saying: "Thou hast stolen my clothes," and how Er Raschid had given his vest and how the fisherman had cut off a third of it, and entirely spoiled it. "And, O Jaafar," said the Caliph, "I am fatigued by my fishing in the river, for I caught a great quantity of fish, and they are on the river bank with my teacher Caliph. He is standing there waiting for me to return to him, and to take to him two great baskets. Then I and he are to go to the market, and we are to sell the fish, and divide the price. Proclaim now, O Jaafar, that to every one who bringeth to me a fish from Caliph my teacher, I will give for it a piece of gold." The crier therefore proclaimed among the troops: "Go ye forth and purchase fish for the Prince of the Faithful."

Accordingly the memlooks went forth to the river bank, and while Caliph the fisherman was waiting for the Prince of the Faithful to bring to him two great baskets, lo, the memlooks pounced upon him like eagles, and took the fish, and put them in gold-embroidered handkerchiefs, and proceeded to beat each other to get at him. So Caliph said: "No doubt these fish are fish of Paradise!" so seizing two of them in his right hand and two in his left, he descended into the water to his throat. And as he stood thus, lo, a black slave advanced to him, and that slave was chief of all the black slaves that were in the palace of the Caliph Haroun Er Raschid. And he saw Caliph the fisherman standing in the water with the fish in his hands, and he took the fish from Caliph, and placed them in a handkerchief, and said: "O fisherman, verily thy fortune is unlucky! I have not with me any money. But to-morrow come thou to the palace of the Caliph, and ask for the eunuch Sandal. Whereupon the eunuchs will bring thee to me, and I will pay thee what I owe," and the slave took the fish and went his way.

And Caliph seeing that his fish were all sold put his net upon his shoulder, and returned home. And on his way he passed by the shop of the tailor of the Prince of the Faithful, and when the tailor saw the fisherman wearing a cloak worth a thousand pieces of gold, of the apparel of the Caliph, he said, "O Caliph, whence obtainedst thou this cloak?" "I received it from a young man," Caliph replied, "to whom I taught the art of fishing. He stole my clothes, and gave me this cloak instead of them." The tailor then knew that the Caliph Haroun Er Raschid had passed by while Caliph was fishing, and had jested with him and given him the cloak. Then the fisherman went to his own abode.

KOUTELKULOUB, THE BEAUTIFUL SLAVE

NOW when the Lady Zobeide, the wife of the Prince of the Faithful, knew that her husband was gone forth to hunt, she ordered the female slaves to spread the carpets and cushions in the palace, and commanded viands to be prepared, among these a China dish containing sweetmeat of the most dainty kind, in this she put a sleeping potion. She then ordered one of the eunuchs to go to the slave-girl Koutelkuloub and invite her to partake of the feast of the Lady Zobeide, and to say to her: "The wife of the Prince of the Faithful desireth to amuse herself with thy music and sweet melody." And Koutelkuloub replied: "I hear and obey Allah and the Lady Zobeide." She then arose and taking with her musical instruments, went in unto the Lady Zobeide and kissed the ground before her many times.

The Lady Zobeide raised her head, and contemplated the slave-girl's beauty and loveliness. She saw a damsel with smooth cheeks, a brilliant countenance, and large black eyes. Her face was beauteously bright. The splendour of her countenance was like the rising sun, the hair over her forehead like the darkness of the night, her odour like the fragrance of musk, her forehead like the moon, and her figure like the waving branch. She amazed by her beauty every one who beheld her.

And the Lady Zobeide said to her: "A friendly and free and ample welcome to thee, O Koutelkuloub. Sit and amuse us with thy music and art." So she replied: "I hear and obey." She sat, and took the tambourine, and after that the flute, and next the lute, and she played fourteen times, and sang till she moved with delight her hearers. After that she exhibited her skill in juggling and sleights, and every pleasing art. Then the damsel kissed the ground before Zobeide, and sat down. And the slaves presented to her the viands, and afterwards the sweetmeat in which was the sleeping potion. And Koutelkuloub ate of it and fell on the floor asleep.

Then said the Lady Zobeide: "Bring a chest." And

one of the eunuchs brought a chest, and the Lady Zobeide put the damsel in it and said to the eunuch: "Sell
the chest, and make it a condition that the purchaser
buy the chest locked; then give the price in alms."
And the eunuch took the chest, and went forth to do
as he was commanded.

And, lo, the Caliph then came back from the chase,
and his first inquiry was for the damsel Koutelkuloub.
And one of his eunuchs advanced to him and kissed
the ground before him and said: "O my lord, may thy
head long survive, know for certain that Koutelkuloub
hath vanished away."   "May Allah not rejoice thee
with good tidings, O wicked slave!" answered the Caliph;
and he arose and entered the palace and heard of the
mysterious disappearance from every one in it, and he
wept and mourned for Koutelkuloub.   And thus it
happened to the Caliph Haroun Er Raschid.

Now, as to Caliph the fisherman, when the morning
came, and diffused its light, he said to himself: "This
day will I go to the eunuch who bought of me the fish."
He then set forth to the palace of the Prince of the
Faithful, and when he arrived there he found the memlooks and the black slaves and the eunuchs sitting and
standing.   And, lo, the eunuch who took from him the
fish was sitting with the memlooks in attendance upon
him.   When Sandal the eunuch saw Caliph the fisherman, he laughed, and put his hand to his pocket.   But
just then a great clamour arose, and, lo, the Vizier Jaafar came forth from the Caliph's apartments.   When
Sandal saw him he rose to meet him, and walked before him, and they conversed together.

Caliph the fisherman waited a while, during which
the eunuch looked not towards him.   So the fisherman

"GIVE ME WHAT IS MY DUE, THAT I MAY GO"

became impatient, and, placing himself before the Vizier, he made a sign with his hand, and said to the eunuch: "O delayer of the payment of thy debt, may Allah disgrace thee! Give me what is my due, that I may go!" And the eunuch heard him, and was ashamed before Jaafar. "O eunuch," said Jaafar, frowning, "what doth this poor beggar demand of thee?" Sandal the eunuch answered: "Dost thou not know this man, O our lord the Vizier? This is the fisherman whose fish we seized on the banks of the Tigris." Then said Jaafar: "This is the teacher of the Prince of the Faithful, and his partner! Our lord the Caliph hath arisen this day with a mourning heart and a troubled mind, and perchance this fisherman will divert him. So let him not go until I consult the Caliph."

The Vizier Jaafar went in to the Caliph. He saw him sitting, and mourning, and hanging down his head towards the ground, And Jaafar standing before him said: "Peace be on thee, O Prince of the Faithful, and defender of the religion." The Caliph raised his head and answered: "On thee be peace, and the mercy of Allah and his blessings!" Then said Jaafar: "I went forth, O my lord, from thee, and I saw thy master and thy teacher and thy partner, Caliph the fisherman, standing at the gate."

When the Caliph heard Jaafar's words he smiled and his trouble left him. "By my life, Jaafar," he said, "I conjure thee to tell me, is it true that the fisherman is standing at the gate?" Jaafar answered: "By thy life, O Prince of the Faithful, he is standing at the gate." Then said the Caliph: "I will assuredly give him whatever Allah hath ordained, either misery or prosperity!" And he took a piece of paper, and cut it in pieces. "O Jaafar," he said," write on these **papers,** twenty sums of money, from a piece of gold to a thousand pieces of gold; and write also the post of police magistrate to that of Vizier, and twenty different kinds of punishment, from the slightest chastisement to slaughter," and Jaafar said, "I hear and obey, O Prince of the Faithful." He wrote the papers with his own hand as the Caliph commanded him. Then said the Caliph: "Bring in the fisherman and let him take one of these papers and whatever is written upon it will I do unto him accordingly."

Now, when Jaafar heard these words, he trembled at what might befall the fisherman. But he went out, and laid hold of his hand, and brought him surrounded by memlooks, behind and before him, through seven chambers to the apartment of the Caliph; then said he to Caliph: "Woe to thee, O fisherman! Thou wilt now stand before the Prince of the Faithful, and the defender of the religion." He raised the grand curtain, and the eye of Caliph the fisherman fell upon the Caliph Haroun Er Raschid who was sitting upon his couch, with the lords of the empire standing in attendance upon him.

When the fisherman saw the Caliph he knew him, and advancing said: "A friendly and free welcome to thee, O piper. It was not right for thee to leave me sitting to watch over the fish, and go, and not return, so that the memlooks advanced upon beasts of various colours, and snatched the fish from me. All this was caused by thee, for if thou hadst come with the great baskets, we should have sold the fish for a hundred pieces of gold. When I came to demand my due they imprisoned me. Who imprisoned thee also in this place?"

The Caliph smiled, and lifting up the edge of the curtain, put forth his head from beneath it, and said to the fisherman: "Advance and take one of these papers." And Jaafar added, "Take the paper speedily, without talking, and do as the Prince of the Faithful hath commanded thee."

Accordingly Caliph the fisherman approached, and took one of the papers, and handed it to the Caliph, who handed it to the Vizier Jaafar. And Jaafar looked at it, and said: "O Prince of the Faithful, there is written here that the fisherman shall receive a hundred blows with the staff!" Thereupon the Caliph ordered that the fisherman should have a hundred blows with the staff inflicted upon him. And the attendants did as they were commanded and they gave the fisherman a gold piece and sent him away.

And when Caliph the fisherman came to the gate, Sandal the eunuch saw him. "Come hither, O fisher-man," he said, "and bestow on us a part of the present which the Prince of the Faithful hath given thee." "Dost thou desire to share with me, O black-skinned?" Caliph replied, "I have received a hundred blows with the staff and one piece of gold!" and he threw down the piece of gold, and ran forth, the tears running down his cheeks. So when the eunuch saw him in this state he pitied him and called out to the pages, "Bring him back," and they brought him back. And Sandal put his hand to his pocket, and took forth a red purse, and, lo, in it were a hundred pieces of gold. "O fisherman," he said, "take this gold as the price of thy fish and go thy way." So Caliph the fisherman rejoiced and he took the gold, and the Caliph's piece of gold, and went forth, and he forgot his beating.

Returning to his abode he passed through the market for female slaves. And he saw a large ring of people. And he drew near and looked and, lo, there was a sheikh, with a chest before him, on which was sitting a eunuch. The sheikh was crying out: "O merchants, who will buy this chest, of which the contents is unknown, from the palace of the Lady Zobeide?" And Caliph the fisherman called: "Be it mine for a hundred pieces of gold and one." And the merchants thought that Caliph was jesting so they laughed at him, and said: "O eunuch, sell it to Caliph for a hundred pieces of gold and one!" And the eunuch said: "Take it, O fisherman, and give me the gold." And Caliph took forth the gold and gave it to the eunuch and the contract was concluded.

Caliph the fisherman then took the chest upon his head, and carried it to his abode. He laboured to open it, and was not able to do so, therefore he said: "To-morrow I will open it." And he lay down upon the chest and slept. After a while something moved within it and Caliph rose in fear, and said: "It must be a Genie!" He beat the lock with a stone, and broke it, and opened the chest, and, behold, in it was a damsel as beautiful as the moon. She unclosed her eyes, and gazing on Caliph the fisherman said: "I am Koutelkuloub the slave-girl of the Caliph Haroun Er Raschid. The Lady Zobeide stupefied me with a sleeping potion and put me in the chest. But this has happened to me for thy good fortune for the Prince of the Faithful will reward thee richly." "But," said Caliph, "is not this the Er Raschid in whose palace I was imprisoned? I have never beheld anyone more avaricious than he, that piper of little goodness and intellect! For he caused

THE CALIPH SMILED

me yesterday to receive a hundred blows with the staff, and gave me but one piece of gold, although I had taught him the art of fishing!" "Abstain from this foul language," answered Koutelkuloub. "Open thine eyes and behave respectfully when thou seest him, and it will be for thy good fortune." And when Caliph heard her words, it was as though his judgment awoke, and as though scales had been removed from his eyes.

Then Koutelkuloub arose from the chest, and laid herself down to sleep until morning. And when day came they proceeded together to the palace of the Prince of the Faithful. And Koutelkuloub went in unto the Caliph Haroun Er Raschid, and she took Caliph the fisherman with her. When the Caliph saw her he greeted her with great joy and amazement, and Koutelkuloub kissed the ground before him, and related all that had happened, after which she said: "O Prince of the Faithful, this poor fisherman hath told me that he hath a reckoning to make with our lord, the Prince of the Faithful, on account of a partnership in the trade of fishing."

And Caliph the fisherman drew near and kissed the ground before the Caliph Haroun Er Raschid, and prayed for the continuance of his glory and blessings. And the fisherman told the story of the eunuch and how he had given him the hundred gold pieces. He told also of his entering the market and of his buying the chest for the hundred pieces of gold and one, not knowing what was in it, and he related the story from beginning to end.

Then the Caliph gave orders to present Caliph the fisherman with fifty thousand pieces of gold, and he assigned him a monthly allowance of fifty gold pieces. And thus the fisherman acquired great dignity, and high rank, and honour and respect. He purchased a handsome house and took in marriage one of the daughters of the chief men of the city, and continued to live henceforth in happiness, glory and hilarity, enjoying abundant wealth, a pleasant and agreeable life, and pure and grateful delight until he was visited by the exterminator of delights and the separator of companions.

*　*　*　*　*　*　*　*　*

Sheherazade having finished this story, proceeded to relate the story of Ali Baba, and of the forty thieves destroyed by a faithful slave.

Chapter VIII

STORY OF ALI BABA AND THE FORTY THIEVES

THERE lived in ancient times, in Persia, two brothers, one named Cassim, the other Ali Baba. Their father left them scarcely anything, but he divided the little property he had equally between them.

Cassim married a wife, who soon after became an heiress to a large sum, and a warehouse full of rich goods; so that he all at once became one of the wealthiest and most considerable merchants, and lived at his ease.

Ali Baba on the other hand, who had married a woman as poor as himself, lived in a very wretched habitation, and maintained his wife and children by cutting wood, which he carried to town upon his three asses, and there sold.

One day, when Ali Baba was in the forest, and had cut wood enough to load his asses, he saw at a distance a great cloud of dust, and soon he perceived a troop of horsemen coming towards him. Fearing that they might be thieves, he climbed into a large tree, whose branches were so thick that he was completely hidden.

He placed himself in the middle of the tree, from whence he could see all that passed without being discovered. The tree stood at the base of a rock, so steep and craggy that nobody could climb up.

The troop of men, who were all well mounted, came to the foot of this rock, and there dismounted. Ali Baba counted forty of them, and, from their looks, was assured that they were thieves. Nor was he mistaken, for they were a band of robbers, who without doing any harm to the neighbourhood, robbed at a distance. Every man unbridled his horse, tied him to a shrub, and hung about his neck a bag of corn. Then each of them took a wallet from his horse, which from its weight seemed to Ali Baba to be full of gold and silver. One who seemed to be the captain of the band, came, with his wallet upon his back, under the tree in which Ali Baba was concealed, and making his way through the shrubs, he stood before the rock, and pronounced distinctly these words: "Open Sesame." As soon as the captain of the robbers had uttered these words a door opened in the rock, and after he had made all his band enter before him, the captain followed, and the door shut again of itself.

The robbers stayed some time within the rock, and Ali Baba, who feared that one of them might come out and catch him, if he should endeavour to make his escape, was obliged to sit patiently in the tree. At last the door opened again, and the forty robbers came out. The captain came first, and stood to see the others all pass by him, then he pronounced these words: "Shut Sesame," and instantly the door of the rock closed again as it was before. Every man bridled his horse, fastened his wallet, and mounted, and when

ALI BABA AND THE FORTY THIEVES

the captain saw them ready, he put himself at their head, and they returned by the way they had come.

Ali Baba did not immediately quit his tree, but followed the band of robbers with his eyes as far as he could see them. He then descended, and remembering the words the robber captain had used to cause the door to open and shut, he was filled with curiosity to try if his pronouncing them would have the same effect. Accordingly he went among the shrubs, and perceiving the door concealed behind them, stood before it, and said: "Open Sesame." The door instantly flew wide open.

Ali Baba was surprised to find a cavern well lighted and spacious, in the form of a vault, which received the light from an opening at the top of the rock. He saw rich bales of silk stuff, brocade, and valuable carpeting, piled upon one another; gold and silver ingots in great heaps, and money in bags. The sight of all these riches made him suppose that this cave must have been occupied for ages by bands of robbers, who had succeeded one another.

Ali Baba immediately entered the cave, and as soon as he did so, the door shut of itself. This did not disturb him, because he knew the secret with which to open it again. He paid no attention to the silver, but carried out much of the gold coin, which was in bags. He collected his asses, which had strayed away, and when he had loaded them with the bags, laid wood over in such a manner, that the bags could not be seen. When he had done this he stood before the door, and pronounced the words: "Shut Sesame," and the door closed after him. He then made the best of his way to town.

When Ali Baba reached home, he drove his asses into a little yard, shut the gates very carefully, threw off the wood that covered the bags, and carried them into the house, and ranged them in order before his wife. He then emptied the bags, which raised such a heap of gold, as dazzled her eyes, and when he had done this he told her the whole adventure from beginning to end, and, above all, charged her to keep it secret.

Ali Baba found the heap of gold so large that it was impossible to count so much in one night; he therefore sent his wife out to borrow a small measure in the neighbourhood. Away she ran to her brother-in-law Cassim, who lived near by, and asked his wife to lend her a measure for a little while. The sister-in-law did so, but as she knew Ali Baba's poverty, she was curious to discover what sort of grain his wife wanted to measure, and she artfully put some suet in the bottom of the measure.

Ali Baba's wife went home, and measured the heap of gold, and carried the measure back again to her sister-in-law, but without noticing that a piece had stuck to the bottom. As soon as she was gone, Cassim's wife examined the measure, and was inexpressibly surprised to find a piece of gold stuck to it. Envy immediately possessed her breast. "What!" said she, "has Ali Baba gold so plentiful as to measure it? Where has that poor wretch got all his wealth?" Cassim, her husband, was not at home, and she waited for his return, with great impatience.

When Cassim came home, his wife said to him: "Cassim, I know that thou thinkest thyself rich, but thou art mistaken. Ali Baba is infinitely richer than thou. He does not count his money, but measures it!"

Cassim desired her to explain the riddle, which she did, by telling him of the stratagem she had used to make the discovery, and she showed him the piece of money, which was so old that they could not tell in what prince's reign it had been coined.

Cassim, instead of being pleased, conceived a base envy of his brother's prosperity. He could not sleep all that night, and in the morning went to him before sunrise. "Ali Baba," said he, showing him the piece of money, which his wife had given him, "thou pretendest to be miserably poor, and yet thou measurest gold! How many of these pieces hast thou? My wife found this at the bottom of the measure thou borrowedest yesterday."

Ali Baba, perceiving that Cassim and his wife knew all, told his brother, without showing the least surprise or trouble, by what chance he had discovered this retreat of thieves. He told him also in what place it was, and offered him part of his treasure to keep the secret. "I expect as much," replied Cassim haughtily, "but I must know exactly where this treasure is, and how I may visit it myself when I choose; otherwise I will go and inform the Cadi, that thou hast this gold. Thou wilt then lose all thou hast, and I shall have a share for my information."

Ali Baba, more out of good nature, than because he was frightened by the insulting menaces of his unnatural brother, told him all he desired, and taught him the very words he was to use to gain admission into the cave. Cassim, who wanted no more of Ali Baba, left him, and immediately set out for the forest with ten mules bearing great chests, which he designed to fill with treasure. He followed the road which Ali

Baba had pointed out to him, and it was not long before he reached the rock, and found out the place by the tree, and by the other marks which his brother had described.

When he discovered the entrance to the cave he pronounced the words: "Open Sesame." The door opened immediately, and when he had entered, closed upon him. In examining the cave, he found much more riches than he had imagined. He was so covetous, and greedy of wealth, that he could have spent the whole day feasting his eyes upon so much treasure, if the thought that he had come to carry away some had not hindered him.

He laid as many bags of gold as he could carry at the door of the cavern, but his thoughts were so full of the great riches he should possess, that he could not think of the words to make the door open, but instead of Sesame, said: "Open Barley," and was much amazed to find that the door remained fast shut. He named several sorts of grains, but still the door would not open, and the more he endeavoured to remember the word Sesame, the more his memory was confounded. He threw down the bags he had loaded himself with, and walked distractedly up and down the cave, without the least regard to the riches that were around him.

About noon the robbers chanced to visit their cave, and at some distance saw Cassim's mules straggling about the rock, with great chests upon their backs. Alarmed at this the robbers galloped at full speed to the cave. They dismounted, and while some of them searched about the rock, the captain and the rest went directly to the door, with their naked sabres in their hands, and pronouncing the proper words it opened.

Cassim, seeing the door open, rushed towards it in order to escape, but the robbers with their sabres soon deprived him of his life.

The first care of the robbers, after this, was to examine the cave. They found all the bags which Cassim had brought to the door to be ready to load his mules, and they carried them again to their places, without missing what Ali Baba had taken before. Then, holding a council, they deliberated on the occurrence. They could not imagine how Cassim had gained entrance into the cave, for they were all persuaded that nobody knew their secret, little thinking that Ali Baba had watched them. It was a matter of the greatest importance to them to secure their riches. They agreed, therefore, to cut Cassim's body into four quarters, to hang two on one side and two on the other, within the door of the cave, in order to terrify any person, who should attempt to enter. They had no sooner taken this resolution than they put it into execution. They then left the place, closed the door, mounted their horses, and departed to attack any caravans they might meet.

In the meantime, Cassim's wife was very uneasy when darkness approached, and her husband had not returned. She spent the night in tears, and when morning came she ran to Ali Baba in alarm. He did not wait for his sister-in-law to desire him to see what had become of Cassim, but departed immediately with his three asses, begging her first to moderate her anxiety.

He went to the forest, and when he came near the rock was seriously alarmed at finding some blood spilt near the door, but when he pronounced the words, "Open Sesame," and the door opened, he was struck with horror at the dismal sight of his brother's quarters. He entered the cave, took down the remains, and having loaded one of his asses with them, covered them over with wood. The other two asses he loaded with bags of gold, covering them with wood also as before, then bidding the door shut he left the cave. When he came home, he drove the two asses loaded with gold into his little yard, and left the care of unloading them to his wife, while he led the other to his sister-in-law's house.

Ali Baba knocked at the door, which was opened by Morgiana, an intelligent slave, whom Ali Baba knew to be faithful and resourceful in the most difficult undertakings. When he came into the court, he unloaded the ass, and taking Morgiana aside, said to her: "The first thing I ask of thee is inviolable secrecy, which thou wilt find is necessary both for thy mistress's sake and mine. Thy master's body is contained in these two bundles, and our business is to bury him as though he had died a natural death. Go tell thy mistress that I wish to speak to her, and mind what I have said to thee."

Morgiana went to her mistress and Ali Baba followed her. Ali Baba then detailed the incidents of his journey, and of Cassim's death. He endeavoured to comfort the widow, and said to her: "I offer to add the treasures which Allah hath sent me, to what thou hast, and marry thee, assuring thee that my wife will not be jealous, and that we shall be happy together. If this proposal is agreeable to thee, I think that thou mayest leave the management of Cassim's funeral to Morgiana, the faithful slave, and I will contribute all that lies in my power to thy consolation."

What could Cassim's widow do better than accept this proposal? She therefore dried her tears, which had begun to flow abundantly, and showed Ali Baba that she approved of his proposal. He then left the widow, recommended Morgiana to care for her master's body, and returned home with his ass.

The next morning, soon after day appeared, Morgiana, knowing an old cobbler who opened his stall early, went to him and bidding him good-morrow, put a piece of gold into his hand. "Well," said Baba Mustapha, which was his name, "what must I do for it? I am ready!" "Baba Mustapha," said Morgiana, "thou must take thy sewing materials, and come with me, and I will blindfold thee until thou comest to a certain place."

Baba Mustapha hesitated a little at these words, but after some persuasion he went with Morgiana, who, when she had bound his eyes with a handkerchief, led him to her deceased master's house, and never unbandaged his eyes until he had entered the room where she had put the quarters. "Baba Mustapha," said she, "make haste and sew these quarters together, and when thou hast done so, I will give thee another piece of gold."

After Baba Mustapha had finished his task, Morgiana blindfolded him, gave him another piece of gold, and recommending secrecy, led him to his shop, and unbandaged his eyes. She then returned home, and prepared Cassim's body for the funeral, which was held the next day with the usual pomp and ceremony.

Three or four days after the funeral Ali Baba removed his few goods openly to the widow's house, but the money he had taken from the robbers he conveyed thither by night. Soon after his marriage with his sister-in-law was celebrated, and as these marriages were customary in his country, nobody was surprised. As for Cassim's warehouse Ali Baba gave it to his eldest son.

Let us now leave Ali Baba to enjoy the beginning of his fortune, and return to the forty thieves. They came again to their retreat in the forest, but great was their surprise to find Cassim's body taken away, with some of their bags of gold. "We are certainly discovered," said the captain, "and if we do not speedily apply some remedy, shall gradually lose all the riches which our ancestors and ourselves have been many years amassing with so much pain and danger. It is evident that the thief whom we surprised, has an accomplice, and now that one of the villains has been caught we must discover the other. One of you who is bold, artful and enterprising must go into the town, disguised as a traveller. He will thus be able to ascertain whether any man has lately died a strange death. But in case this messenger return to us with a false report, I ask you all, if ye do not think that he should suffer death?" All the robbers found the captain's proposal so advisable that they unanimously approved of it. Thereupon one of the robbers started up and requested to be sent into the town. He received great commendation from the captain and his comrades, disguised himself and taking his leave of the band, went into the town just before daybreak. He walked up and down until accidentally he came to Baba Mustapha's stall, which was always open before any of the other shops.

Baba Mustapha was seated with an awl in his hand.

The robber saluted him, and perceiving that he was old, said: "Honest man, thou beginnest work very early. Is it possible that one of thine age can see so well?" "Certainly," said Baba Mustapha, "thou must be a stranger, and do not know me. I have extraordinary eyes, and thou wilt not doubt it, when I tell thee that I sewed a dead body together, in a place where I had not so much light as I have now."

The robber was overjoyed at this information, and proceeded to question Baba Mustapha until he learned all that had occurred. He then pulled out a piece of gold and putting it into the cobbler's hand, said to him: "I can assure thee that I will never divulge thy secret. All that I ask of thee is to show me the house where thou stitchedst up the dead body. Come, let me blind thine eyes at the same place, where the slave girl bound them. We will walk on together, and perhaps thou mayest go direct to the house, where occurred thy mysterious adventure. As everybody ought to be paid for his trouble, here is a second piece of gold for thee." So saying he put another piece of gold in Baba Mustapha's hand.

The two pieces of gold were a great temptation to the cobbler. He looked at them a long time, without saying a word, thinking what he should do, but at last he pulled out his purse, and put them into it. He then rose up, to the great joy of the robber, and said: "I do not assure thee that I shall be able to remember the way, but since thou desirest it, I will try what I can do."

The robber, who had his handkerchief ready, tied it over Baba Mustapha's eyes and walked by him until he stopped, partly leading him, and partly guided by him. "I think," said Baba Mustapha, "that I went no farther," and he had now stopped before Cassim's house, where Ali Baba lived. The robber before he pulled off the bandage from the cobbler's eyes, marked the door with a piece of chalk, which he had ready in his hand, and finding that he could discover nothing more from Baba Mustapha, he thanked him for the trouble he had taken, and let him go back to his stall. After this the robber rejoined his band in the forest, and triumphantly related his good fortune.

A little after the robber and Baba Mustapha had departed, Morgiana went out of Ali Baba's house upon an errand, and upon her return, seeing the mark that the robber had made, stopped to observe it. "What can be the meaning of this mark?" said she to herself, "somebody means my master no good!" Accordingly she fetched a piece of chalk, and marked two or three doors on each side, in the same manner, without saying a word to her master or mistress.

Meanwhile the robber captain had armed his men, and he said to them: "Comrades, we have no time to lose, let us set off well armed, but without its appearing who we are. That it may not excite suspicion, let only one or two go into the town together, and join our rendezvous, which shall be the great square. In the meantime I will go with our comrade, who brought us the good news, and find the house, that we may decide what had best be done."

This speech and plan were approved of by all, and soon they were ready. They filed off in parties of two each, and got into the town without being in the least suspected. The robber who had visited the town in the morning, led the captain into the street where he had marked Ali Baba's residence, and when they came to the first of the houses, which Morgiana had marked, he pointed it out. But the captain observed that the next door was marked in the same manner. The robber was so confounded that he knew not what explanation to make, but was still more puzzled when he saw five or six houses similarly marked.

The captain finding that their expedition had failed, went directly to the place of rendezvous, and told the members of the band that all was lost, and that they must return to their cave. He himself set them the example, and they all returned secretly as they had come. When they were gathered together, the captain told his comrades what had occurred, and the robber spy was declared by all to be worthy of death. The spy condemned himself, acknowledging that he ought to have taken more precaution and he received with courage the stroke from him who was appointed to cut off his head.

But as the safety of the band required that an injury should not go unpunished, another robber offered to go into the town and see what he could discover. His offer being accepted, he went, and finding Baba Musta-pha, gave him a gold piece, and, being shown Ali Baba's house, marked it, in an inconspicuous place, with red chalk. Not long after Morgiana, whose eye nothing could escape, went out, and seeing the red chalk, marked the other neighbours' houses in the same place and manner.

The second robber spy, on his return to the cave, reported his adventure, and the captain and all the band were overjoyed at the thought of immediate success. They went into the town, with the same precautions as before, but when the robber and his captain came to the street, they found a number of houses marked alike with red chalk. At this the captain was enraged, and retired with his band to the cave, where the robber spy was condemned to death, and was immediately beheaded.

The captain, having lost two brave fellows of his band, and being afraid lest he should lose more, resolved to take upon himself the important commission. Accordingly he went and addressed himself to Baba Mustapha who did him the same service he had done for the other robbers. The captain did not mark the house with chalk, but examined it so carefully, that it was impossible for him to mistake it. Well satisfied with his attempt, he returned to the forest, and when he came to the cave, where the band awaited him, said: "Now, comrades, nothing can prevent our full revenge, as I am certain of the house." He then ordered the members of the band to go into the villages round about, and buy nineteen mules, and thirty-eight large leathern jars, one full of oil, and the others empty.

In two or three days' time the robbers had purchased the mules and the jars. The captain, after putting one of his men into each jar, rubbed the outside of the vessels with oil. Things being thus prepared, when the nineteen mules were loaded with the thirty-seven robbers in jars, and the jar of oil, the captain, as their driver, set out with them, and reached the town by the dusk of the evening, as he had intended. He led the mules through the streets, until he came to Ali Baba's house, at whose door he stopped. Ali Baba was sitting there after supper to take a little fresh air, and the captain addressed him and said: "I have brought some oil a great distance, to sell at to-morrow's market, and it is now so late that I do not know where to lodge. If I should not be troublesome to thee, do me the favour to let me pass the night in thy house." Though Ali Baba had seen the robber captain in the forest, and had heard him speak, it was impossible to know him in the disguise of an oil merchant. He told him that he should be welcome, and immediately opened his gates for the mules to pass through into the yard. At the same time he called a slave, and ordered him to fodder the mules. He then went to Morgiana, to bid her prepare a good supper for his guest.

Supper was served, after which the robber captain withdrew to the yard, under pretence of looking after his mules. Beginning at the first jar, and so on to the last, he said to each man: "As soon as I throw some stones out of my chamber window, cut the jar open with the knife thou hast for that purpose, and come out, and I will immediately join thee." After this he returned to the house, and Morgiana, taking a light, conducted him to his chamber, where she left him.

Now, Morgiana, returning to her kitchen, found that there was no oil in the house, and, as her lamp went out, she did not know what to do, but presently be-thinking herself of the oil jars, she went into the yard. When she came nigh to the first jar, the robber within said softly: "Is it time?" Though the robber spoke low, Morgiana heard him distinctly, for the captain, when he unloaded the mules, had taken the lids off the jars to give air to his men, who were ill at ease, and needed room to breathe.

Morgiana was naturally surprised at finding a man in a jar instead of the oil she wanted, but she immediately comprehended the danger to Ali Baba, and his family, and the necessity of applying a speedy remedy without noise. Collecting herself, without showing the least emotion, she answered: "Not yet, but presently." She went in this manner to all the jars, giving the same answer, until she came to the jar of oil.

By this means, Morgiana found that her master, Ali Baba, who thought that he was entertaining an oil-merchant, had really admitted thirty-eight robbers into his house, including the pretended oil-merchant, who was their captain. She made what haste she could to fill her oil pot, and returned to her kitchen, and, as soon as she lighted her lamp, she took a great kettle, went again to the oil jar, filled the kettle, set it upon a large wood fire, and as soon as it boiled, went, and poured enough into every jar to stifle and destroy the robber within. She then returned to her kitchen, put out the light, and resolved that she would not go to rest, until she had observed what might happen, through a window which opened into the yard.

She had not waited long before the captain of the robbers gave the appointed signal, by throwing little stones, several of which hit the jars. He then listened, and not hearing or perceiving any movement among his companions, became uneasy and descended softly into the yard. Going to the first jar he smelt the boiled oil, which sent forth a steam, and examining the jars one after the other he found all of his band dead, and by the oil that he missed out of the last jar, guessed the means and manner of their death. Hence he suspected that his plot to murder Ali Baba and plunder his house was discovered. Enraged to despair at having failed in his design, he forced the lock of a door that

"AS SOON AS I THROW SOME STONES OUT OF MY CHAMBER WINDOW,
COME OUT"

led from the yard to the garden, and climbing over the walls, he made his escape. Morgiana satisfied and pleased to have succeeded so well, in saving her master and his family, went to bed.

The next morning Morgiana took Ali Baba aside and communicated to him the events of the preceding night. Astonished beyond measure Ali Baba examined all the jars, in each of which was a dead robber. He stood for some time motionless, now looking at the jars, and now at Morgiana, without saying a word, so great was his surprise. At last, when he had recovered himself, he said: "I will not die without rewarding thee as thou deservest! I owe my life to thee, and, as the first token of my gratitude, I give thee thy liberty from this moment, and later I will complete thy recompense! I am persuaded with thee that the forty robbers had laid snares for my destruction. Allah by thy means hath delivered me from their wicked designs, and I hope he will continue to do so, and that he will deliver the world from their persecution and from their cursed race. All we now have to do, is to bury the bodies of these pests of mankind."

Ali Baba garden's was very long, and there he and his slaves dug a pit in which they buried the robbers, and levelled the ground again. After which Ali Baba returned to his house and hid the jars and weapons, the mules he sold in the market. While Ali Baba was thus employed, the captain of the forty robbers returned to the forest, and entered the cave. He there sat down to consider how he could revenge himself upon Ali Baba.

The loneliness of the gloomy cavern became frightful to him. "Where are ye, my brave comrades," cried he, "old companions of my watchings, and labours? **What** can I do without you? Did I collect you only to lose you by so base a fate, and so unworthy of your courage? Had ye died with your sabres in your hands, like brave men, my regret had been less! When shall I enlist **so** gallant a band again? I will truly revenge you **upon** this miserable Ali Baba, and will provide new masters for all this gold and treasure, who shall preserve and augment it to all posterity!" This resolution being taken, the captain feeling more easy in his mind, and full of hopes, slept all night very quietly.

When he awoke early next morning, he disguised himself as a merchant, and going into the town, took a lodging at an inn. He gradually conveyed, from the cavern to the inn, a great many rich stuffs, and fine linens. He then took a shop opposite to Cassim's warehouse, which Ali Baba's son had occupied since the death of his uncle. Within a few days the pretended merchant had cultivated a friendship with the son, caressed him in the most engaging manner, made him small presents, and asked him to dine and sup with him.

Ali Baba's son did not choose to lie under such obligations to the pretended merchant, without making the like return; he therefore acquainted his father with his desire to return these favours. Ali Baba, with great pleasure, took the entertainment upon himself, and invited his son to bring his friend to supper; he then gave orders to Morgiana to prepare a fine repast.

The pretended merchant accompanied the son to Ali Baba's house, and after the usual salutations, said: "I beg of thee not to take it amiss that I do not remain for supper, for I eat nothing that has salt in it, therefore judge how I should feel at thy table!" "If that be all," replied Ali Baba, "it ought not to deprive me of thy company at supper, for I promise thee that no salt shall be put in any meat or bread served this night. Therefore thou must do me the favour to remain."

Ali Baba then went into the kitchen, and commanded Morgiana to put no salt in the meat that was dressed that night. Morgiana, who was always ready to obey her master, was much dissatisfied at this peculiar order. "Who is this strange man," she asked, "who eats no salt in his meat? Does he not know that the eating of salt by host and guest cements forever the bond of friendship?" "Do not be angry, Morgiana," said Ali Baba, "he is an honest man, therefore do as I bid."

Morgiana obeyed, though with reluctance, and was filled with curiosity to see this man who would eat no salt with his host. To this end she helped Ali Baba to carry up the dishes, and looking at the pretended merchant, she knew him at first sight, notwithstanding his disguise, to be the captain of the forty robbers, and examining him carefully, she perceived that he had a dagger under his garment.

Thus having penetrated the wicked design of the pretended merchant, Morgiana left the hall, and retiring to her own chamber, dressed herself as a dancer, and girded her waist with a silver girdle, to which there hung a poniard. When she had thus clad herself she said to a slave: "Take thy tabour, and let us go, and divert our master and his son's guest." The slave took his tabour, and played all the way into the hall before Morgiana, who immediately began to dance in such a manner as would have created admiration in any company.

After she had danced several dances with equal grace, she drew the poniard, and holding it in her hand, began a dance of light movements, and surprising leaps. Sometimes she presented the poniard to one breast, then to another, and oftentimes seemed to strike her own. At length Morgiana presented the poniard to the breast of the pretended merchant, and with a courage worthy of herself, plunged it into his heart.

Ali Baba and his son shocked at this action, cried out aloud. "Unhappy wretch!" exclaimed Ali Baba, "what hast thou done to ruin me and my family!" "It was to preserve, not to ruin thee," answered Morgiana, opening the pretended merchant's garment, and showing the dagger. "See what an enemy thou hast entertained! Look well at him, and thou wilt find both the false oil-merchant, and the captain of the band of forty robbers. Remember too that he would eat no salt with thee, and wouldest thou have more to persuade thee of his wicked design?"

Ali Baba, overcome with gratitude, embraced Morgiana, and said: "Morgiana, I gave thee thy liberty, and now I will marry thee to my son, who will consider himself fortunate to wed the preserver of his family." Ali Baba then turned and questioned his son, who far from showing any dislike, readily consented to the marriage, not only because he wished to obey his father, but because it was agreeable to his inclinations. A few days after, Ali Baba celebrated the nuptials of his son and Morgiana, with great solemnity, a sumptuous feast, and the usual dancing.

Ali Baba and his son buried the captain of the robbers with his comrades, and at the end of a year, seeing that he had not been molested by any other robbers, Ali Baba mounted his horse, and set out for the cave. When he arrived there he pronounced the words: "Open Sesame," and the door immediately opened. From the condition of the treasures, he judged that no one had visited the cave since the band of forty robbers had been destroyed. He put upon his horse as much gold as he could carry, and returned home.

Afterwards Ali Baba took his son to the cave, taught him its secret, which they handed down to their posterity, who ever after, using their good fortune with moderation, lived in great honour and splendour.

* * * * * * * * *

"All the preceding tales are indeed wonderful," said Sheherazade, "but I will now relate the most wonderful of all my stories," and she forthwith began the story of Aladdin and the Princess Badroulboudour.

Chapter IX

STORY OF ALADDIN AND THE WON-DERFUL LAMP

THERE lived in ancient times, in the capital of China, a tailor named Mustapha, who was so poor that he could scarcely support his wife and son. Now, his son, whose name was Aladdin, was idle and careless and disobedient to his father and mother, and he played from morning till night in the streets, with other bad and idle lads. Mustapha chastised him, but Aladdin remained incorrigible, and his father was so much troubled that he became ill and died in a few months. His mother finding that Aladdin would not work did all she could by spinning cotton to maintain herself and him.

Now Aladdin, who was no longer restrained by fear of a father, gave himself over entirely to his idle habits. As he was one day playing, according to custom, with his vagabond associates, a stranger passing by stood and regarded him earnestly. This stranger was a sorcerer, an African magician. By means of his magic, he saw in Aladdin's face something necessary for the accomplishment of a deed in which he was engaged. And the wily magician, taking Aladdin aside from his companions, said: "Boy, is not thy father called Mustapha, the tailor?" "Yes," answered the boy, "but he has been dead a long time."

At these words, the African magician threw his arms about Aladdin's neck, and kissed him several times, with tears in his eyes. "Alas, O my son," he cried, "I am thine uncle. I have been abroad for many years, and now I am come home with the hopes of seeing thy father, but thou tellest me that he is dead! I knew thee at first sight because thou art so like him, and I see that I was not deceived!" Then putting his hand into his pocket, he asked Aladdin where his mother lived, and gave him a small handful of money, saying: "Go, O my son, to thy mother, and give her my love, and tell her that I will visit her to-morrow."

As soon as the African magician had departed, Aladdin ran to his mother overjoyed. "Mother," he said, "I have met my uncle!" "No, my son," answered his mother, "thou hast no uncle by thy father's side or mine." Then Aladdin related to her all that the African magician had told him.

The next day, Aladdin's mother made ready a repast, and when night came some one knocked upon the door. Aladdin opened it, and the African magician entered, laden with wine and various fruits. He saluted Aladdin's mother, and shed tears, and lamented that he had not arrived in time to see his brother Mustapha. "I have been forty years absent from my country," said the wily magician, "travelling in the Indies, Persia, Arabia, Syria, and Egypt. At last I was desirous of seeing, and embracing my dear brother, so I immediately prepared for the journey, and set out. Reaching this city I wandered through the streets, where I observed my brother's features in the face of my nephew, thy son."

The African magician perceiving that the widow began to weep at these words, turned to Aladdin, and asked him what trade or occupation he had chosen. At this question Aladdin hung down his head, blushing and abashed, while his mother replied that he was an idle fellow, living on the streets. "This is not well," said the magician. "If thou hast no desire to learn a handicraft, I will take a shop for thee, and furnish it with fine linens and rich stuffs." This plan greatly flattered Aladdin, for he knew that the owners of such shops were much respected, so he thanked the African magician, saying that he preferred such a shop to any trade or handicraft. Aladdin's mother, who had not till then believed that the magician was the brother of her husband, now could no longer doubt. She thanked him for his kindness to Aladdin, and exhorted the lad to repay his uncle with good behaviour.

The next day, early in the morning, the African magician came again, and took Aladdin to a merchant, who provided the lad with a rich and handsome suit, after which the magician took him to visit the principal shops, where they sold the richest stuffs and linens. He showed him also the largest and finest mosques, and entertained him at the most frequented inns. Then the magician escorted Aladdin to his mother, who, when she saw her son so magnificently attired, bestowed a thousand blessings upon his benefactor.

Aladdin rose early the next morning, and dressed himself in his elegant, new garments. Soon after this the African magician approached the house, and entered it, and, caressing him, said: "Come, my dear son, and I will show thee fine things to-day!" He then led the lad out of the city, through magnificent parks and gardens, past fine palaces and buildings; enticing him beyond the gardens, across the country, until they arrived at some mountains. He amused Aladdin all the way by relating to him pleasant stories, and feasting him with cakes and fruit.

When at last they arrived at a valley, between two mountains of great height, the magician said to Aladdin: "We will go no farther. I will now show thee some extraordinary things. While I strike a light, do thou gather up loose sticks for a fire." Aladdin collected a pile of sticks, and the African magician set fire to them, and, when they began to burn, he muttered several magical words, and cast a perfume upon the fire. Immediately a great smoke arose, and the earth, trembling, opened, and uncovered a stone with a brass ring fixed in the middle.

Aladdin became so frightened at what he saw that he would have run away, but the magician caught hold of him, and gave him such a box on the ear that he knocked him down. Aladdin rose up trembling with tears in his eyes, and inquired what he had done to merit such a punishment. "I have my reasons," answered the magician harshly, "thou seest what I have just done! But, my son," continued he softening, "know that under this stone is hidden a treasure destined to be thine. It will make thee richer than the greatest monarch in the world. Fate decrees that no one but thou mayest lift the stone, or enter the cave, but to do this successfully thou must promise to obey my instructions."

Aladdin was amazed at all he saw, and, hearing

that the treasure was to be his, his anger was appeased, and he said quickly: "Command me, uncle, for I promise to obey." The magician then directed him to take hold of the ring and lift the stone, and to pronounce at the same time the names of his father and grandfather. Aladdin did as he was bidden, and raised the heavy stone with ease, and laid it on one side. When the stone was pulled up there appeared a cave several feet deep with a little door, and with steps to go further down.

"Observe, my son," said the African magician, "what I direct. Descend and at the bottom of these steps, thou wilt find a door open. Beyond the door are three great halls in each of which thou wilt see four large brass cisterns, full of gold and silver. Take care that thou dost not touch any of the wealth. Before thou enterest the first hall, tuck up thy vest, and pass through the first and the second and the third hall without stopping. Above all things do not touch the walls, not even with thy clothing, for if thou do so, thou wilt die instantly.

"At the end of the third hall, thou wilt find a door which opens into a garden planted with fine trees, loaded with fruits. Walk directly across the garden by a path that will lead thee to five steps which will bring thee to a terrace, where thou wilt see a niche, and in that niche a lighted lamp. Take down the lamp, extinguish the flame, throw away the wick, pour out the oil, and put the lamp into thy bosom, and bring it to me. If thou shouldst wish for any of the fruits of the garden, thou mayest gather as much as thou pleasest."

The magician then took a ring from his finger, and

placed it upon Aladdin's hand, telling him that it would preserve him from all evil. Aladdin sprang into the cave, descended the steps, and found the three halls just as the African magician had described. He passed through, taking care not to touch the walls, crossed the garden without stopping, took down the lamp from the niche, threw away the wick, poured out the oil, and placed the lamp in his bosom.

But as he came down from the terrace, he stopped to observe the fruits. All the trees were loaded with extraordinary fruits, of different colours. Some trees bore fruit entirely white, and some clear and transparent as crystal; some red, some green, blue, purple and others yellow, in short there were fruits of all colours. The white were pearls; the clear and transparent, diamonds; the red, rubies; the green, emeralds; the blue, turquoises; the purple, amethysts; and those that were yellow, sapphires. Aladdin was altogether ignorant of their worth, and would have preferred figs and grapes, or any other fruits. But though he took them for coloured glass of little value, yet he was so pleased with the variety of bright colours, and with the beauty and extraordinary size of the seeming fruits, that he gathered some of every sort, and filled the two new purses his uncle had given him, and crammed his bosom as full as it could hold.

Aladdin, having thus loaded himself with riches, he knew not the value of, returned, through the three halls, to the mouth of the cave, where the magician was expecting him with the utmost impatience. Now the African magician intended, as soon as he should receive the lamp from Aladdin, to push the lad back into the cave, so that there should remain no witness of the affair. But as soon as Aladdin saw him he cried out: "Pray, uncle, lend me thy hand to help me out." "Give me the lamp first," said the magician, "it will be troublesome to thee." "Indeed, uncle," answered Aladdin, "I am unable to give it to thee now, but I will do so as soon as I am up." But the African magician was obstinate and insisted on having the lamp, and Aladdin, whose bosom was so stuffed with the fruits that he could not well get at it, refused to give up the lamp until he was out of the cave. The magician provoked at this refusal, flew into a rage, threw some incense into the fire, pronounced two magical words, and instantly the stone, which had covered the mouth of the cave, moved back into its place. Then the African magician, having lost all hope of obtaining the wonderful lamp, returned that same day to Africa.

When Aladdin found himself thus buried alive, he cried, and called out to his uncle that he was ready to give him the lamp, but in vain, since his cries could not be heard. He descended to the bottom of the steps, desiring to enter the garden, but the door, which had been open before by enchantment, was now closed by the same means. He then redoubled his cries and tears, and sat down upon the steps, without any hopes of ever seeing the light again.

Aladdin remained in this state for two days, without eating or drinking. On the third day, clasping his hands in despair, he accidentally rubbed the ring which the magician had placed upon his finger. Immediately a Genie of enormous size, and frightful aspect, rose out of the earth, his head reaching the roof of the cave, and said to him: "What wouldest thou have? I will obey thee as thy slave, and the slave of all who may

IMMEDIATELY A GENIE OF ENORMOUS SIZE ROSE OUT OF THE EARTH

possess the ring on thy finger, I and the other slaves of that ring!"

At any other time Aladdin would have been frightened at the sight of so extraordinary a figure, but the danger that he was in made him answer without hesitation: "Whoever thou art, deliver me from this place!" He had no sooner spoken these words than he found himself on the very spot, where the magician had caused the earth to open.

Thankful to find himself safe, he quickly made his way home. When he reached his mother's door, the joy at seeing her, and the weakness due to lack of food, made him faint, and he remained for a long time as dead. His mother did all she could to bring him to himself, and the first words he spoke were: "Pray, mother, give me something to eat." His mother brought what she had, and set it before him.

Aladdin then related to his mother all that had happened to him, and showed her the transparent fruits of different colours, which he had gathered in the garden. But though these fruits were precious stones, brilliant as the sun, the mother was ignorant of their worth, and she laid them carelessly aside.

Aladdin slept very soundly till the next morning, but on waking he found that there was nothing to eat in the house, nor any money with which to buy food.

"Alas, my son," said his mother, "I have not a bit of bread to give thee, but I have a little cotton, which I have spun, and I will go and sell it." "Mother," replied Aladdin, "keep thy cotton for another time, and give me the lamp I brought home with me yesterday. I will go and sell it, and the money I shall get for it will serve both for breakfast and dinner, and perhaps for supper also."

Aladdin's mother brought the lamp, and as it was very dirty she took some fine sand and water to clean it, but she no sooner began to rub, than in an instant a hideous Genie, of gigantic size, appeared before her, and said in a voice like thunder: "What wouldest thou have? I am ready to obey thee as thy slave, and the slave of all those who hold the lamp in their hands, I and the other slaves of the lamp!"

Aladdin's mother, terrified at the sight of the Genie, fainted, but Aladdin snatched the lamp out of her hand, and said to him: "I am hungry. Bring me something to eat." The Genie disappeared immediately, and in an instant returned with a large silver tray, holding twelve covered dishes of the same metal, which contained the most delicious viands; six large, white bread cakes, two flagons of wine, and two silver cups. All these he placed upon a carpet, and disappeared. This was done before Aladdin's mother recovered from her swoon.

Aladdin fetched some water and sprinkled it in her face, and she recovered. Great was her surprise to see the silver tray, twelve dishes, six loaves, the two flagons and cups, and to smell the savoury odour which exhaled from the dishes. When, however, Aladdin informed her that they were brought by the Genie, whom she had seen, she was greatly alarmed and urged him to sell the enchanted lamp and have nothing to do with the Genie. "With thy leave, mother," answered Aladdin, "I will keep the lamp as it hath been of service to us. Thou mayest be sure that my false and wicked uncle would not have taken so much pains, and undertaken such a long journey, if he had not known that this wonderful lamp was worth more than all the gold and silver which were in those three halls. He knew too well the worth of this lamp not to prefer it to so great a treasure. Let us make profitable use of it, without exciting the envy and jealousy of our neighbours. However, since the Genie frightens thee I will take the lamp out of thy sight, and put it where I may find it when I want it." His mother, convinced by his arguments, said he might do as he wished, but for herself she would have nothing to do with Genii.

The mother and son then sat down to breakfast, and when they were satisfied, they found that they had enough food left for dinner and supper, and also for two meals for the next day. By the following night they had eaten all the provisions the Genie had brought, and the next day, Aladdin, putting one of the silver dishes under his vest, went to the silver-market and sold it. Before returning home he called at the baker's and bought bread, and on his return gave the rest of the money to his mother, who went and purchased provisions enough to last for some time.

After this manner they lived, till Aladdin had sold all the dishes and the silver tray. When the money was spent he had recourse again to the lamp. He took it in his hand, rubbed it, and immediately the Genie appeared, and said: "What wouldest thou have? I am ready to obey thee as thy slave, and the slave of all those who hold that lamp in their hands, I and the other slaves of the lamp!" "I am hungry," said Aladdin, "bring me something to eat." The Genie immediately disappeared, and instantly returned with a tray containing the same number of dishes as before, and he set them down, and vanished. And when the provisions were gone, Aladdin sold the tray and dishes as before. Thus he and his mother continued to live for some time, and, though they had an inexhaustible treasure in their lamp, they dwelt quietly with frugality.

Meanwhile Aladdin frequented the shops of the principal merchants, where they sold cloth of gold, and silver, linens, silk stuffs, and jewellery, and oftentimes joining in their conversation, he acquired a knowledge of the world, and a polished manner. By his acquaintance among the jewellers, he came to know that the fruits, which he had gathered in the subterranean garden, instead of being coloured glass, were jewels of inestimable value.

One day as Aladdin was walking about the town, he heard an order proclaimed, commanding the people to close their shops and houses, and to keep within doors, while the Princess Badroulboudour, the Sultan's daughter, went to the baths and returned. When Aladdin heard this he became filled with curiosity to see the face of the Princess. So he placed himself behind the outer door of the bath, which was so situated that he could not fail to see her.

He had not long to wait, before the Princess came, and he could see her plainly through a chink in the door, without being discovered. She was attended by a great crowd of ladies, and slaves, and eunuchs, who walked on each side, and behind her. When she came near to the door of the bath she took off her veil, and Aladdin saw her face.

The Princess was the most beautiful brunette in the world. Her eyes were large, lively and sparkling, her looks sweet and modest, her nose without a fault, her mouth small, and her lips vermilion red. It was not surprising that Aladdin, who had never before seen such a blaze of charms, was dazzled, and that his heart became filled with admiration and love.

After the Princess had passed by, Aladdin returned home in a state of great dejection, which he could not conceal from his mother, who was surprised to see him thoughtful and melancholy. She inquired the cause of this, and Aladdin told her all that had occurred, saying: "This, my mother, is the cause of my melancholy! I love the Princess more than I can express, I cannot live without the beautiful Badroulboudour, and I am resolved to ask her in marriage of the Sultan, her father."

Aladdin's mother listened in surprise to what her son told her, but when he spoke of asking the Princess in marriage, she burst into a loud laugh. "Alas, my son," she said, "what art thou thinking of? Thou must be mad to talk thus!" "I assure thee, my mother, " replied Aladdin, "that I am not mad, but I am resolved to demand the Princess in marriage, and thy remonstrances shall not prevent me, instead I will expect thee to use thy persuasion with the Sultan." "I go to the Sultan!" answered his mother, amazed and surprised, "I assure thee I cannot undertake such an errand. And who art thou, my son, " continued she, "to think of the Sultan's daughter? Hast thou forgotten that thy father was one of the poorest tailors in the city? How can I open my mouth to make such a proposal to the Sultan? His majestic presence, and the lustre of his court would confound me! There is another reason, my son, which thou dost not think of, which is that no one ever asks a favour of the Sultan without taking him a fitting present."

Aladdin heard very calmly all that his mother had to say, then he replied: "I love the Princess, or rather I adore her, and shall always persevere in my design to marry her. Thou sayest that it is not customary to go to the Sultan without a present. Would not those fruits, that I brought home from the subterranean garden, make an acceptable present? For what thou and I took for coloured glass, are really jewels of inestimable value, and I am persuaded that they will be favourably received by the Sultan. Thou hast a large porcelain dish fit to hold them, fetch it, and let us see how the stones will look when we have arranged them according to their different colours."

Aladdin's mother brought the porcelain dish, and he arranged the jewels on it according to his fancy. But the brightness and lustre they emitted in daylight, and the variety of colours, so dazzled the eyes of both mother and son, that they were astonished beyond measure. After they had admired the beauty of the jewels, Aladdin said to his mother: "Now thou canst not excuse thyself from going to the Sultan, under the pretext of not having a present for him!" But his mother did not believe in the beauty and value of the stones, and she used many arguments to make her son change his mind. Aladdin, however, could not be changed from his purpose, and continued to persuade her until out of tenderness she complied with his request.

The next morning, Aladdin's mother took the porcelain dish, in which were the jewels, and, wrapping it in two fine napkins, set out for the Sultan's palace.

She entered the audience chamber, and placed herself just before the Sultan, the Grand Vizier, and the great lords of the court, who sat in council, but she did not venture to declare her business, and when the audience chamber closed for the day she returned home. The next morning she again repaired to the audience chamber and left when it closed without having dared to address the Sultan, and she continued to do thus daily, until at last one morning the chief officer of the court approached her, and at a sign from him, she followed him to the Sultan's throne, where he left her.

Aladdin's mother saluted the Sultan, and kissing the ground before him, bowed her head down to the carpet, which covered the steps of the throne, and remained in that posture until he bade her rise, which she had no sooner done, than he said to her: "My good woman, I have observed thee to stand for a long time, from the opening to the closing of the audience chamber. What business brings thee hither?"

When Aladdin's mother heard these words, she prostrated herself a second time, and when she arose said: "O King of Kings, I will indeed tell thee the incredible and extraordinary business that brings me, but I presume to beg of thee to hear what I have to say in private." The Sultan then ordered all but the Grand Vizier to leave the audience chamber, and directed her to proceed with her tale.

Thus encouraged Aladdin's mother humbly entreated the Sultan's pardon for what she was about to say. She then told him faithfully how Aladdin had seen the Princess Badroulboudour, and of the love that the fatal sight had inspired him with, and she ended by formally demanding the Princess in marriage for her son. After which she took the porcelain dish, which she had set down at the foot of the throne, unwrapped it, and presented it to the Sultan.

The Sultan's amazement and surprise were inexpressible, when he saw so many large, beautiful, and valuable jewels. He remained for some time motionless with admiration. At length, when he had recovered himself, he received the present from the hand of Aladdin's mother, crying out in a transport of joy: "How rich, how beautiful!" After he had admired and handled all the jewels, one by one, he turned to his Grand Vizier, and showing him the dish, said: "Behold, admire, wonder! Confess that thine eyes never beheld precious stones so rich and beautiful before! What sayest thou to such a present, is it not worthy of the Princess, my daughter?"

These words agitated the Grand Vizier, for the Sultan had for some time intended to bestow the Princess his daughter upon the Vizier's son. Therefore going to the Sultan the Vizier whispered in his ear and said: "I cannot but own that the present is worthy of the Princess, but I beg thee to grant me three months' delay, and before the end of that time, I hope that my son may be able to make a nobler present than Aladdin, who is an entire stranger to thy majesty."

The Sultan granted his request, and turning to Aladdin's mother said to her: "My good woman, go home, and tell thy son that I agree to the proposal thou hast made me, but that I cannot marry the Princess, my daughter, until the end of three months. At the expiration of that time, come again." Aladdin's mother, overjoyed at these words, hastened home and informed Aladdin of all the Sultan had said. Aladdin thought himself the most happy of all men at hearing this news. He waited with great impatience for the expiration of the three months, counting not only the hours, days, and weeks, but every moment.

When two of the three months were passed, his mother, one evening, finding no oil in the house, went out to purchase some. She found in the city a general rejoicing. The shops were decorated with foliage, silks, and gay carpets; the streets were crowded with officers, magnificently dressed, mounted on horses richly capari- soned, each attended by numerous footmen. Aladdin's mother asked the oil-merchant what was the meaning of all this festivity. "Whence comest thou, my good woman!" he answered, "know that to-night the Grand Vizier's son is to marry the Princess Badroulboudour, the Sultan's daughter!"

Aladdin's mother hastened home, and related all the news to Aladdin. He was thunderstruck on hearing her words, and hastening to his chamber, closed the door, took the lamp in his hand, rubbed it in the same place as before, and immediately the Genie appeared, and said to him: "What wouldest thou have? I am ready to obey thee as thy slave, and the slave of all those who hold that lamp in their hands, I and the other slaves of the lamp!" "Genie," said Aladdin, "I have demanded the Princess Badroulboudour in mar- riage of the Sultan her father. He promised her to me, only requiring three months' delay. But instead of keeping his word, he has this night married her to the Grand Vizier's son. What I require of thee is this, as soon as the bride and bridegroom are alone, bring them both hither."

"Master," said the Genie, "I hear and obey!" The

Genie then disappeared, flew to the palace, took up the bed with the bride and bridegroom in it, returned, and set it down in Aladdin's room. The Genie then took the bridegroom, who was trembling with fear, and shut him up in a dark closet. Aladdin then approached the Princess, and said most respectfully: "Adorable Princess, thou art here in safety! The Sultan thy father promised thee in marriage to me, and as he has now broken his word I am thus forced to carry thee away, in order to prevent thy marriage with the Grand Vizier's son. Sleep in peace until morning, when I will restore thee to the Sultan thy father." Having thus reassured the Princess, Aladdin laid himself down, and slept until morning.

Aladdin had no occasion the next morning to summon the Genie, who appeared at the hour appointed. He brought the bridegroom from the closet, and placing him beside the Princess, transported the bed to the royal palace. The bridegroom pale and trembling with fear sought the Sultan, related to him all that had happened, and implored him to break off his marriage with the Princess. The Sultan did so and commanded all rejoicings to cease.

Aladdin waited until the three months were completed, and the next day sent his mother to the palace to remind the Sultan of his promise. The Sultan no sooner saw her than he remembered her business, and as he did not wish to give his daughter to a stranger, thought to put her off by a request impossible of fulfilment. "My good woman," he said, "it is true that sultans should keep their promises, and I am willing to do so as soon as thy son shall send me forty trays of massy gold, full of the same sort of jewels, thou hast already made me a present of. The trays must be carried by a like number of black slaves, who shall be led by as many young and handsome white slaves magnificently dressed."

Aladdin's mother prostrated herself a second time before the Sultan's throne, and retired. She hastened home laughing within herself at her son's foolish ambition. She then gave him an exact account of what the Sultan had said to her, and the conditions on which he consented to the marriage. Aladdin immediately retired to his room, took the lamp, and rubbed it. The Genie appeared, and with the usual salutation offered his services. "Genie," said Aladdin, "the Sultan gives me the Princess his daughter in marriage, but demands first forty large trays of massy gold, full of the fruits of the subterranean garden; these he expects to be carried by as many black slaves, each preceded by a young and handsome white slave, richly clothed. Go, and fetch me this present as soon as possible." The Genie told him that his command should be instantly obeyed, and disappeared.

In a short time the Genie returned with forty black slaves, each bearing upon his head a heavy tray of pure gold, full of pearls, diamonds, rubies, emeralds, and every sort of precious stone, all larger and more beautiful than those already presented to the Sultan. Each tray was covered with silver tissue, richly embroidered with flowers of gold. These together with the white slaves quite filled the house, which was but a small one, as well as the little court before it, and a small garden behind. The Genie having thus fulfilled his orders, disappeared.

Aladdin found his mother in great amazement at

seeing so many people and such vast riches. "Mother," he said, "I would have you return to the palace with this present as a dowry, that the Sultan may judge by the rapidity with which I fulfil his demands of the ardent and sincere love I have for the Princess his daughter." And without waiting for his mother's reply, Aladdin opened the door into the street, and made the slaves walk out, each white slave followed by a black with a tray upon his head. When they were all out his mother followed the last black slave, and Aladdin shut the door and retired to his chamber, full of hopes.

The procession of slaves proceeded through the streets, and the people ran together to see so extraordinary and magnificent a spectacle. The dress of each slave was rich in stuff and decorated with jewels, and the noble air and fine shape of each was unparalleled. Their grave walk, at an equal distance from each other, the lustre of the jewels curiously set in their girdles of gold, the aigrets of precious stones in their turbans, all filled the spectators with wonder and amazement. At length they arrived at the Sultan's palace, and the first slave, followed by the rest, advanced into the audience chamber, where the Sultan was seated on his throne, surrounded by his viziers and the chief officers of the court. After all the slaves were entered, they formed a semicircle before the Sultan's throne, the black slaves laid the golden trays upon the carpet, and all the slaves prostrated themselves, touching the ground with their foreheads. They then arose, the black slaves uncovering the trays, and stood with their arms crossed over their breasts.

In the meantime Aladdin's mother advanced to the foot of the throne and prostrated herself before the

Sultan. When he cast his eyes on the forty trays filled with the most precious and brilliant jewels, and gazed upon the fourscore slaves so richly attired, he no longer hesitated, as the sight of such immense riches, and Aladdin's quickness in satisfying his demand, easily persuaded him that the young man would make a most desirable son-in-law. Therefore he said to Aladdin's mother: "Go and tell thy son, that I wait with open arms to embrace him, and the more haste he makes to come and receive the Princess my daughter, the greater pleasure he will do me."

Aladdin's mother hastened home, and informed her son of this joyful news. He, enraptured at the prospect of his marriage with the Princess, retired to his chamber, again rubbed the lamp, and the obedient Genie appeared as before. "Genie," said Aladdin, "provide me with the richest and most magnificent raiment ever worn by a king, and with a charger, that surpasses in beauty the best in the Sultan's stable, with a saddle, bridle, and other caparisons worth a million of gold pieces. I want also twenty slaves, richly clothed, to walk by my side and follow me, and twenty more to go before me in two ranks. Besides these, bring my mother six female slaves to attend her, as richly dressed as any of the Princess Badroulboudour's, each carrying a dress fit for a sultan's wife. I want also ten thousand pieces of gold, in ten purses. Go and make haste."

As soon as Aladdin had given these orders, the Genie disappeared, but returned instantly with the horse, the forty slaves, ten of whom carried each a purse containing ten thousand pieces of gold, and six female slaves, each carrying on her head a dress for Aladdin's mother, wrapped in silver tissue. The Genie presented all these to Aladdin and disappeared.

Of the ten purses, Aladdin took four, which he gave to his mother, the other six he left in the hands of the slaves who brought them, with an order to throw the gold by handfuls among the people, as they went to the Sultan's palace. The six slaves who carried the purses he ordered likewise to march before him, three on the right hand, and three on the left.

Aladdin then clad himself in his new garments, and mounting his charger, began the march to the Sultan's palace. The streets through which he passed were instantly filled with a vast concourse of people, who rent the air with their acclamations. When he arrived at the palace everything was prepared for his reception. He was met at the gate by the Grand Vizier, and the chief officers of the empire. The officers formed themselves into two ranks at the entrance of the audience chamber, and their chief led Aladdin to the Sultan's throne.

When the Sultan perceived Aladdin, he was surprised at the elegance of his attire, and at his fine shape, and air of dignity, very different from the meanness of his mother's late appearance. Rising quickly from the throne, the Sultan descended two or three steps, and prevented Aladdin from throwing himself at his feet. He embraced him with demonstrations of joy, held him fast by the hand, and obliged him to sit close to the throne.

The marriage feast was begun, and the Sultan ordered that the contract of marriage between the Princess Badroulboudour and Aladdin, should be immediately drawn up; he then asked Aladdin if he wished the ceremony solemnized that day. To which Aladdin answered: "Though great is my impatience, I beg leave to defer it until I have built a palace fit to receive the Princess, therefore, I pray thee, give me a spot of ground near thy palace, where I may build." "My son," said the Sultan, "take what ground thou thinkest proper," and he embraced Aladdin, who took his leave with as much politeness as though he had always lived at a court.

As soon as Aladdin reached home, he dismounted, retired to his own chamber, took the lamp, and called the Genie as before, who in the usual manner offered him his services. "Genie," said Aladdin, "I would have thee build me, as soon as possible, a palace near the Sultan's, fit to receive my wife, the Princess Badroulboudour. Build it of porphyry, jasper, lapis lazuli, or the finest marbles of various colours. On the terraced roof build me a large hall, crowned with a dome. Let the walls be of massy gold and silver. On each of the four sides of this hall let there be six windows. Leave one window lattice unfinished, but enrich all the others with diamonds, rubies, and emeralds. I would have also a spacious garden, and a treasury full of gold and silver. There must be kitchens, offices, storehouses, and stables full of the finest horses. I want also male and female slaves, and equerries and grooms. Come and tell me when all is finished."

The next morning before break of day, the Genie presented himself to Aladdin and said: "Master, thy palace is finished, come and see if it pleaseth thee." Aladdin had no sooner signified his consent, than the Genie transported him thither in an instant, and led him through richly furnished apartments, and Aladdin found nothing but what was magnificent. Officers, slaves and grooms were busy at their tasks, and the treasury was piled to the ceiling with purses of gold, and the stables were filled with the finest horses in the world. When Aladdin had examined the palace from top to bottom, and particularly the hall with four and twenty windows, he found all beyond anything he had imagined. "Genie," he said, "there is only one thing wanting, which I forgot to mention, that is a carpet of fine velvet for the Princess to walk upon, between my palace and the Sultan's." The Genie disappeared, and instantly a carpet of fine velvet stretched across the park to the door of the Sultan's palace.

When the porters of the Sultan's palace came to open the gates, they were amazed to see a carpet of velvet stretching from the grand entrance across the park, to a new and magnificent palace. The Grand Vizier, who arrived soon after the gates were opened, being no less amazed than the others, hastened to acquaint the Sultan with the wonderful news. The hour of going to the audience chamber put an end to their conjectures, but scarcely were they seated before Aladdin's mother arrived, dressed in her most sumptuous garments, and attended by the six female slaves, who were clad richly and magnificently. She was received at the palace with honour, and introduced into the Princess Badroulboudour's apartment, by the chief of the eunuchs. As soon as the Princess saw her, she arose, and saluted her, and desired her to sit beside her upon a sofa. A collation was served, and then the slaves finished dressing the Princess, and adorning her with the jewels which Aladdin had presented to her.

The Sultan immediately ordered bands of trumpets,

cymbals, drums, fifes, and hautboys, placed in different parts of the palace, to play, so that the air resounded with concerts which inspired the city with joy. The merchants began to adorn their shops and houses with fine carpets, and silks, and to prepare illuminations for the coming festival.

When night arrived the Princess took tender leave of the Sultan her father, and, accompanied by Aladdin's mother, set out across the velvet carpet, amid the sound of trumpets, and lighted by a thousand torches. Aladdin received her with joy, and led her into the large, illuminated hall, where was spread a magnificent repast. The dishes were of massy gold, and contained the most delicious viands, and after the supper there was a concert of the most ravishing music, accompanied by graceful dancing, performed by a number of female slaves.

The next morning Aladdin mounted, and went in the midst of a large troop of slaves to the Sultan's palace. The Sultan received him with honours, embraced him, placed him upon the throne, near him, and ordered a collation. Aladdin then said: "I entreat thee to dispense with my eating with thee this day, as I came to invite thee to partake of a repast in the Princess's palace, attended by thy Grand Vizier, and all the lords of thy court." The Sultan consented with pleasure, rose up immediately, and, followed by all the officers of his court, accompanied Aladdin.

The nearer the Sultan approached Aladdin's palace the more he was struck with its beauty, but he was much more amazed when he entered it, and could not forbear breaking out into exclamations of wonder. But when he came into the hall of the four and twenty windows enriched with diamonds, rubies, emeralds, all large and perfect stones, he was so much surprised that he remained for some time motionless. "This palace," exclaimed he at length, "is surely one of the wonders of the world, for where in all the world besides shall we find walls built of massy gold and silver, and diamonds, pearls, and rubies adorning the windows!"

The Sultan examined and admired all the windows, but on counting them he found that there were but three and twenty so richly adorned and that the fourth and twentieth was left imperfect, and in great astonishment he inquired the reason of this. "It was by my orders that the workmen left it thus," said Aladdin, "since I wished that thou shouldest have the glory of finishing this hall." The Sultan was much pleased with this compliment, and immediately ordered his jewellers and goldsmiths to complete the four and twentieth window. When the Sultan returned to his palace he ordered his jewels to be brought out, and the jewellers took a great quantity, which they soon used without making any great advance in their work. They worked steadily for a whole month, but could not finish half the window, although they used all the jewels the Sultan had, and borrowed of the Vizier.

Aladdin, who knew that all the Sultan's endeavours to complete the window were in vain, sent for the jewellers and goldsmiths, and commanded them not only to desist but to undo the work they had done, and to return the jewels to the Sultan, and to the Grand Vizier. They undid in a few hours what they had accomplished in a month, and retired, leaving Aladdin alone in the hall. He took the lamp, which he carried about with him, rubbed it, and the Genie appeared.

"Genie," said Aladdin, "I order thee to complete the four and twentieth window." And immediately the window became perfect like the others.

Scarcely was the window completed when the Sultan arrived to question Aladdin, as to why the jewellers and goldsmiths had desisted from their work. Aladdin received him at the door, and conducted him directly to the hall, where he was amazed to see the window perfect like the rest. "My son," exclaimed the Sultan, embracing him, "what a man thou art to do all this in the twinkling of an eye! Verily, the more I know thee the more I admire thee!" And the Sultan returned to his palace content.

After this Aladdin lived in great state. He visited mosques, attended prayers, and returned the visits of the principal lords of the court. Every time he went out he caused two slaves, who walked by the side of his horse, to throw handfuls of money among the people, as he passed through the streets and the squares; and no one came to his palace gates to ask alms, but returned satisfied with his liberality, which gained him the love and blessings of the people.

Aladdin had conducted himself in this manner for several years, when the African magician, who had undesignedly been the instrument of Aladdin's prosperity, became curious to know whether he had perished in the subterranean garden. He employed his magic arts to discover the truth, and he found that Aladdin, instead of having perished miserably in the cave, had made his escape, and was living splendidly, and that he was in possession of the wonderful lamp, and had married a princess. The magician no sooner learned this than his face became inflamed with anger, and he cried out in a rage: "This miserable tailor's son has discovered the secret and the virtue of the lamp! I will, however, prevent his enjoying it long!"

The next morning he mounted a horse, set forwards, and never stopped until he arrived at the capital of China, where he alighted, and took up his residence at an inn. The next day his first object was to inquire what people said of Aladdin, and, taking a walk through the town, he heard them talking of the wonderful palace and of Aladdin's marriage to the Princess. He went instantly and viewed the palace from all sides, and he doubted not but that Aladdin had made use of the lamp to build it, for none but Genii, the slaves of the lamp, could have performed such wonders. Piqued to the quick at Aladdin's happiness and splendour, he returned to the inn, where he lodged.

As soon as he entered his chamber, he ascertained by the means of his magic arts, that Aladdin was absent on the hunt, and that the lamp was in the palace. He then went to a copper-smith's and bought a dozen copper lamps. These he placed in a basket, which he bought for the purpose, and with the basket on his arm, went directly to Aladdin's palace. As he approached he began crying: "Who will change old lamps for new ones? Who will change old lamps for new ones?" And all who passed by thought him a madman or a fool to offer to change new lamps for old.

Now the Princess Badroulboudour who was in the hall with the four and twenty windows, heard a man crying: "Who will change old lamps for new ones?" and remembering the old lamp, which Aladdin had laid upon a shelf before he went to the chase, the Princess, who knew not the value of the lamp, commanded a

"WHO WILL CHANGE OLD LAMPS FOR NEW ONES?"

eunuch to take it and make the exchange. The eunuch did so, and the African magician, as soon as he saw the lamp, snatched it eagerly from his hand, and gave him a new one in its place.

The magician then hastened away, until he reached a lonely spot in the country; when he pulled the lamp out of his bosom, and rubbed it. At that summons the Genie appeared, and said: "What wouldest thou have? I am ready to obey thee as thy slave, and the slave of all those who hold that lamp in their hands, I and the other slaves of the lamp!" "I command thee," replied that magician, "to transport me immediately, and the palace, which thou and the other slaves of the lamp have built in this city, with all the people in it, to Africa." The Genie disappeared, and immediately the magician, and the palace, and all its inhabitants, were lifted up, and transported from the capital of China and set down in Africa.

As soon as the Sultan arose the next morning, he went according to his custom to the window to contemplate and admire Aladdin's palace. When he looked that way, instead of a palace, he saw an empty space. He thought that he was mistaken, and looked again in front, to the right and left, and beheld only empty space where formerly had stood the palace. His amazement was so great that he remained for some time turning his eyes towards the spot, and at last convinced that no palace stood opposite his own, he returned to his apartment, and ordered his Grand Vizier to be sent for with expedition.

The Grand Vizier came with much precipitation. "Tell me," said the Sultan, "what has become of Aladdin's palace." "His palace!" exclaimed the Vizier, "is it not in its usual place?" "Go to my window," answered the Sultan, "and tell me if thou canst see it." The Grand Vizier went to the window, where he was struck with no less amazement than the Sultan had been. When he was well assured that there was not the least appearance of the palace, he returned to the Sultan. "Well," said the Sultan, "hast thou seen Aladdin's palace?" "Alas," answered the Grand Vizier, "it has vanished completely! I have always thought that the edifice, which was the object of thy admiration, with all its immense riches, was only the work of magic and a magician."

At these words the Sultan flew into a passion. "Where is that impostor, that wicked wretch," cried he, "that I may have his head taken off immediately? Go thou, bring him to me loaded with chains!" The Grand Vizier hastened to obey these orders, and commanded a detachment of horse to meet Aladdin returning from the chase, and to arrest him, and bring him before the Sultan.

The detachment pursued their orders, and about five or six leagues from the city met Aladdin returning from the chase. Without explanation, they arrested him, and fastened a heavy chain about his neck, and one around his body, so that both his arms were pinioned to his sides. In this state they carried him before the Sultan, who ordered him to be put to death immediately. But a multitude of people had followed Aladdin, as he was led in chains through the city, and they threatened a riot, if any harm should befall him. The Sultan, terrified at this menace, ordered the executioner to put up his sabre, to unbind Aladdin, and at the same time commanded the porters to declare unto the people that the Sultan had pardoned him, and that they might retire.

When Aladdin found himself at liberty, he turned towards the Sultan, and said: "I know not what I have done to lose thy favour! Wilt thou not tell me what crime I have committed?" "Your crime, perfidious wretch!" answered the Sultan. "Dost thou not know it? Where is thy palace? What has become of the Princess my daughter?" Aladdin looked from the window and perceiving the empty spot where his palace had stood, was thrown into such confusion and amazement, that he could not return one word of answer. At length breaking the silence he said: "I know not whither my palace has vanished! Neither can I tell thee where it may be! Grant me but forty days in which to make inquiry, and if, at the end of that time, I have not the success I wish, I will offer my head at the foot of thy throne, to be disposed of at thy pleasure." "Go," said the Sultan, "I give thee the forty days thou askest for, but if thou dost not find my daughter, thou shalt not escape my wrath. I will find thee out in whatsoever part of the world thou mayest conceal theyself, and I will cause thy head to be struck off!"

Aladdin went out of the Sultan's presence in great humiliation, and filled with confusion. For three days he wandered about the city making inquiries, but all in vain, he could find no trace of the vanished palace. At last he wandered into the country, and, at the approach of night, came to the banks of a river, where he sat down to rest. Clasping his hands in despair he accidentally rubbed the ring, which the African magician had placed upon his finger, before he went down into the subterranean abode to fetch the precious lamp. Immediately the same Genie appeared, whom he had seen in the cave, where the magician had left him. "What wouldest thou have?" said the Genie, "I am ready to obey thee as thy slave, and the slave of all those who have that ring on their fingers, I and the other slaves of the ring!"

Aladdin, agreeably surprised at an apparition he so little expected, replied: "Save my life, Genie, by showing me the place where the palace I caused to be built now stands, or immediately transport it back where it first stood." "What thou commandest is not in my power," answered the Genie, "I am only the slave of the ring, thou must address thyself to the slave of the lamp." "If that be the case," replied Aladdin, "I command thee by the power of the ring, to transport me to the spot, where my palace stands, in what part of the world soever it may be, and set me down under the window of the Princess Badroulboudour."

These words were no sooner out of his mouth, than the Genie transported him into Africa, to the middle of a large plain, where his palace stood, and placing him exactly under the window of the Princess Badroulboudour's apartment, left him. The next morning when the Princess looked out of her window she perceived Aladdin sitting beneath it. Scarcely believing her eyes, she opened the window, and motioned to him to come up. Aladdin hastened to her apartment, and it is impossible to express the joy of both at seeing each other, after so cruel a separation.

After embracing and shedding tears of joy, they sat down, and Aladdin said: "I beg of thee, Princess, both for thine own sake, and the Sultan thy father's, and mine, tell me what became of an old lamp which I left upon a shelf in my robing-room, when I departed for the chase?" "Alas! dear husband," answered the Princess, "I was afraid our misfortune might be owing to that lamp, and what grieves me most is that I have been the cause of it!" "Princess," replied Aladdin, "do not blame thyself, but tell me what has happened, and into whose hands it has fallen."

The Princess then related how she had changed the old lamp for a new, and how the next morning she had found herself in an unknown country, which she was told was Africa, by the traitor, who had transported her hither by his magic arts. She also told how the wicked magician visited her daily, forcing upon her his unwelcome attentions, and how he daily tried to persuade her to take him for a husband in the place of Aladdin. "And," added the Princess, "he carries the wonderful lamp carefully wrapped in his bosom, and this I can assure thee of, because he pulled it out before me, and showed it to me in triumph."

"Princess," said Aladdin, "this magician is a most perfidious wretch, and I have here the means to punish him, and to deliver thee from both thine enemy and mine. To accomplish this thou must obey my directions most carefully. When the African magician comes to-night, place this powder in his cup of wine, offer him the cup, and he will esteem it so great a favour that he will not refuse, but will eagerly quaff it off. No sooner will he have drunk than thou wilt see him fall backwards." After the Princess had agreed to the measures proposed by Aladdin, he took his leave, and spent the rest of the day in the neighbourhood of the palace till it was night, and he might safely return by a private door.

When the evening arrived the magician came at the usual hour, and as soon as he was seated, the Princess handed him a cup of wine, in which the powder had been dissolved. The magician reclined his head back to show his eagerness, drank the wine to the very last drop, turned his eyes in his head, and fell to the floor dead. At a signal from the Princess, Aladdin entered the hall, and he requested her to retire immediately to her own apartment.

When the Princess, her women, and eunuchs, were gone out of the hall, Aladdin shut the door, and going to the magician opened his vest, took out the lamp which was carefully wrapped up, and unfolded and rubbed it, whereupon the Genie immediately appeared. "Genie," said Aladdin, "transport this palace instantly to China, to the place from whence it was brought hither." The Genie bowed his head in token of obedience, and disappeared. Immediately the palace was lifted up and transported to China.

The morning of the return of Aladdin's palace, the Sultan stood at his window absorbed in grief. He cast his eyes towards the spot where the palace had once stood, and which he now expected to find vacant, but to his surprise and amazement, there stood Aladdin's palace in all its former grandeur. He immediately ordered a horse to be saddled and bridled, and brought to him without delay, which he mounted that instant, thinking that he could not make haste enough to reach the palace.

Aladdin received the Sultan at the foot of the great staircase, helped him to dismount, and led him into the Princess's apartment. The happy father embraced her with his face bathed in tears of joy, and the Princess related to him all that had happened to her from the time the palace was transported to Africa, to the death of the African magician.

Aladdin ordered the magician's body to be removed, and in the meantime the Sultan commanded the drums, trumpets, cymbals, and other instruments of music to announce his joy to the public, and a festival of ten days to be proclaimed for the return of the Princess and Aladdin.

Now the African magician had a younger brother who was equally skilful in magic, and who surpassed him in villainy and evil designs. Some time after the African magician had failed in his enterprise against Aladdin, this younger brother, who had heard no tidings of him, resorted to his magic arts. He learned that his brother was no longer living, and that the person who had caused his death was Aladdin, and he learned also that Aladdin resided in the capital of the Kingdom of China.

When the magician had informed himself of his brother's fate, resolving to revenge his death, he departed for China, where after crossing plains, rivers, mountains, deserts, and a long tract of country, without delay he arrived after incredible fatigue. As soon as he came to the capital of China, he went to the cell of a holy woman, called Fatima, murdered her, and disguised himself in her habit, he then went immediately to Aladdin's palace, and inquired for the Princess Badroulboudour. The Princess, who had long heard of Fatima but had never seen her, was very desirous to converse with her, and sent four eunuchs to bring the holy woman. When the magician, who, under a holy garment, disguised a wicked heart, was

introduced into the great hall, and perceived the **Prin-**
cess, he began a prayer for her health and prosperity,
and that she might have everything she desired. When
the pretended Fatima had finished his long prayer,
the Princess thanked him for his good wishes, and requested him to sit beside her. After some conversation,
the Princess said: "My good mother, I am overjoyed
to have the company of so holy a woman as thyself,
who will bestow a blessing upon this palace. And now
that I am speaking of the palace, pray how dost thou
like it? And before I show it to thee tell me first what
thou thinkest of this hall."

Upon this question the counterfeit Fatima affected
to hang down the head, and, at last looking up, sur-
veyed the hall from one end to the other. When he
had examined it well, he said to the Princess: "This
hall is truly admirable and most beautiful; there wants
but one thing! If a Roc's egg were hung in the middle
of the dome, this hall would have no parallel in the
four quarters of the world, and thy palace would be
the wonder of the universe." "My good mother,"
said the Princess, "what bird is a Roc? And where
may one find an egg?" "Princess," replied the pretended Fatima, "the Roc is a bird of prodigious size,
which inhabits the summit of Mount Caucasus. The
architect, who built thy palace, can get thee an egg."

The Princess thanked the False Fatima, and conversed with him upon other matters, but could not
forget the Roc's egg, which she resolved to request of
Aladdin, when he returned from hunting. He had been
gone six days, which the magician knew, therefore
he had taken advantage of his absence. The Princess
invited the false Fatima to remain for the night, and

scarcely had he retired to the apartment assigned to him, when Aladdin returned from the chase.

As soon as he arrived he went directly to the Princess's apartment, saluted and embraced her, but she seemed to receive him coldly. "My Princess," said he, "has anything happened during my absence, which has displeased thee, or given thee trouble?" "I have always believed," answered the Princess, "that our palace was the most superb, magnificent, and complete in the world, but I tell thee now what I find fault with, upon examining the hall of the four and twenty windows. Dost thou not think that it would be complete if a Roc's egg were hung up in the midst of the dome?" "Princess," replied Aladdin, "it is enough that thou desirest such an ornament. I will supply the deficiency immediately, for there is nothing which I would not do for thy sake."

Aladdin left the Princess Badroulboudour that moment, and went up into the hall of the four and twenty windows, where pulling out of his bosom the lamp, which he now always carried with him, he rubbed it, upon which the Genie immediately appeared. "Genie," said Aladdin, "this hall is imperfect without a Roc's egg hung up in the midst of the dome. I command thee, in the name of the lamp, to repair the deficiency." Aladdin had no sooner uttered these words, than the Genie gave so loud and terrible a cry, that the hall shook, and Aladdin could scarcely stand upright. "What, wretch!" said the Genie, in a voice like thunder, "is it not enough that I and my companions have done everything for thee, but thou, ungrateful one, must command me to bring my master, and hang him up in the midst of this dome? Well it is that this request does not come from thee, or else I would reduce thee, thy wife, and thy palace immediately to ashes! Know then that the true author is the brother of the African magician, thy enemy. He is now in thy palace, disguised in the habit of the holy woman Fatima, whom he has murdered, and it is he who suggested to thy wife to make this pernicious demand. His design is to kill thee, therefore take care of thyself!" After these words the Genie disappeared.

Pondering on the words of the Genie, Aladdin returned to the Princess's apartment, and without mentioning what had happened, requested her to send for the false Fatima. When the pretended holy woman entered, he advanced towards Aladdin with his hand on a dagger, concealed in his girdle under his gown. Aladdin, observing this, seized his hand before he could draw his dagger, and pierced him to the heart with a sword.

"Alas!" cried the Princess in horror, "What hast thou done! Thou hast killed the holy Fatima!" "No, my Princess," replied Aladdin, "I have not killed Fatima, but a villain, who would have assassinated me, if I had not prevented him. This wicked wretch," he added, "is the brother to the African magician!" Aladdin then ordered the body of the false Fatima to be removed, and related to the Princess all that had happened.

Thus was Aladdin delivered from the persecution of two brothers, who were magicians. Within a few years the Sultan died in a good old age, and the Princess Badroulboudour, and her husband Aladdin succeeded him. They reigned together many years, and left a numerous and illustrious posterity.